THINKWEI

WAGENKI

Jeff Weston was born in 1970, in Bolton, Lancashire. He graduated in 1999 from Manchester Metropolitan University with a degree in English literature and commenced a career in stockbroking the following year. He is the middle son of an electrical engineer and barmaid/housewife and author of three novels (*The Leaf Blower, Mutler, Wagenknecht*), three plays (*The Relationship, Directions, The Broken Heart Ward*) and a collection of short stories (*Homage to Hernandez & Other Stories*). His writing has crossed over into sports journalism and book reviews for psychotherapy magazines.

'The underlying premise here is imaginative'
          -Sophie Lambert, *Conville and Walsh*

'You write well'
          -Tibor Jones & Associates

'From start to finish, very difficult to put down, desperate as the reader is to salvage and assemble the bits of meaning percolated through the narrative. *Wagenknecht* is a courageous, bold and inventive piece of modern literary fiction'
          -Ade Kolade

'The earthy and intellectual gab of William Wagenknecht shows irreverence, revelry and bite'
          -Patricia Khan

'As if Roth, Bellow and Salinger have risen from the grave and, together, planned one final project designed to purge modern culture of its vacuousness'
          -Sean Thomas

'Charlie Parker (*Birdland*). John Williams (*Stoner*). And now Jeff Weston (*Wagenknecht*). The 29th August is a date when maternity wards around the country are on high alert for the first distinctive cries of new born artists'
          -Robert Perrin

Jeff Weston

WAGENKNECHT

THINKWELL BOOKS

Copyright © 2019 Jeff Weston.

All rights reserved. No part of this publication may be reproduced, distributed, or transmitted in any form or by any means, including photocopying, recording, or other electronic or mechanical methods, without the prior written permission of the publisher, except in the case of brief quotations embodied in critical reviews and certain other noncommercial uses permitted by copyright law. For permission requests, contact the publisher.

Any references to historical events, real people, or real places are used fictitiously. Names, characters, and places are products of the author's imagination.

Written by Jeff Weston 2013-16.

Support and proofreading by L Hernandez.

Cover design & interior formatting by Rachel Bostwick.

Published by Thinkwell Books, U.K.

First printing edition 2019.

For my parents
who raised me in a simple, loving way

"Awareness was his work; extended consciousness was his line, his business…vigilance."
- Saul Bellow
Herzog (1964)

Prologue: *THE WAGON* 1
Part 1: *THE FALL* 3
Part 2: *THE PAST* 53
Part 3: *THE CRAWL* 167

Prologue: *THE WAGON*

Whoever heard of a confident man that wasn't a shyster? thought William Wagenknecht. If he was to write for the nerds, the diffident then he would gladly accept such a mighty role; shepherd them from the big mouths, the bullies, the prosaic piss artists, the slime-ridden careerists.

People claimed he was an estranged capitalist, a sanctimonious sack of shit, an existentialist, a raging and indignant hypocrite. Well – he was happy with all those titles; anything but sycophant, laugh-along truckler or impressionable coot.

He had played the role of 21st century man and it hadn't tasted so good. Now, he was looking around for bigger answers, storms which had been quelled, the noble lie in its underwear.

Do you think you know about life? Do you think you know a damn thing? Beyond the pleasant, neighbourly mirth and vocational rigour?

The words de-frosted his brain. They infused his metaphysical tendencies. He had heard that something in the 17th century was truer than now but that the big project had been halted, the red button pressed.

He pictured the back of a refuse wagon and wondered what was in there, how this had come about. Peering inside…

Part 1: *THE FALL*

All the Wagenknechts cracked up at forty. Some hung on for another two years, peddled an unconvincing face, but inside they were similarly mashed, dead from modernity's heat, its puerile dust, its gravel-like ideas.

It was a step up from a bar mitzvah, a christening at three months, a twenty-first to signal one's coming of age. Forty was to bring less optimism though – rather a hard look at the horizon.

Wagenknecht. *What* was he? *Who* was he? An immigrant? Only in name. The clothes – a little bit of Ellis Island, but only because he hated wool suits, their harsh fibres roughing up his skin, failing to let him settle. And settle he couldn't. The old strategies of swimming under water, cycling, long, quick-striding walks no longer worked. He was motoring in his head, running over his mistakes, blunders, poor choices. Work. Women. Investments. *Everything* was an investment. God – he knew it now. He had let the Romantics addle his brain, tip-toe and escort him across Blake's murals and through Whitman's beard.

The fall. The collapse. It had been precipitous, sudden - wondrous in a twisted way. Wagenknecht. William Wagenknecht – beholder of Adorno's melancholy science – had lost all direction, stuttered, stumbled, ungraciously bowled into fellow citizens asking, perhaps demanding, that they guess his age.

'How old? Go on. Much torment in this face?'

They stared back, offered different forms of woe, avoided him, retreated from his mad gaze.

Wagenknecht, the old warrior, dreamer, beckoner of life, stood there on the dirty pavement edge thinking, pondering. *This. This is who I am now. I can hear the buzzards overhead.* Arms outstretched, he looked up above the rim of his glasses – away from the soiled stone.

A suit that had given him ten years, the singed eyebrows inherited from his father, the bald calves – he seemed to slip them all, dance with the gods for a moment.

Normally, when around this city – Salchester, his economic home – he would dim his nostrils, breathe in a certain restricted way, be wary of the carcinogens congregating around him.

Something had freed him though – he had seen the line through the fog, seen that he had passed it months ago. Probably when he was with *her* – Lysette, his ex-wife. The crack up had started then. Better to crack up on his own, flee the conjugal scene, empty the tanks, try to fill his soul with something else, he thought.

But the sufferance he could not shake off. If anything, it had intensified. You give a woman too much, she hates you. You ask her to go Dutch, she throws you an unyielding stare. You show willing - understand that the marital show is over - and you are forever persecuted.

Dear Mr Locke – You assert that the mind is initially a blank canvas. Well, I cannot agree. The female sex surely begins life braced in a seething, boiling manner. I have seen too many full specimens for this not to be the case. I wandered down a maternity ward very recently and it was noticeable that the pink-clad cherubs were sullen, immediately able to pick off and trouble their blue peers.

Focus, he couldn't. The patterns in his head were wilting, breaking up. Clear thought eluded him. The bustle of the city was on a separate plain, in a different sphere. He could see out but was suddenly unable to move.

Wagenknecht's thoughts multiplied, his eye lids flickered. It felt like the stage *after* humanity's automaton period. Gone were his concerns about being up to date, behaving judiciously, looking graceful. Much of what passed through his mind was indecipherable, the fuzz of a vacant station, yet in it were answers, turns and doors he had been incapable of accessing.

He seemed to be looking *through* the people now, the rushing hordes, *at* the shifting sky. *That is our natural speed*, he mused. *Strolling with the clouds*. The internal-combustion engine has sped us up – added a ludicrous velocity. We're all trying to run with it, explode our hearts, burn out our shins. *Stop, you bastards. Stop!*

Sometimes he shook. His lower arms and hands took on a pre-Parkinson's rumble. There was a quiver which rippled through him. Wagenknecht did not fear such a state, but rather wondered what else it brought. A different mindset? A forced allegiance to the sick, the fallen?

When epilepsy sufferers did their jerking on the floor, lost consciousness, for a moment unstrapped the central nervous system, perhaps they were travelling a little towards heaven, escaping the manufactured calm.

The tundra before Wagenknecht – this piece of urbanity with its tall buildings and filthy canals – struck him as outdated, the choked sentence of a desperately hurried breed of man. The steel and glass were spreading more each week, turning Salchester into a sci-fi destination, but one's public land, one's self-destiny seemed to be receding with it. They were cobbling over the rough, spillages of his soul – offering sleekness and elegance for freedom.

This, Wagenknecht had difficulty with, but he could not work out if it was the looming future which agitated him or the absence of his family.

Scotty, his son. Jasmine, his daughter. He was trying to organise their lives, find them each a track, hunt down their futures. His base, his mission control, his retreat had initially been his ageing parents' house – a generous front bedroom but with the overspill of their wardrobe haunting it, a slight horse manure whiff emanating from his father's sweaters.

He, at first, felt ridiculous – like a child again, stripped of numerous faculties and functions. Only the top front room was truly his, although his mother made a great effort in accommodating his projects and plays; the back living room table his to exploit, spread his papers over and be seated at whilst staring out through the patio doors at the overgrown field.

The field had represented his youth – its two football pitches and artery-like paths now long since superseded by couch grass, bluebells, rose willow, buttercups and wild oaks. In it, he had learned to mark a player properly, hit a golf ball, kiss, run a zigzag escape route from bees, jump over the brook at the bottom and contemplate life on top of a disused bunker.

The isolation and solitude was a 1970s dream that would not return. He looked out now and saw a carpeted nothingness; a kestrel's lair, but otherwise unattended land neglected by the local kids. While they were sat hooked up to technology, completely unsuitable women had ransacked his life, drawn blood, labelled him a bastard for living.

Two months in at his childhood home after watching his well-meaning parents count their pills at the dining table, Wagenknecht decided that he wished to buy the pock-marked garage at the rear. He could extend out – down to a foot short of a canine burial site. The timber roof was tiled, high. He figured he could use the existing west side for a walk-in kitchen and the newly built drop as a two-level living room/bathroom with overhead sleeping quarters.

Perhaps the morning sun would rouse him. Perhaps such desperately sought privacy would have him reborn. The wall space that Lysette had implicitly colonized would be his here. His to educate Scotty and Jasmine through maps, Impressionism, pictures of great, distant relatives, recent endeavours and their own growing up.

'My tools are in there. My lawnmower. Chairs for the summer.'

'Can't we re-house them?'

'Where?'

Wagenknecht hesitated. He could not upset a 77-year old man.

'My bird box.'

'It's on the outside, Dad. That'll be OK.'

'I'm not so sure.'

There was a sense that he thought himself to be Marlon Brando at times. The cooing and chirping of

8 | Jeff Weston

domestic and wild birds *his* responsibility, *his* unique parentage.

The following day, Wagenknecht's mother came to him. Told him they had found a large, suitable outdoor storage box. This is how it was. She was the negotiator, the whisperer behind closed doors, the altruistic glue. Douglas and Leonard, his brothers, could afford to sidestep such generosity, but William was somehow in its thrall, aware of his sluggish last twenty years.

He had gotten in some retired workers on the cheap, given them the spec, asked for nothing other than smoothly plastered walls and good joinery and pointing. A form of minimalism would follow – again, regeneration of a sort, the pulling away from Lysette's increasing clutter.

If only her mind hadn't wobbled with its poor-girl fury. Christ – he recalled them at their height: salting the ratatouille and then back to bed, her South American nipples slightly out of place on the breast but lingering, large, perfect. Near the end though, his penis a faded actor, his mind rattled with uncertainty and unnatural begging. What becomes of the great couples?

Dear Mr Freud – Shouldn't we just aim for kindness? The high sex is liberating yet if lost a permanent tormentor. You talk of the predominantly erotic person giving priority to his emotional relations with others, and then bound into the finer narcissistic model being self-sufficient, reliant on his own internal mental processes. Perhaps marriage is the crazed merchant tying up all his capital in one place. But polygamy – can it really rise? Man's decision to adopt an upright gait – the genitals thus becoming visible and in need of protection – you attach to a new sense of shame, the start of the fateful process of civilization. I think we might have surpassed this – fallen into a pretend-virtuous world.

Wagenknecht, at times, slumped in the reclining chair. His body felt wrong. He appeared to be pinned down by solipsism's finest army. He thought of his ailments – asthma, geographic tongue, the pre-Parkinson's shakes, mild bipolarism, hiatus hernia, Asperger's (undiagnosed), Dupuytren's contracture, the occasional tweak of the heart, anxiety. He had been born with a lack of energy. It was said that the dummy rolled out when parking the pram and that his future as a labourer of any kind would be severely limited. Hiked up on his former rickety legs, he considered what else he might offer the world.

The small lump discovered on his left palm made him doubly wonder. Sometimes he saw the beginning of a potentially serious diagnosis as an escape route long sought. His doc, a charming, breezy man of a similar age rolled into a speech about John the Baptist and how eventually William would be unable to extend the fingers on his left hand but that it certainly wasn't cancer. Wagenknecht's fingers would bend, become claw-like, possibly fuse together.

Dupuytren's – the name he liked. It sounded mighty, worthy of a special breed of man. He would read up on John the Baptist – compare character traits.

The shooting pains in his hand, he could bear, cope with. Removing his wedding ring had had the odd effect of mitigating such agony as if part conductor or administrator of the dreadful choir. The slipping off of the metal band and placing it on his key fob was somehow timely, appropriate, the precursor to the true fall.

A man on public transport suddenly without his symbolic 'ball and chain' can be drawn into philandering, embraced by adultery in a single glance. Wagenknecht, a dark-haired, attractive man, exchanged thirsty looks, for a second unzipped the breasts before him. But then, blinking back into life, understood the enormity of taking on another woman. Nothing was for free. The Sisyphean aftermath of indulgence had driven men to murder, had extinguished what stability they had. Rage lay beneath the primmest of prim dresses. Women wanted full-time protectors, chauffeurs, docile shop accompaniers. And those damn tattoos that they held in esteem (a modern day blemish inking over the great creation) – not many saw through the wheeze, the con trick, the permanent fancy dress.

Wagenknecht had to steer around the suckers, not be pulled along by the ordinary pillars of the world. Too many had been tainted – great men in cameo performances of their intended lives; brains rotting, *nothing real to carry home*.

Unlike Chomsky, I cannot excuse mankind, thought Wagenknecht. Revolutions, I don't expect. Weakness I can understand. But not to be high-minded – discuss why we are here, be fascinated by the skies. That takes a certain type of individual – a twitching, short-term, 'live for the moment' ruffian. Wagenknecht did not recognise society's faces anymore. In them he saw disinterest, quickness, a panoply of dubious concerns. Dead. They were dead already. And yet they had not planned their funeral – the guest list, the hymns, the speeches, the engraving on the tombstone.

Such particulars were vital to Wagenknecht. They gave him a sense of peace. On a single sheet of A4, he had written so far: STRICTLY NO BOSSES, *MORNING HAS BROKEN*, SPEECHES: BOTH BROTHERS PLUS ROUTCLIFF AND HESELGLASS, TOMBSTONE: PLAYWRIGHT – SON – FATHER – TERRIBLE HUSBAND.

The engraving he would have to discuss with the church. He was not sure if they allowed the pejorative. As much as he criticised Lysette, he knew his shortcomings, he traversed their inner flutterings almost hourly. And therefore felt such an inclusion necessary – a wink, if anything, a tip off that, yes, he had failed her, not fully read up on the needs of a wife.

Wagenknecht, despite his occasional snobbishness, had a left-wing heart. In that prognosis lay Lysette's loneliness, her underperformance, her eventual fury. *You wish to make the world better, your own home falls.*

Within weeks – fixed up in his new abode – Wagenknecht began to dedicate his Sundays to a silent protocol of diazepam and shaving cream. After the tablet at noon, he shaved. Somehow, it was a fresh beginning, a fearless looking around. The calm it instilled was relatively inexpensive. Clean-faced and serene, his thoughts no longer unduly wavered. Or if they did the inaction, the deliberation did not frighten him. Sometimes choices took time. Direction needed mulling over.

The stash of medication had been left over from a prescription for his neck. Worse than Dupuytren's, the asthma, the heart, was his chimney-like neck. Stacked with a network of nerves and circuitry, the plinth for his head often tortured him from inside, left him immobile – wedged and separated from his body.

Lay there, it felt like a cryogenics experiment. Two or three decades later – maybe a century – there would be a new body through which he would restore a certain harmony. For now, as in *Cold Lazarus*, there was desperation, a jutting of tears. The weariness and pleading induced by such a state pushed him into new worlds, along paths with a psychedelic tremor, an extra dimensional paroxysm.

The condition rarely returned but the drugs to a previously 'clean' individual like Wagenknecht gained a certain respect. Life's woes vanished. He was never far enough out of it that people knew and so Sunday became a church of sorts, a set up for the week. The small, yellow 10mg parcels were relaxants. They coated the world with less cynicism. They did not reduce his intelligence but rather brought the sky closer - mixed its fantastic blue with the greens, greys and browns that surrounded him.

When, eventually, his stock ran out, he did not immediately panic. He still shaved, still tried to make out the shrubs in the garden beyond the smoked glass. Wagenknecht wondered if he could kid himself, take an ibuprofen instead, do what they do in experiments and play to the power of the mind.

At first, he bought it – believed that his patterns were the same, chose to comprehend the not-as-tiny chemical bullet as his saviour, a pre-lunch tonic, a giver of streaks of happiness and composure.

But then something inside him sat up. The old agitation returned. Not to resolve that before him in a matter of seconds made him shake. And they were mostly simple dilemmas, simple situations. His finger and thumb repeatedly straightened the stem of his glasses, he continually adjusted the trousers around his thighs, he rubbed his left palm against the back of his neck even though it was without pain.

Fidgety. He was fidgety, restless, twitching in a way. There could be no direction, no future while he was like this.

He lay down, tried to enter a dream state, recalled the conversations and therapy he had had since the initial drag on his mind. Work. Work had defeated him. He was twenty years in, twenty to go, but…the reverberations, the echo of pointlessness had him. He had stopped enjoying things. Seen the grind. Tuned out.

A broker. He was a broker. A facilitator. The man with the clicks and charm to buy and sell shares. At first it had seemed exciting, a crucial snippet of the world, a way of understanding personalities, motivations and hubris. People mostly have no game plan, Wagenknecht quickly learned. They chase the numbers, jump in fully clothed, misinterpret information and patterns. And some of these very same people were running the world, unchecked, in a mandatory vacuum of applause.

Noise suggested money in broking. The excited rush of voices and shouts gave the illusion of profit. Wagenknecht – a fifteen-year veteran of the dealing floor – had been one of about fifty dealers originally. That was now down to four. The computers had taken over. Less bodies were required. Only the quick-moving stocks and large deals were phoned through to Cockney HQ.

Despite continual resistance and an obvious wish to stay in the corn-earning part of the firm, Wagenknecht was thought reasonably highly of and thus seduced from time to time into considering greater roles.

Such managerial interviews or positions he declined. They would buy his opinions if he moved there. He suspected the floors, the people, the politics were booby trapped. There would be an overhang if he accepted – time would no longer be time, but rather a watch of their making. The one example of a man rising the ranks that he could see was Shilp. Shilp. He did a great line in dishonesty and regulation. He generally went for a jog each lunch time, fortunate to dodge the assassins. Looking at the man square on, you saw a trainee bastard, a pillar of society, invidious ascendency in all its folds.

Wagenknecht was unable to speak normally after certain days in the job. His lines took on a staccatoed air, a frenzied nothingness. You didn't have conversations with market makers. The words were sparingly assembled alongside the principal aim. 'Does the bid work in forty, Tommy?' 'Just about, Bill.' 'You good?' 'OK, sir, OK.'

Some of them he'd known for a decade and a half now, had met over sea bass, beers and chardonnay. There had been vigorous handshakes, merriment and a drop of profundity, but to Wagenknecht it felt like a winding-up order. They were all scrappers like him – harmless souls caught in a profession that perversely demanded profit and integrity – and yet something in them he could not forgive.

Dear Mr Kierkegaard – You were onto something. Man must indeed stand alone. The general rules of life are not so overbearing that we stop making decisions. The turning points must be in our minds – even a mind that is flaking like an old painted wall. Self-determining agents, you say? Can I at least fall on my younger brother who seems to have landed himself a plum deal? That is still a decision, right?

Wagenknecht had once packed when nobody was there - taken home the personal items from his drawers, his books, the lists pinned up around his desk. He wanted a clean, inconspicuous exit the following day – had planned the next three months in a life-altering, yet still haphazard way: sickness; a new woman and home; a different job.

He would sit in front of his doctor, look glum, flail around, become uncoordinated – part of it an act, part of it the gruesome weight of what he had been carrying around. Past therapy would be mentioned – both marriage guidance and cognitive behavioural (CBT). He hadn't had the courage to leave his wife and so the CBT was the next logical step. Opposite him had been a highly suitable replacement – a brunette with a beauty spot on the sloped incline of her left breast. Wagenknecht suffered in those six sessions – gazed at her welcoming demeanour and caring manner and contrasted it with what he had: a fireball, a woman who censored herself in the bedroom, a woman who juggled and distorted his history before throwing it back at him.

Why was he still here in this lesser world, with a woman who tidied only her half of the bed? Because of them. Because of Scotty and Jasmine; his daughter, the sweet girl who liked to grab his hand and run; his son, utterly lacking deference – geared up beautifully for the bastards he would inevitably come across.

The new woman, Maria he had been seeing for perhaps a season. They would scamper to the same pub during their lunch hours, sit opposite, immerse themselves in Wagenknecht's woes and her incomplete life. They had been lovers twenty years ago and wondered if a part of that youthful joie de vivre could be revived.

Wagenknecht would look at her, take in her high cheek bones, her slender arms, the facts surrounding her failed relationships. She was still easy going – less puritanical than Lysette, less dominant. Her white blouse was usually one button too low, a glimpse of her tastefully-coloured brassiere afforded the old stomper – accentuated curves appreciated, celebrated, given their mid-life due.

It remained an unconsummated affair. Talking. Talking. Laughing. Simplifying life. Perhaps a sweep of the lips but nothing improper, nothing that could indict him or be called an offence. Once, on departing, she had patted his rear. It was innocuous, unobjectionable, yet it had the effect of moving them on, gave Wagenknecht the mettle to want more.

A tram would sometimes rattle past as they were saying goodbye. Wagenknecht, out of the sticks in the nearest big city, feared being seen by a neighbour. But then something in him enjoined or urged a type of fatalism. It would be quicker this way. It would speed up or rather bypass their romantic deliberations.

Maria had prepared half a wardrobe for him. Their brief talk of money had resulted in her suggestion of 'payment in kind' given Wagenknecht's intention not to destroy his old household through pecuniary oppression.

It sounded extraordinarily sultry. And unlike Lysette, Wagenknecht deemed his ageing body the absolute property of his partner. If Maria wished to toy with him, yank out his jewels, in exchange for free heat, water and rent, then the floundering playwright had no objections – none at all.

Despite his basin of ailments and the madness that occasionally intercepted his frontal artery, Wagenknecht had the spring of a young man. He looked at life through baby eyes, with hope, trust and the manacled glee of Charlie Parker.

Family Christmases delayed their union. Pre-booked January shows sought to collude with the idea that a wardrobe somewhere – Wagenknecht could not vividly picture it – would never hang his decade-old clothes. School parents' evenings gave Wagenknecht new eyes – eyes that would cut out his own happiness, yet be there to witness the plaudits afforded his offspring, the incremental changes in them and a bond that would have remained a seed but for his full-time presence.

Amidst the shouting and pushing of parents deluded by the nuclear dream, the Wagenknecht children would blossom, swerve the fracas, be sustained.

Like a mushroom cloud. Like a pyrocumulus fallout.

By then Maria had met someone else. She had waited eleven months, shown patience and fortitude amid Wagenknecht's excuses, his withered and pusillanimous display. The lunches had grown fewer. His being between two worlds but in neither had demolished him, seen off his naïve and wishful hope.

The job. If he could have nothing else, then the job. A way out of this vocational cesspool. Avoid passing the wasteful baton of broking to the next generation. Into the white, unwrinkled hands of Scotty, his blonde angel.

Wagenknecht arranged a meeting, an informal interview with his younger brother, Douglas. It was winter, the roads icy, saplings bent by the weight of snow. Douglas was to pick him up outside the train station – his 4x4 capable of traversing the terrain over the Pennines to his warehouse.

'Get in,' were the bludgeoned first words of his stockier sibling, his hair once gone but then abracadabrad back. Wagenknecht stood on the metal grill, slid into the passenger seat and then swung to the thick, cumbersome door. It was a tank, a road-crushing leviathan of a car. Wagenknecht didn't entirely hate it. He at least felt warm, looked after, happy to be driven somewhere.

You make enough money, society leaves you alone, he thought. From the plush, leather upholstery, Wagenknecht felt like he had risen a class, joined the ranks of a special diaspora.

'Why the panicked call? Why do you need me?'

'To see if there's a position at the warehouse.'

'Who for?'

'Me.'

'You can look after my licences. Find me some sellers. I can pay you twenty or twenty-five plus bonuses. It's all the same to me.'

He was a middle man – the shipper of electronic goods from Europe to Hong Kong. He had plagiarized the idea from his former employer, earned thirty thousand tax free on the side and was now self-made, VAT registered, a big man.

God certainly mucks around, thought Wagenknecht. His brother was clever yet gruff – used to consorting with a table of brutes.

Wagenknecht had had nine bosses during his working life. Eight of them had read *The Sun*. He'd imagined Verdi and the coiffured crowning of apt leaders and had gotten Murdoch instead.

He suspected Douglas had made it in life because his face didn't change when people offended him. The usual tics and blood moving around seemed absent – beaten back by a porpoise-like skin and inexpressiveness.

'What do you think?'

'You're ok if I see the set up?'

'Yes. Yes.'

Much of the five mile journey was in silence, muteness, an appreciation of the crisp snow around them. The white stuff could be harsh, hostile but also like a thick snug blanket, not strangling life, but slowing it, adding poignancy.

'You were the original entrepreneur in the family. What was it - W Enterprises?'

'It was.'

Wagenknecht couldn't tell if Douglas was jesting or tracing back, trying to mine and understand some of his doomed youth.

'Why did it not grow?'

There was still a fondness, a rapturous sense that Wagenknecht had ideas, but executing them, fine-tuning them, taking risks – he wasn't built that way. Douglas, on the other hand, firmly had his 'skin in the game', a decade's worth of accounts and tax returns that demonstrated his astuteness, an almost blasé reading of the world.

'I wasn't keen on speaking to people. Picking up the phone. I think I had my stationery printed up with just an address on. I hoped my letters to people would be sufficient…'

'What?! Whoever heard of a shy entrepreneur? Listen, William…'

'I know. It doesn't look good. But consider me a pioneer of international trade. We've done business in the same regions. Perhaps – somehow – I cleared the way for you.'

'What did you import and sell?'

'Old master replicas from Taiwan. Ugandan raincoats.'

'How many?'

'How many imported?'

'No – sold.'

'One.'

'Who to?'

'A friend.'

'For how much?'

'Four pounds.'

'William…'

The conversation was becoming too much. Wagenknecht looked out of the window – hoped the car wouldn't stop. He needed its rhythm right now, needed to be away from his old world, his current plight, the buttered hands of humanity.

What was real anymore? Had his younger brother slipped into such rich pastures without effort or was there hurt and a side to him that Wagenknecht had missed?

Not here, God. Not here. Can't feel myself.

'Are you saying you want me to carry you? Give you a non-productive job?'

There was nothing touching in the sentence, nothing obviously bountiful or benevolent. And yet Wagenknecht chose to imagine they were playing as kids again – candid and earnest, without portentous layers.

'Yes. Exactly that. Restore my pride, my nerves. I don't want it real. There's something ugly about it being real. Find me a profession which shields me, keeps the maulers away.'

Only when it was said did Wagenknecht realise the depth of his begging, the sulphuric stench of his words. The car had come to a halt. He was surrounded by similar looking vehicles on a modest, relatively old-fashioned business park. A giant bay formed the entrance to Douglas's premises.

He could never have imagined such enormity housing his raincoats, his oil paintings, the varied pallor of his questionable imports. No. Thinking big had eluded him. And yet he'd been confident that the public would hand him money, buy his goods.

Wagenknecht had been partly seduced by his own business cards – their grey and red and a fashionable shadow font for the time. But really – had he ever been a business man? Could he honestly call himself that? Business without people is what he'd wanted. It had been a form of leisure, recreation, an unhurried eulogizing of his ideas.

He got out, crunched his way around on the fresh snow. Douglas looked across with a wisp of pity.

'Through here.'

'No. I'm sorry – no.'

'What do you mean?'

Wagenknecht scampered away – ran in the opposite direction. From his brother. His own brother! But a man he had probably lost several years ago. What is worse than embarrassment, he thought? Forbearance. Commiseration. The downward look of an uncultured man.

'William!'

He heard the shout, the semi-plea but was already shuffling along. *Let God judge me through the antennae in my head, but nobody else*, Wagenknecht mused. He would race back to his plays, his scripts, the replacement worlds he created in order to breathe, see a future and have purpose.

The ageing mortar in the terraced streets around him hinted of struggling occupants, 'Stand still' people that gave their lives to commerce.

"He who wishes to know the truth about life in its immediacy must scrutinize its estranged form, the objective powers that determine individual existence in its most hidden recesses."

Wagenknecht couldn't help but think of Adorno, his *Minima Moralia,* life "dragged along as an appendage of production". Even on a Friday night, out of its clutches, he felt the ball bearing roll down its track, leading them once more to the starting line, their mouse trap Monday.

Dear Mr Murdoch – When you took over Clay Felker's New York magazine in 1976, I think it signalled that life had become a business. We could grieve such a thing. We could kit ourselves out in fencing garb and allow the winner to shape all that follows, but may I just inform you instead of Felker's words after the coup – his staff gathered in a restaurant across the road: "Rupert Murdoch's ideas about friendship, about publishing and about people are very different than mine. He should know that he is breaking up a family, and he does so at his peril." Peril – what do you think he meant by that? Have you ever been afraid, have you ever cowered? Were we meant to begin the killings, the assassinations?

Wagenknecht's own family was crumbling. He could not remember if the therapy had come between or after the births of Scotty and Jasmine. What he recalled was Lysette's umbrage at having to sit in the presence of an obviously middle-class woman. This was an unacceptable bias before they had begun. Such an adjudicator would clearly back the better-spoken horse.

'You have your actor,' she announced, getting up just ten minutes into the session, ready to storm out, play the diva, embrace the nihilistic world Wagenknecht had paid for.

'Sit down, Lysette. Let me assure you that, one – I am not easily taken in, and two – you have the wrong idea about what we're trying to achieve. There is no winner, no placing the onus for change on one side of the relationship. We're simply trying to draw out feelings, make connections and understand the path forward. Without argument. Without recriminations.'

This is what I have to contend with, thought Wagenknecht, hoping for a tiny gesture from Ms Lenov. This truculence. This crazed hopping around. Culturally, socially, politically, sexually Lysette was not enough. She had failed to embrace civil society – a now 250-year experiment.

Lenov was a woman Wagenknecht could not screw but who knew about tolerance, dialectics, the civilized crater that humanity attempted to wander around in. Any high understanding in front of – and he used the word sparingly – his wife, had gotten to be dangerous, within range of her black-and-white-ometer, her dismissiveness, her bitch list.

And the list was expanding – mostly teeming with unimpeachable bystanders. Wagenknecht had dared to engage in conversation with a petite woman of Swedish origin while watching Scotty play football. He had made the same error indulging a shy and pleasant, fair-haired lady via Jasmine's gymnastics class. When roller-skating had rattled into town allowing Wagenknecht to watch a graceful, rose-cheeked specimen, the game was suddenly up.

Jasmine, not under her own volition, had been quizzed regarding her father's morning activities when present; an hour too early for Lysette's bones.

'Women,' his daughter had replied, not realising her role as star witness. 'He talks to women.'

"Not only does the individual advance from infancy to manhood, but the species itself from rudeness to civilization."

Wagenknecht was fulfilling his primary role in life – leaving barbarism behind. Yes – he waited for the pretty ones and sidestepped the bounding, Hercules-like maidens but what exactly was his crime?

'William – do you have anything to add?'

Wagenknecht blinked. He had lost the thread of the room, but would roll out what was on his mind anyway, take advantage of the amnesty.

'She busts me. For nothing. Expects the world to conform to her requirements. Thinks that I should be home each evening at 5pm. My entire career has been subtly controlled by the woman before you who herself has not worked for fifteen years. My chief responsibility is to relieve her of her tough housewife duties. Forget commerce, business trips, unusual train rides, clients, the money that keeps us from penury. All hail, Lysette!'

'William. William. You are not in a court. And employing sarcasm will not help matters.'

Lenov had given him a rap, had firmly indicated where the lines of warfare should be and yet Wagenknecht had managed to trundle out words which had been shadowing his heart for years.

He leaned forward, looked down, awaited the conflagration, the inferno, the tempest that was his wife. He could not look at her face when it came, could not wilfully interpret the revenge that would scythe him behind closed doors.

'Lysette?'

Wagenknecht had a photo of her from ten years ago that he still occasionally showed off. In blue Lycra joggers with zips at the calf and a thick, winter turtleneck sweater, she had beamed a contented, joyous smile. The pebbled beach around her had served to lift and contrast what he deemed to be her beautiful rabbit teeth. And the face – it was without concern, warm, articulate – ready to delight him, plunder his finer side.

Dear Mr Cameron – What chance the homeless man, a rueful human conquered by his emotions?

'The family was always too big an engine for him. He lost his humour, his empathy. If only he'd explained his work commitments in a less forceful manner.'

Aaah – the cool metaphor. A rare treat, thought Wagenknecht. If only such control, such grace was prevalent toe to toe. Women. Wo-men. Woe-men. How had he fallen into this sham marriage, this rag-and-bone parlance? Perhaps his error had been not following stocks anymore – their jaunty simplicity. Instead, he followed women – their heels, hips, breasts, eyes. Foolishly, he had imagined a portfolio of tender women – each ready to link his arm, see him as a prototypical man (one who had bypassed the traditional curriculum).

Maria. (Before their reunion.) He had laughed at her suggestion, her vow of love. *Love?! What the hell was love?!* He was a kid – a mere twenty. Maybe that was their downfall – unrecognisable under the meagre light of a pub car park; his reaction blundering, careless, indelicate.

With Lysette, six years on, Wagenknecht had wanted to just horse about, hold her tight and do nothing but criticize the world. That had been their bond, their raison d'être, the intimate wiring of their scheme. There had been no preliminary talks regarding the turning off of the taps. Long walks. Cinema. Chicken tikka Balti. Theatre. Sundays in bed. Country pubs. Current affairs. Tolerating his love of boxing, football, ping pong and tennis. All of it had stopped.

Dear Mr Hume – You say knowledge cannot go beyond experience. Well, I have fallen into something very dark which makes me think otherwise. This psychological dressage has me wailing over the jumps. I am suddenly in a world of no possibilities, hindrances everywhere, my naturalness treated as unnatural. Next to me lies a stranger – one I am not permitted to wake before 8am. Randomness, spontaneity and desire are seen as old modes of love. If I place my hand on her, she treats it as a criminal act.

'You sub-contracted our love. Shooed it out through the cat flap. Did you imagine that masturbation was a suitable surrogate? Did you imagine that I no longer needed your contours or a bit of culture? Christ – you became cold.'

They were far from an armistice. Those last words would come back at him in the form of a slap, possibly a feeble kick. He would be reminded of his disrespect, his honesty, the audacious swing of his exchange.

Lenov intervened: 'William – you're off the point. Lysette made mention of family...work.'

'Isn't it all connected?' The truth commission was in full flow. 'Too big an engine, you say? Perhaps your unwillingness to rev up in bed killed me. Perhaps the motions of family life were a dreadful harbinger.'

'William. We don't speak that way. You need to moderate your language. "Rev up" is offensive used in that context. Tactless.'

'Led by his dick. Pushing his morning erection against me. What a seductive *tool*! Subtlety dead. Everything I used to see in you – gone.'

Wagenknecht accepted some of the clamour, the disgust. A woman's joy changed, shifted, teetered dizzyingly towards a pre-menopause land of overripeness.

But Maria – five years older. Lysette – eight years older. The theory was that *they* could imagine a pre-responsibilities world, draped around a younger man, but that he – Wagenknecht – had to age according to the laws of science, adjust his animalistic and sensual needs.

He had coincidentally chosen women who did not have an escape plan. Maria – no father. He had smoked himself to death. Lysette – that same paternal inadequacy. In and out of jail. Mysteriously dead before his daughter's first birthday. Wagenknecht, a liker of big families – their protective net, their warmth, their Christmas inebriation – hadn't minded. Such paltry numbers did not send him down another path. It was just that years into each relationship, he began to see the added weight. Not a burden. Not an encumbrance. But the realisation that he was to be friend, father and partner – a noxious mix.

'What is man to do? I played the role you assigned me. Sometimes I wouldn't express a *real* opinion for a month. But still – no kissing. No want or need.'

'That always had to be your motive.'

'Well, y…' Wagenknecht pulled back – couldn't say the word. It would cost him. Lenov would switch corners. Unbundling the truth was a form of voodoo.

"The question of the human has become hopelessly tethered to a thoroughly rational, self-determining subject…Thinkers have plotted the failures and blind spots of the modern, autonomous self. The philosophical project of Enlightenment modernity has long since been revealed as a fiction grounded in the ruse of a Cartesian Cogito that, even in its doubt, was always naïve about the power of reason… the modern self has been scattered amidst the ruins of an

Enlightenment reason that imagined itself pure and autonomous."

Myth. Romance. Existentialism. They were all missing, in too short supply, depleted. Wagenknecht had them all under the duvet and that is what Lysette did not understand. This was not the phallicism she imagined, but a getting to the right place – the home of laughter, frankness, cursing, wit, warmth. In the graceful kneading of her contours, he found more of himself – most of it ungrudging, generous and begotten.

'Why did you stop?'

'It became unnatural, a little forced. I still cared, but…'

'You lost interest in me. Stopped asking questions.'

'*You* lost interest in you.'

A quiet filled the air. He had hit the bell on the pinball machine, plugged or rather drawn out her biggest regret. There was nowhere to look. For a moment they were in three separate spheres.

After ninety seconds, she spoke: 'Yes. I did…'

There is no progress! he felt like shouting. It is as Diderot proclaimed. The whole game is just probability. And so humanity scrambles around in its pit, people perplexed. Is there a type of cooperation and amelioration that we missed? Dialectics had supposedly cured the pre-17th century thirst for winners. The duel, whether mental or physical, had been superseded. Misplaced deference was no more. "Toleration of a degree of moral uncertainty was the condition of the collective production of any future moral certainty." We had gotten lost so soon though. $E=mc^2$. The scientists had given us warfare, not values. Lysette was the atomic weapon that now wondered over its shell.

Surveillance. We were all under surveillance. Diderot, for his 'Letter on the Blind' and *Encyclopedie*, and Wagenknecht for pushing a branch of human knowledge that lent him pleasure: the great bust and feral hair of the female. Modern economists gazed down at their prettified work but knew it could not save us. Only a lick, a kiss at the side of the clitoris could do that.

Some of Wagenknecht's old school pals had been caught – not by surveillance but by modernity's crib, the weight of its blanket, expectations in exchange for comfort. Godledge, the large-brained mammal but with absolutely no ambition had turned his back on a career. Better to be free of politics, nepotism, the arraigning laws of the land (triggered when you put your head too far above the parapet). He could only look at life in one way – with frankness. And such engagement proffered little. It frustrated the finest minds on the block today.

Austoff – he had been a different case. Brilliant at chemistry (Wagenknecht had sat on the bench next to him – bathed in some of their 'teamwork'). Biology – down with the worms and photosynthesis. Physics – incredibly in tune with its formulae, its rainbows, the world-changing effrontery central to its quantitative thinking. Austoff had gotten the job his talents warranted – programming computers – but the speed of the role had wiped him out. He had no wish to surge through life, no wish to upset his internal rhythms. The masters liked to gorge on efficiency, but Austoff could not give them that. It was a form of bullying – the same as when his side-parting was slapped out of place. Too many years of that already. This was meant to be civilized, wasn't it?

They – his employers – could only quote Bellow: "Depressives cannot surrender childhood." 'This is the big world now, Austoff. Smile and run. Smile and run.'

'No – that is not me.'

'Then walk.'

Wagenknecht knew many more – clever, thought-wielding individuals, capable men and women cut down, not understood, loaded aboard a forgotten ship. Big dreams, big depression: the psychopaths in charge. Was dreaming now illegal? Wagenknecht often watched them – the princes of the day; willing servants really. Their gift? Memory. Lifeless, phlegmatic impassiveness. A whimpering collection of words which bloodied the English language: traction; granular; comfort; going forward; belter; high level; on board; drill down. What if we shot them, slowly shifted towards a world where we could bring into harbour the forgotten ship? Subcommando Marcos would approve. Plenty would revel on witnessing the picnic of corpses. But not enough. More would be outraged. 'How dare you shoot these fine men!' 'Fine to whom?' 'Their families. International trade.' 'They help us survive, do they?' 'Yes – I think they do. Did. And look at them now…'

"Humankind cannot stand much reality." Wagenknecht knew the quotes, knew that the poets had lost their place. He tried to inhabit the midway point – between hardness and softness. Dallied in both camps when needed. His justification? Scotty and Jasmine. Always them. And he had his mecca – a place for prayers, silence, deeper thoughts.

Here. Here it is. Where he used to live. Braggy Boredman. On this stinking corner of a four-lane junction in an old semi with a too-steep driveway. This proves you can succeed. Boredman – not two, three or four like Austoff and Godledge but number one. The don. The brain. And an August baby like Wagenknecht – the youngest in the class. Brown, maybe reddish hair – a slight curl to it. Angelic features. Witty, but not cruel. An example – a pure example – of conceitedness not embraced, vainglory pushed back. His nickname – Braggy – merely a title from others, a warning perhaps, that such a brain could easily harness itself up to the economic circus, the trampling elite whose faces were smothered in cake.

Last seen in a pub in Choton when they were twenty-two. Wagenknecht's handshake twisted into something quite fashionable, yet the warm eyes of Boredman still there, the cheery *University Challenge* buoyancy very evident – not yet serviced by Mammon.

Were entrepreneurs exempted? Did their genius have comforters around it – dependants less inclined to exploit and misuse? Could they play *and* be accommodated – the invisible leash loosened? Wagenknecht had seen a resilient humour in such people. Although not necessarily in control, their flailing body of ideas and sharpness warmed people, beguiled and inveigled them.

Was Wagenknecht sharp, full of silky reasoning – more than a canapé to the stiff bosses above him? When the temperature was right – yes. When the mood of the brokerage took on a slightly nihilistic, free-swinging air – yes. But he was losing his manners fast, his lightheartedness, and such traits were the entrée, the fixing of ears. The kids (the pre-35 crowd) coming through the ranks still had them. Their joyfulness was even regenerative at times. It also served to isolate him though. His great concern was that he had nothing in common with a huge proportion of mankind.

Consequently, he forgot people's names. Stood at the photocopier, the drinks machine, entering reception, exiting the building – casual colleagues would call him: "William." He would nod back, loosen his language ("Y'alright?") but fail to remember who they were. He had a rough idea of what they did, but their names eluded him – sometimes for days. It was vaporous, impolite. Even if they were nondescript or disinteresting, he ought to know. He…

Dear Mr Darwin – This natural selection business. Are you saying that the lazy, idle and those that don't adapt are left behind? Society must inevitably reflect the harshness of nature, I believe were your words. But doesn't this lead to a bastard colony where the good are shunned? What are we chasing or running towards if that is the case? And not to have a transcendent goal for fear of it being a threat? Your studies are appreciated. They have uncovered important areas of man's evolution. But they are limited, unchallenging and obedient in the manner of Heidegger. True human nature should not dance with nothingness – risk its vitality falling into a dark pit – but instead make decisions that bring light and dampen rage. You need to step aside, sir. It is time for the weak to rise. We need to alter the imprint of the human.

He had pulled them backwards in the pram (Scotty and Jasmine) – kept the sun off them. The hot summers in Choton had tried to unsettle them, burn their temples, have them blinking at nature's mighty force. The routes were mostly polluted with the exception of the canal, and the roundhouse which took you through fields with cows and sheep.

An early fill of animals, thought Wagenknecht. Good. That is how it should be. Added to their cats and the ducks, it felt like they were tracing their way around the world – absorbing expressions; behaviour, rivalry and foolishness.

Jasmine, when they had driven out to a park, would simply clamber all over his reclined frame – sometimes go beyond the picnic blanket, onto the fresh grass, sometimes pause on his chest and sweetly look at the landscape surrounding her like a miniature Stegosaurus. Her features were those of a cherub. Her strawberry cheeks and fine hair encapsulated an essence and wonder that were tapered down when you grew up. Adapt. Adapt! He hoped she didn't. He hoped the world would be ready to take on her foibles, her idiosyncrasies, the slow, almost languishing beat within her which sought truth.

You grind things out for *two* generations when you become a father, thought Wagenknecht. You're running *two* tracks – dipping at the tape for the kids as well. The bond is much greater, to you, than the previous bond of father/son, mother/son. It's a taxi ride up the family hierarchy.

Wagenknecht wished to halt or slow the day when he would be at the top. He didn't wish to peer out and have no protection, no comforting arm in the form of a place to go, eyes to meet, history to depend on.

Scotty had begun to sense his fear, the anxiety which sometimes lit up inside him. He looked at his father still with hope but it was declining, transmogrifying into disappointment. This faded lump before him – was he to mimic everything about him, listen to the better words that came his way?

Wagenknecht had begun to shout a little. His frustration with Lysette was finding outlets. The wrong outlets. He expected something of Scotty that he did not expect of Jasmine: consistency.

'Stop scootering through those flies!' He thought the dark patch on the floor was a silhouette at first, but then realised what Scotty was doing – speeding amongst them, thousands of them in the hot sun, this filthy gathering of shit-orbiters.

'What are you doing?!' Wagenknecht had grabbed the scooter from off the path, released it from Scotty's soft grip and flung it onto the grass.

'You bastard! He's only…'

'Only bathing in flies! Washing his hair in winged filth.'

'Give it him back.'

'So we don't take a stand? We don't speak in concert?' Wagenknecht was losing himself as he said it, but this was Lysette in top gear – frustrating him, not agreeing with anything mandatory, logical, pulling his 'lack of romance' into the public sphere and taking great delight from distortion.

'An eight-year-old boy. You would threaten an eight-year-old boy.'

It wasn't even a question. Lysette did not deal in questions. Just facts. Statements. Insane observations.

What could Wagenknecht say to such a thing, such mendacity, such rotten fallaciousness?

Jasmine was behind them, on her small bike, perhaps wondering over her parents, taking in the scene, using the same paints as her mother.

This is what happened, thought Wagenknecht. Errors could not be resolved in a fleeting way, corrected on all sides, placed where they ought to be and surpassed. There had to be a dossier, a thesis, a rinsing of the last ten years.

Only Heselglass had it worse. Heselglass – his fine friend from work, an old Trojan and stout, three-marriage pro. He claimed to have been bumped out of life. Car, house, bank balance, jewellery, pride – his first wife had taken them all. Heselglass, for all his duties to society – he had served in the 2nd battalion army, guarded the seemingly invisible Rudolf Hess at Spandau Prison – had been reduced to a level just one up from a tramp.

'Man leaves a marriage with a smaller vocabulary, William. Of that I am certain. Expletives take over. Squabbling becomes the norm. And yet, I did it again – twice.'

Having this man around eased Wagenknecht's pain. Whether literal or not, Heselglass's words were pitched in the manner of a permanent comedy sketch. The lack of a smile added to their power. These were deep rolls of thunderous experience handed out like nibbles to a consuming few.

Heselglass – the man with the 38-inch waist, thick, thick spectacles, jellyfish hands, a slightly reddened face from his Cointreau obsession, but charming; a rough, working-class raconteur.

Women had preyed on this, sought out his generosity, the smudged bank notes which bought them meals, gave them travel, hung glittering studs from their ears.

Heselglass was not quite the archetypal sugar daddy given his modest earning potential, yet the seeking of companionship did a man in. And that is all he wanted. Companionship. A few trimmings, but mostly company. Someone to warm his furniture – perhaps welcome him home.

After the second marriage or *fait accompli*, Heselglass vanished from work. The great stories needed holding, crying over. A second divorce was a capable executioner. It looked man in the eye and asked him to fall or step into the sweet shop once more. Heselglass, hoping for a long-lasting gobstopper, somehow pulled himself out of the thick mire, examined his face closely in the bathroom mirror aided by the weekend morning light.

'At least there were no children. I believe it's harder with children. You're able to fight more without little ones – defend your crop. All the same, I didn't imagine I'd be here aged forty-six. I thought life was kinder.'

It was nourishing to Wagenknecht – to hear this, to have a template in place. To know that someone was further on than him. Yes – further on. WORK. HOUSE. MARRIAGE. KIDS. DIVORCE. WISDOM. Even though Heselglass had skipped procreation, he was a man you listened to, a man you stopped for. His jowled expression batted out story after story – tales that spared you the hurt. Because Heselglass was the man running across No Man's Land with a bunch of flowers sprouting from his sleeve. Heselglass was a cavalier, the bravest man in the north of England, prepared to be cut down at the feet of a woman.

'They compared notes, you know – wives one and two – held me up to ridicule. One of them would phone me, tell me what I wasn't good at and then pass the receiver to the other who would add to the list. I felt like a perverse head of development. I had brought through the ranks two wives – now in the senior squad – not afraid to tackle.'

'I try to remember the good stuff about mine – Lysette – from years ago,' Wagenknecht offered. 'She used to hang her tits over the bannister. No particular time. She'd shout me into the hallway and then watch – weigh up my reaction. What can a man do in that situation except hurtle up the stairs? Sometimes we'd screw on the landing in broad daylight. Sometimes she'd have candles dotted around the bedroom, oils waiting. That is why man works. That is the only reason man works – to pay for the linen.

'But then the sourness. I still don't know why. Not properly. Age? Familiarity? Man doesn't mind that, but women…'

'You get a better no.2 than me.'

'Hesel – I don't think I can. She's exhausted me. I see paranoia in every one of them now.'

The Renaissance – a break from feudalism, the noble summit of perfect existence. The Enlightenment – advances in science, the industrial revolution. Romanticism – the cynical study of humanity's underside. Transcendentalism – let imagination be the defining characteristic of consciousness.

You took one, the others came after you. There was no settling down, no shutting the world out. Wagenknecht recalled the therapy – surely fixed in such a period. He still had Lenov's handouts, now scattered on a desk in his garage abode: Marital stages – Dependence, Independence, Interdependence. From romance, to reality, the power struggle, finding oneself, reconciliation and mutual respect. There were stick men and women in various poses – your eyes drawn to the staircase you were meant to climb. Lysette had pushed him off during the power struggle. He was sure of it. Broken the spindles. Caused chaos. Made it clear that her eight-year seniority mattered. Even whilst selling him fairness, equality and that deadly invention, romance.

'Weak, strong, weak, strong,' Wagenknecht muttered. 'Which am I?' To love, to breathe, to evolve he needed his plays. Worlds had to be formed, his pen had to stroke the page in a certain manner. *Creation on the cheap!* No set, no instruments, no real people (cluttering things up), no costumes – just his lined *Scholar* books, his extensive use of colons, his head directing affairs.

Do you know how important it is that I put these words in order, give them life? he imagined having to stress to an intruder. Do you know?! Forget what is outside. Look here! At the Biro'd scrawl. Try to understand its magnificence, its ability to travel around man's mind.

His completed five plays by now had a little dust on them. They were protected from the light, however, encased gracefully in a handmade walnut bookshelf. *Directions. The Broken Heart Ward. The Accurate Man. Georges Debil. The Diffident Society.* Graft. A trajectory that Wagenknecht welcomed. What would he be doing otherwise? Boozing? Pawning his mind to the television? Exercising in one of those steel-laden, sorrowful caverns?

He was hanging on. To the old life. To a world less dressed up in ostentatious clobber.

Dear Socrates – What I don't get and what must have troubled you also is man's failure to dream. I know that you often lapsed into other worldliness, felt the clouds, but these brutes around us – even 2400 years on – seem to uncouple their subconscious, give laughter too high a rating. The panacea is philosophy not politics – some of us know that. But the interlocutors – they march on. I do not see them giving swords to the opposition or unenlightened as you did – an honourable gesture aimed at prolonging debate. Instead, these incomplete beings seem to trample that before them. Academics say you were at the forefront of the West's whole intellectual tradition. Well, as a modern sceptic, I would like to brief you on the continued popular confidence in the new order. Meletus, Lycon and Anytus are alive and well in the form of Hunt, Morgan and May. They have none of your doubt. We answer their questions, but they are above ours.

Those bloody Athenians! They had you down as what? A destroyer of laws. Sometimes I run with Hobbes myself, but let us not invent convenient, unprovable schmaltz – say that you were pushing the wrong gods, poisoning the minds of youth. Religious sedition? Was it that? The powerful have an unhealthy aversion to sedition. Personally I like a bit of disorder. There aren't many left, Socrates. There aren't many to carry the torch for you. Today, you would be sacked from many a boardroom – shunted out for not embracing a cheap decisiveness. They would peer at you from the end of the table and shake their heads, suggest that you find another gig – perhaps as Father Christmas with that overflowing beard. Just make sure the Elves have a good, working knowledge of the cash register!

Elenchus. And dialectic. They are no more, I am afraid to say. The latter is not as I thought. It is not really argument or debate but something more profound: the justification of man's deep-rooted beliefs. You would be shot for that now. Not to sense the mood in the room is a common crime. You must immediately un-frame your argument and join the filthy conga...

The chairs – that is what Wagenknecht had noticed. Counsellors or therapists had the finest collection of chairs – salubrious homes for the injured, reclining dens for those that wished to drift off, feel relaxed, unburden themselves of knots. Wagenknecht had sat in three – two of them out in the country, branches from mighty oaks almost reaching in and steadying his hand. The shifting light in these places – the homes of his counsellors, Lenov and her successor - was sustaining, invigorating. Wagenknecht's eyes were swimming, refracting the luminous particles. Austoff would be proud. The bipolar giant would approve of his impromptu physics experiment and the flood of light leading to photosynthesis. Growth – whether in plants or from the comfort of a shrink's padded chair was essential. Those that had stopped listening to its pulse – in whatever form – were doomed.

Wagenknecht feared that his youth – his teens, his twenties – had interfered with such growth. The women or girls that he had dated were sub-standard. Promise had shown itself to be a masked deceiver. Always one to link up with a luscious smile, Wagenknecht had thrown his hand in with a varied assortment of unsuitable chicks. Katy: Wagenknecht had turned up with a Chinese takeaway. Not two, but one. He didn't wish to stuff himself. In that meagre portion, however, his fate had been decided instantly. She plated up the food and then plonked him down to watch *Top Cat*. It was unusual, perhaps a punt at his emotional level. Either way, Wagenknecht wondered if this was to be it – being steered away from real involvement, misunderstood.

Natalie, a girl six years his junior, had been next – a rare blonde, firm all over with a permanently chapped top lip. The straw, flaxen hair felt marvellous. It was a prelude of sorts. They had met in a pub. He had spluttered her age ('Sixteen?!') while the landlord had been collecting glasses. Such buffoonery had endeared her. And hooking up with a blonde felt to Wagenknecht a little dangerous – where men ought to do a little national service. Her ability to kiss though had been woeful. Instead of mystery, she gave him a plodding march. Perhaps the chapped lip – delightful in its own way – was prone to a bungling interpretation of others' jaunts and needs. Its retreat, Wagenknecht soon noticed, was ice cream. Natalie preferred the kitchen to the bedroom – a dollop here, a dollop there.

Wagenknecht lay low after that. The textbooks on women had been wrong. A special island was required for them in their 40s and 50s – certainly. But just starting out and still messed up (unable to read the landscape) – Wagenknecht despaired. *Don't ask for me, if...if...you don't know yourself! Walk on by! Leave my troubled heart!*

If there was nothing single to track, to 'dig', to fascinate over, then Wagenknecht had a duty to explore existing nests – mull over those taken mothers, wives, girlfriends, partners, cohabitants.

Serena had been leggy with black hair – her body scooped into her clothes well, her face optimistic. Her eye lashes seemed to fan her very being – bring an out-of-kilter ease and insouciance. The backstory though. Wagenknecht knew by now there was a backstory. In the handing over of the day's sandwiches – Wagenknecht's small, Choton office using the services of Serena's family – it was not just money for bread, but money for chatter, connections, titillation and rolls.

Wagenknecht had been the employee pushed forward to conclude the daily deal and as much as his burgeoning prejudice and stereotyping had warned him to avoid this class of individual, his curiousness had been reawakened.

Serena – the upfront delivery girl, with a friendliness that *had* to be interpreted. As flirtation. As wonder for this 'other world'. As a need to experience something outside of her usual zone.

Where could Wagenknecht possibly take her? To his parents' house away from her council dwelling? Out drinking in the middle class pubs familiar to him? To pleasant cafes? The kid though. She had a two-year-old boy. He would be hauled along. At least to a) and c). It was a compromise which would enable him to stand face to face with this woman before indulging. Serena was clearly a giver – unlike Katy and Natalie. She actively held hands, kissed in public, was courteous in a way that intrigued Wagenknecht. She was leaning into his world but not in a grabbing sense. Everything she did was perhaps modelled on TV actresses because Wagenknecht was certain that her own world was troublesome – full of the usual cast of raging partner, directionless parents, and low culture.

Wagenknecht had to blank this out. It was just the woman before him – her hair like a Chinese doll's, her smile full and gleaming. They had laid the child down in the front parlour – his Koala bear and its eucalyptus leaf clutched tightly – and skipped up to Wagenknecht's room. Ready. For the unveiling. For his first association with infidelity, adultery, the act or denuding which damned us all.

'Take them off,' she insisted.

'No – you first,' Wagenknecht countered.

He slipped off her top and handled her bra – lowering the famed piece of cloth until it was at her belly button, unhinged, de-coupled and ready to be thrown aside. What Wagenknecht saw next was not the chest he'd imagined, not the separate, beautiful identity that usually stirred him, but rather a nebulous and amorphous concoction, a splodge without shape or fullness.

What a *let down,* fired into his head. Such a bust gave him nothing to run his hand down, over. He could not weave in and out and around because there was no magnificence or proudness to celebrate or dance over. No great sphere at the lower edge.

He held her – tried to re-engage by kissing her neck, smelling her hair. He offered up a half or three-quarter erection – something she would look to bolster.

Why? Why the con? There had been no padding, no overt manipulation but the unwrapping...it had led to him being duped, disappointed.

Think! Think of the girls or women that you declined! Nadia. Kim. Mia. All of them sweet, likely to have a longer fuse (in terms of craziness). *Sexiness versus kindness? Was that the deal, God? No having both?* What was Serena then? What was she now?

They moved onto the bed – Wagenknecht's slim, single mattress, his early twenties' retreat. He stroked her. The ends of his fingertips played along the crevices, but he wished to usher her out, re-clothe her, send her on her way. His kiddish understanding of perfection had been shattered. The longer they lay down together, the more he wished to roll her frame off the bed. Into a rug. Into a giant piece of wrapping or delivery paper – despite her willingness, despite her ardour.

'Fuck me then.'

'I don't have a condom.'

'It doesn't matter.'

I think it does, Wagenknecht said to himself. I have no wish to father your second child. *Christ!* There was an immediacy with these types, a short term, gallivanting nut swirl of an agenda. You fuck. You get pregnant. Life works itself out. *Really?!*

One wrong fuck and you join a cast of people, an extended family, who instantly have a stake in you – a posse of individuals whose chief characteristic is anger.

Wagenknecht, still the gent, still a flamethrower of sensitivity, held her for twenty minutes. She whispered encouragement, tried to pull him off his track, grabbed at his member, but Wagenknecht had the image fixed in his mind. Of deranged in-laws. Of Radio 1 instead of Radio 3. Of a pan-beating race never out of it, never calm.

Dear Ms Torgerson – you talk of a "thick old head" in what must be one of the most grand, melancholic lines ever dueted. What a voice can do! How a few words in the right chord can lift two decades of a man's life and leave them trembling, prostrate. But the unspoken. It shapes our life, doesn't it – slots its mood into our expression. That is where the real worry resides. Thank you for your art though. Do thank Mr Staples as well. He knows more than most – is able to decipher human warblings.

Wagenknecht tipped himself off the bed, reached for his pants and stared at Serena for a moment. There was no on-loan smile or well-researched grin. In that respect she was genuine. Nor did she have the face of a woman whistled at too many times. What lay before him, still writhing a little – begging for an erection or finger – was a woman looking to jump a class. Could he blame her for that? An attempt to re-house her child? Not entirely. But she had gotten the wrong brother. Wagenknecht was the polite one – sure. Yet such a quality was not on the middle class tick list.

'Come back…'

'I can't. Another time.'

Leonard. Douglas. They wouldn't land themselves in such a situation. They didn't *do* mothers, those that had already started a family. Something unsavoury about it. Something that reflected the poor judgement of the woman at hand. *Terrible of her not to find security for the next fifty years!*

How great then that a week later when the archetypal Ford Sierra pulled up outside the house – Serena's scrawny partner pointing and bawling (working class women always spilled the beans) – that he should pick out Leonard as the culprit! Leonard – home for the weekend, a flourishing career as a chartered accountant and tax specialist – answering the door, thus becoming the default shagger of this little man's Chinese doll. Incredible what probability does – frames a man in seconds (twenties, reasonably good looking, well spoken...*the real crime*).

'You go near her again! You touch her and...'

William and Douglas had wondered at the noise, crowded into the porch, unknowingly frightened him off – the kid's father. A final few cries as he backed up the drive to his souped-up car with the double exhaust. But nothing physical, apart from a strange kick at the holly tree. Those were the days when the porch was a straightened '7' shape into the house, not the door followed by door that now prevailed (re-developed by madcap Uncle Terry).

Nobody stormed such a house, thought Wagenknecht – risked taking a man down, before having to turn to his right. It was in the Navy SEAL manuals. Thank God for the old porch – its decaying frame, its pre-brick structure.

'You choose some rotten women!' Leonard had claimed years later, in his fancy shoes, his expensively-assembled garb. 'I nearly took a beating for you. *For you!*'

Wagenknecht knew it was a story which ingratiated clients, which levelled Leonard and entertainingly catapulted his grumbling. Leonard - with his straight, sensible wife; her frankness borne from her husband's salary. *And what a haul, what a booty it was!* Wagenknecht understood that Leonard was twenty times the man he was.

Before the double-Puritan wife, Wagenknecht's elder brother had dated well – flaunted sex goddesses with tight curls, run with slim-fingered, wild flowers who would flick ash over his torso. The 'settling down' stage had either evolved or been tragically prompted by the tight curl girl leaving for Australia; the same woman he had howled with, danced to the *Jungle Book* with in Burningham jazz clubs.

Now, he was a business man. He had grown in a way Wagenknecht found difficult to quantify. Something in him had turned to ice – become phlegmatic. Most business men talked, had a breaking point – bowled their secrets to someone. Not Leonard. His cheeks had puffed out. His closed-door world had strangely silenced him.

'A courageous brother stepping into the fold.'

'These hands need to use calculators, William – spreadsheets. You could have risked my career.'

'What could he have done?'

'These people like to get their heads close to yours – show you who's in charge. I bought myself out of that vile world – took a percentage of the police force.'

'You're saying the police have been privatised?'

'Not officially. De facto – yes. Sweeping the world for the rich. Most of their work low-level crowd control, intimidation.'

'But why London? You know Mum and Dad miss you. And their nephew, Garrett – they never see him.'

'Are you a hick? You expect me to hang around here with no ambition? It's *all* in London. Half of the world is in London.'

'You'll come back though? Once you've made enough? Retire up north?'

'No chance. It's too cold. I like the temperature down there. We'd struggle to readjust.'

'What are you – camels?'

'William. We all make decisions. These are mine. I think something in you might have lagged behind because you left the nest later, were coddled more.'

'What do you mean?'

Leonard looked at him squarely – weighed him up, saw sentiment edged with idealism. 'You still carry around this...sensitivity. Speak to the anthropologists, the historians, William. The landscape has changed, but people are the same. Vicious. Unyielding. I don't know what kind of office you're in, but the way you talk, you must be protected, kept at a safe distance from the scrap.'

'I buy and sell. I negotiate.'

'But not like Douglas. There are no physical goods. I think that makes a difference.'

'Hang on – you're an accountant.'

'I'm not talking about me.'

'But you're placing yourself and Douglas above me.'

It wouldn't come – wouldn't arrive. Any elaboration concerning his *own job*, his role in the big scrap. He was just a suit. A suit that walked floors, opened his mouth. There was almost something spectral about him. Leonard – his own brother, his square face seized up with avarice. How he "prospered in the belly of Leviathan". How the literary maestro, Bellow had pitched these types correctly.

'Perhaps because we're both still true. We're both still Forrests. Leonard Forrest. Douglas Forrest. Ma Forrest. Pa Forrest. The whole pack. Except you – William...what is it?'

'Wagenknecht.'

'*Vagen*knecht. What is that?'

'You know what it is. It's like constantly asking me what meat I eat.'

'But this *reverse migration*, taking someone else's name by deed poll – why would you do that? It's like you've left the family.'

90% of his dreams were dead. That is why. It was a way of holding onto something, embracing something more than himself. He knew there would be upset, a look of astonishment from his father, bewilderment from his brothers, incomprehension from his mother, but Forrest was giving him nothing. It had turned Leonard and Douglas into well-off citizens, but seemingly mocked his own efforts (no room for a third millionaire!). William – the daft ideas machine, the Ugandan raincoat specialist, the unfulfilled or naff entrepreneur.

Opinions. *He knew that if he didn't have an opinion, a strong opinion, then he had nothing.* Others would squeeze him, hold his life up to ridicule. Chuck the theories at them though and - despite the quizzical expressions - something happened. An embedded switch inside them tilted the other way. A light went on. It was Edison all over again. And how Wagenknecht respected such a man (if you ignored the elephant). When the cold reared itself up against him, then he thanked the glow in the distance, the glow above his head.

So he *could be* realistic. Praise inventors. Desire progress. It was just that the bullshitters had taken over, were driving the sleigh, whipping the reindeer, when the erstwhile scene had been one of tranquility, equality – *genuine* effort for cash.

Part 2: *THE PAST*

Wagenknecht, upset at the shifting topography, had obtained the necessary signatures, run as an independent parliamentary candidate in the 2010 General Election, felt and sprung around on the Choton School stage during the count. Routcliff and Heselglass had dropped leaflets for him – extolled and lauded his campaign, held him up as a torpedo ready to blow up murky dealings and destroy wilted ideas. WAGENKNECHT – A MAN OF THE TIMES, NOT FORGETTING TIMES PAST. It was a plea to the oldies, a slightly convoluted slogan but one which saved a portion, a favourite chunk of their lives. Why surge forward? he was saying. Why have the dust fly up behind us when we'd like to stop and enjoy – reminisce?

Even then, in this small town, the smear campaign began. Labour could not afford to lose voters. Certainly not to a foreign crack pot. And that is how they portrayed him – Wagenknecht, the commie. Where did such a man come from? How had he landed here on such pleasant shores? Forget the birth certificate. Forget Forrest – for rest. This was him now. The miscreant. The infiltrator. An accent surely put on. And the call. They had quite remarkably managed to get a copy of his call to the doctors, pre-marriage guidance, pre-CBT – a sobbing, moaning "I'll only ever be worth 23k…I forget things" spectacular.

They were playing it over the tannoy. DON'T LET A BABY RUN YOUR CONSTITUENCY. It was McGovern's running mate (Thomas Eagleton) from Missouri all over again, but worse. Christ. And people lapped it up, did not question the sauce or source or context. It was there – running on a loop. Wagenknecht: he couldn't hack it, couldn't handle his own life, never mind theirs. Entrust the direction of the community to this...wet...this pickled egg? No chance. *De ninguna manera!*

There was a momentary humiliation. People answered their doors – mostly the younger crowd – by shouting upstairs or to the other occupants: 'It's Baby Wagenknecht – here to garner our support. What shall we do?' A mock cry would follow, a small piece of am-dram – 'I'm only worth 15k...12k...30k...17k'; different values depending on the house he was knocking at.

It was harming him. His leaflets weren't even being read. The general public – this morass of half-intelligence – much preferred the Labour alternative of him (superimposed) sucking a dummy. Ah, the Neanderthal pit – the fighting, laughing masses.

'You should screw him like he's screwing you,' Heselglass had forcefully suggested back at campaign HQ.

'Hasn't he got a woman's name?' Routcliff had enquired, knowing the answer, knowing the realpolitik.

'Yes – Lindsay.'

'Well, then – dress him up in a bonnet. Have a few speech bubbles coming out of his mouth. Not incriminating stuff, but simple facts – differentiation. "I don't blah, blah, blah, blah...I leave that for Baby." Play to his crowd, laugh at yourself, but show him to be negligent.'

'Yes, capital 'B' – make an ass of him. Assume the identity he's given you. You'll lose the Leslies, but I don't think they're going to swing this election.'

'I know him to have four faces,' Wagenknecht ventured. 'His House of Commons "I'm out of my depth" on economics look, his Derek Hatton "dodgy deals" face in our Henry VII local pub, his sat on a train "wondering at the state of mankind" look (not getting it) and his campaign face, milking his local accent, shifting his jaw in time with the punters.'

'Too erudite,' Routcliff claimed. 'Bits of it we can use, but we can't come in high and mighty.'

'Toffs lose,' Heselglass confirmed. 'Certainly in this environment – a Labour stronghold.'

'OK,' Wagenknecht acknowledged. 'OK.'

He felt he was in safe hands. Routcliff he had known for a decade now. He could be a hard, deceptively temperate concoction but you wanted him in your corner. Anger at such an altitude he had never witnessed before. With most people it seemed to be a fleeting distress call, but with Routcliff – it was acute intolerance, despair in the company of imbeciles. He could bite you, figuratively bruise your very being. His nose resembled a rocket launcher, his tall frame the mad shell of a bygone, steel-like politician. And yet, he liked birds (the winged variety) - Kingfishers, Grey Herons, Coots, Great Crested Grebes; was fascinated by their craft, their movement, their habits. He would stop, mid-walk, home in on a darting colour, forget where he was - almost become frenzied.

Wagenknecht had to read extra periodicals and weeklies to keep up with him. He was already devouring the *London Review of Books*, the *Observer*, the *Weekend FT*, *Le Monde Diplomatique*, *Project Syndicate* and a regrettable subscription to *Forbes* (the home of the millionaire twit), yet he seemed to be lacking in natural history, Galapagos wonder. *National*

Geographic followed. Beautiful pictures. A parade of finches.

Wagenknecht still had to bluff it, hesitate poetically, allow Routcliff to fill in the spaces, but – crucially – they needed each other. Behind them was the guff that mankind laundered – numbers stripped of any meaning, a brokerage which paid their bills, the sad countenance of mercantilism.

Routcliff touted the hard, literary lines of Bellow ("a readiness to answer all questions is the infallible sign of stupidity") whereas Wagenknecht remembered the vulnerable ("the time of life when...the blemishes of ancestors appear – a spot, or the deepening of wrinkles...Death, the artist, very slow, putting in his first touches").

Heselglass was relief from this. No one could stay in Routcliff's company for more than three hours without a timely interruption, without a burst of gaiety. This was not entirely the fault of Routcliff – his seriousness steered, prompted, aroused – but partly Wagenknecht who valued their time together, saw it as a necessary development of their verbal manifesto.

And so laughs were secondary – left for the stumped and dumbfounded pallor of Heselglass; his frame and block-like cheeks daily victims, his lifelong support of Elton John ("seems to me you lived your life like a candle in the wind") staggering yet fantastic. Heselglass only needed to turn his face at a certain angle – the victim ready to absorb life's hurt for us – and the day was broken up, the mindless stabilising of reality didn't seem half bad.

Everywhere he went – women's cribs, trains, restaurants – he was the victim, benevolently exempting others, taking the blow, a walking Yin and

Yang. Sometimes you looked into him and saw a shattered hulk of a man, an exhausted individual. Then, you stopped...using him as a prop for laughter, a route out of the gloom. Limits. Breaking points. We all had them. No wonder he needed Elton John – the dynamic piano, the fluttering to another place, the multi-mood spectacular.

There was something colourful in such music, something that reached down and pulled up the earth, the tarmac. Heselglass – the fall guy. But he had seen things: Spandau Prison (with its silhouette of Hess); every continent (the bacon and eggs aboard cruise ships now the only seduction he needed); women's undergarments (his three marriages proving that *some* knowledge was derived from disaster).

His roll of words in doing his job, resolving dealing disputes wasn't always canny, concise or clear – the latter his principal duty. Overheard Heselglass conversations ("We'll see what's what...Take it from there...Give it a go") had helped the firm reach a new level of opaqueness, a semi-mystique which had the boys chuckling.

'You *can't* do that. You've left the client with nothing. He's no further on.'

'My words are great adjourners. I feel like a judge.'

Dear Mr Sartre – "Man is condemned to be free"? I sense a certain sadness in your expression. Must we fully understand the world in order to be content? Or was your concern around guidance? I know the default setting for existentialists is 'despair' – the universal human condition – and that is something I can respect, but the notion of decision-making and responsibility weighing on a man...yes, I wake up to such a state most mornings, however, what is the alternative?

Incarceration? Handing over the keys to someone else? Work is a kind of prison ten, twenty years in already in that you need it to maintain the life around you. "Man first of all exists, encounters himself, surges up in the world – and defines himself afterwards" you said. Mr Sartre – I don't know that I ever surged up. Where does that leave me? Needing guidance? What if madness is sanity? You start to read this world and realise that the moral keepers are drunk. How do you forge your way ahead then when you know that you need a certain amount of people?

Leonard. Leonard. He was back with Leonard. 'Why am I William Wagenknecht and not William Forrest?'

'Yes.'

'Because the name 'Wagenknecht' needs me. I can't improve 'Forrest' – you've already draped it in money.'

'I don't get you, William. You want me to stop earning?'

For a moment, Wagenknecht froze, looked at his brother, studied him. Environments really do take you, he thought – grapple with your insides.

'The show. I want you to stop the show. Find something different for Garrett.'

'Don't you bring my child into this. You don't know a thing about our lives.'

Only from the pictures, the photographs, Wagenknecht thought – the mass of calendars hung around his parents' house (facing him when he came across for tea, walked the ten yards from his spruced-up garage). Smiles, poses, bits of California in the background – their August retreat. He had never seen a kid decked out in such splendour – wet suits so he could swim with the dolphins, chinos, slacks, tailored sweaters, open trainers, T-shirts not on show in the high street, even tuxedos. *An eight-year-old in a tuxedo!*

Was this the world? Was it a real world? And Leonard – the Eleven Plus king, the O-level and A-level don, ducking comprehensive schooling, sucking on the grammar marrow. Sure, he had fought his way through, pissed on every exam put before him, but *buying privilege* – now he was buying the private jam for Garrett: Latin tests, rugby, attentive teachers, piano lessons, expectation.

'Who opened the gates, Leonard?'

'What do you mean?'

'Who opened the gates to this speed, this new mentality?'

'Don't go chucking in Thatcher as if she screwed you, wrecked your life. There was opportunity before *and* after.'

'But the grammar school. I was there, with you – four years behind. And what does she do? 1982 – it merges with two high schools.'

'I don't know about that.'

'What do you mean?! Because you'd *fucking fled*? You got out the month it was announced. You were the last of the 'golden' generation. And I was left with the hordes...the dribbling masses disrupting things – wrecking my classes. I should have sued. Four years stolen! Why didn't Mum and Dad sue?'

'Come on, William. We didn't have the power. We were a modest family. Was it really so bad?'

'They were on top of me – clambering everywhere. I was suffocated overnight. Three buildings became two. We were crushed in. The old Choton Grammar blazer with the elephant on it was retired and replaced with…something…I can't remember. But she – our badge, our motto – was out-stampeded. Magnificence was given its notice – told to depart.'

'Sometimes I think you want the perfect trajectory. Everything in place. No ugliness. A scripted life.'

'Why, you arrogant…You had the best of it and you want me to settle for less! A change orchestrated by *your* party. *Quick – shut the doors, we have enough leaders!* I thought the Conservatives were pro-grammar?'

'I don't know. It was a different era.'

'Selective amnesia!'

'William. William. Stop this. This is why you've struggled to get on. Accusing people. Trying to rip them apart.'

'Having a voice.'

'Douglas tells me you've had the same, single desk for twelve years. No change of department. No change of firm.'

'And?'

'Familiarity. It compounds a person's dogma. It can be dangerous.'

'What? I read. I know the world.'

'But experience, William. The empirical. Without it…'

Leonard was trying to do a job on him – fold him up, away. Travel broadens the mind. *It also softens it*, thought Wagenknecht. He knew plenty of packaged holiday frauds who claimed to have visited a country, when they hadn't even left the hotel grounds. Ninions. They were ninions. Or ninnies – whatever that meant. *Chicanery at full pelt!*

Wagenknecht was conscious that his own kids had not been on a plane, were marginalised in class because of it. Every fucker travelled these days, every little runt. But he had taken Scotty and Jasmine to Cilan, Marazion, Llanbedrog – the little haunts. Better for their soul. Away from the airport. *Better that Mowgli doesn't ride the carbon elephants.*

'Who are you? Hume? Who have you chatted to exactly?'

'No one of great importance. But there's been a range. A better range than yours.'

'So you and Douglas felt the need to discuss this? How? Where?'

'That doesn't matter.'

'Where?!'

'The golf course.'

'Ah, so you trounce about, trundle down the golf course, meeting a perfect sample of mankind and then worry about my direction in life?'

'William – I'm just telling you...'

'Leonard – what is it you're trying to invite me to? Where is this select club?'

'It's not a club. It's an attitude.'

'So I currently have it wrong?'

'*Listen!* I'm protecting you. Protecting my nephew and niece – Scotty and Jasmine...even Lysette.'

'From what? From fucking what?'

'From people. Shaft them before they shaft you. It's moving. The world's moving. Don't you feel it, William?'

Wagenknecht felt grief, sorrow, heartache. Who was this man at the side of him? Rockefeller? Darth Vader? Was this really the script, the only script?

'No. No, I don't. I see the news terrible in its portrayal of the planet, but neighbours – we have some good neighbours…'

'Neighbours won't feed you, William. Keep you out of the cold. Pleasantries are all well and good, but underneath that…Do you know about the Figwort family?'

'I can't say I've heard of them.'

'Plants. They're a group of *plants* – some of them semi-parasites. Great to look at – cow wheat, eyebright, yellow rattle, lousewort – but thieves. They tap in to the roots of nearby plants, steal food, weaken the opposition's growth, lessen the competition. Humans have different manoeuvres but it amounts to the same thing. Do you see now?'

'I…' Something in Wagenknecht had stopped functioning. He recalled Leonard's visit two or three summers ago – wife, Poppy and son, Garrett in tow. Wagenknecht had only just moved, forty miles from Choton to Fleetpool (further west) – given Lysette thirteen miles of coastline, the kids a bedroom each. Finally – space. Finally, a vestibule – no open staircase in his living room. Part of him felt commanding, able to look out through the thick, white-framed windows with a sense of accomplishment. Was this it? Had he made it? Were the solid 1962 walls his castle, his calcium, the springboard to happiness with Lysette?

She had been begging for the room, criticizing him, comparing their Choton existence to that of fictional families. Irrespective of his income, he needed to provide more, procure, replenish. As a father. As a husband. A semi-grand property was what she deserved. It was why she had allowed his penis to perish.

So long as I provide, she doesn't want the numbers, thought Wagenknecht. This was at least reasonably comforting – no joint bank account, just a standing order to her on the 20th of each month; pin money. And if his honesty for a second stepped forth – ignored the barren antics in the bedroom – then he would admit she was frugal. Beyond the house, her habits were almost World War Two-esque, ration-like. Comfort inside their new home, a good diet, a practical kitchen but not one for shops. Lysette – a rare breed. Still tough, irrational, unforgiving but not a hugger of plastic.

Leonard had called round on a wonderful day – his sideburns too short, his cheeks fuller each time Wagenknecht saw him. The sun was baking this comparatively cheap part of England, lighting up the pavements, giving Fleetpool a benevolent gloss. Simple plans. There were simple plans – cricket on the park before the beach; the passing trams adding a quaintness, the Forrests' position on the grass able to absorb or push their eyes towards the fine architecture on the promenade road (sumptuous detached houses).

The women found a bench next to the tree-trunked zip wire – Lysette and Poppy trying for common ground (easier with the interjections of Jasmine) but mostly watching 'the boys', scrutinising the gladiatorial run-ups and sweeping of the bat.

Two batsmen and a bowler-cum-fielder or wicket keeper-cum-fielder. William and Scotty versus Leonard and Garrett. Wagenknecht wasn't entirely sure why the beamers raged from his right hand perilously close to the face of his piano-playing young nephew, but it felt…important, honest, like a strike at Callicles before his tough streak was inevitably born.

'Leonard! Leonard! Why is he doing that?' came the cry from Poppy, the early fortification, the protective arm around her future Napoleon.

'Go a bit easier, William,' was the muttered response from Leonard – a raised hand to his wife signalling his intended tackling of things.

Garrett – when would his mindset begin to feel entitlement? When would the Latin kick in and the bêtes noires increase in number? Wagenknecht supposed that the high, fast bowling was for Scotty. He wished to show him valour in the face of stacked odds, fight in the face of privilege. He *was* aiming for the wicket, but the top of it – the bails. If he was to bowl Garrett out then he wished style to accompany him.

Another ball. Above the two sculpted wooden pieces lying horizontally in their home. Garrett – not his forte, otherwise he'd pick the loose balls off, send them for fours and sixes.

'To a woman, that looks like malice, William. Go easy.'

'Cricket. I'm merely playing cricket.'

'A succession of no-balls, I would say.'

'Bombing streaks of potency, I prefer.'

'Just look at who's before you – a little lad.'

Wagenknecht could see it, even the ungainly, too-academic poise of Garrett around the stumps, but he also saw the tuxedo, the penguined-up protégé, someone inching ahead of Scotty in brain power.

For that, for the sake of equality, he had to go down. Wagenknecht loved his nephew, saw him as a disciplined, well-balanced kid who walked like Pinocchio – yet he had to protect something. "Act as if the maxim from which you act were to become through your will a universal law." Kant's Categorical Imperative gave him conviction. The beamers were for Garrett as much as him. Wagenknecht was training him to pull back in time – take the occasional tennis ball to the skull, but mostly adjust his rigid body and engage in warfare away from his desk.

'Oww!'

'Jesus, Will.'

'Garrett…'

Rushing in. They came rushing in. As if Kennedy had been shot.

'You're OK, Garrett. You're OK, yeh?' They were Wagenknecht's words above the din and panic – a civilised crop of syllables designed to calm matters.

Poppy examined her son sat stricken on the floor. 'Follow my finger, Garrett…'

'Yes, I can do it, Mum.'

'Where did it get you?'

'Here.' Garrett lightly touched the corner of his temple. He wasn't groggy but certainly dazed, taken aback by his uncle's wild deliveries.

'We're pulling you out,' Poppy stated.

Pulling him out? thought Wagenknecht. Oh, come on – this isn't pro football, this isn't The Ashes. 'Poppy – let him carry on.'

A woman's stare. Disapproval. She didn't even wish to speak to her errant brother-in-law. Just a little bit of code between her and Leonard.

Leonard approached him. His face was safely away from the minors. 'Too aggressive. Too aggressive,' he half-mouthed, half spoke softly. Wagenknecht wasn't keen on the control, the taking of the high ground.

'It was just a ball.'

'Another no-ball. Thrown with something off-key.'

'He'll have to face them eventually. I'm prepping him.'

'Prepping him?'

'Yes – showing him bits of the world.'

'Don't dress it up. Don't do that. As if you're writing one of your f'ing plays. Take responsibility.'

Wagenknecht looked around. They were all waiting for something from him. Scotty wanted him to keep the peace. Lysette – hater of *all* sports – wished to stroll to the beach, stop this competitiveness, this brotherly bullshit.

'Alright. How is he? How is Garrett?'

'There'll be a bruise,' came the stark, cold words from Poppy, the ultimate non-contact benefactor.

The world is made from paper, thought Wagenknecht. Poppy – the ex-accountant, now guard to his brother's assets, not wanting it dirty or likely to impact the levees in *any way*. *A safe passage!* There must be a safe passage for Garrett. *Do not touch my son!*

She had sexless eyes – a Modigliani face. The nose seemed to lack nostrils. Wagenknecht could never break into a life like hers, handle her officialdom, her encumbered ways. And her habit of always staying in hotels when visiting relations – implicit in such a gesture was her transformation into a panjandrum. Lower relations housed themselves in flea pits. How could she slum it again? How could this former working class Irish girl hope to adjust her fluctuating thighs to the gamey residences of family?

Fleetpool had a Hilton one mile away – generous lawns, safe parking, comfortable, even stylish rooms but Leonard and Poppy had had a hotel recommended to them fifty miles further on in Blackrington. It meant leaving early, preparing for the stiff drive home in the morning, but the luxuries – the waxing of beavers, the port night caps – meant it made sense to them. Leonard would climb into his Jaguar, be obedient to his SatNav and away they would go; a double insult – not staying over, but also failing to utilise the area's splendour.

Wagenknecht gripped Garrett's shoulder. 'You're OK, Gary?'

'Garrett,' Poppy corrected him.

'I'm OK, Uncle Will.'

'How about you put one on me?' Wagenknecht prompted, tilting his head a shade, suddenly rotating his fists in the air.

You could see he wanted to, but Garrett's instinctive glance to his mother sought unlikely approval.

Set him free, Wagenknecht thought. For God's sake take his fingers off the piano for a moment.

'Leonard…'

Wagenknecht's brother was the butler. Passing on messages. Signalling the retreat of the troops. Risk – it was to be low. Garrett could loiter on the edges of his private school rugby field – stay clear of the ball as per Poppy's instructions – but boxing, even pretend stuff with the traffic all one way…it could not be condoned. Genes were a dangerous business, picking up environmental cues, and so even a pose, the hint of old-style racketeering, rough-house tactics were ominous magnets to a form of barbarism.

'Best not, William.'

'But I'm the receiver.' He raised both his palms so that they were vertically facing Garrett – waiting for a few shots.

Garrett's face flashed with a need for adrenaline. 'Can I, Dad?'

'No, Son. One mistimed shot and bye, bye concerto.'

It was said heavily. At least Leonard knew the value of physical interaction, thought Wagenknecht. But he had opted to raise his son in the manner of Karl Wittgenstein. Cultured. Ready for industry. In time, an intellectual bully. A taste, even a taste of the 'other' world, would pull him down, oxygenise the ape within him. And apes did not lead. Not in the big dens – the 'Waldorf' offices behind the city's walls.

The vacuous sheen of the Hamptons – Poppy loved it, liked to be stroked and pampered by its maids and servants. Perhaps because of that, her 'tour' of Wagenknecht's house had been sniffy, contemptuous, soaked in boredom and brine. The kitchen was old, needed replacing, but the structure, the location (300 yards from the beach) – couldn't she appreciate that? Leonard too had breezed through the house, considered nothing, stopped not even for an interesting photo or piece of art.

Who were these higher forms so far away from the soil, so bubbled up in their London dwelling? It amused Wagenknecht, but he also felt sorrow – the word that travelled with him the most. He had failed to reinvent himself; William had entered the fancy dress shop – an exercise each decade – but had exited with little more than a change of socks. He couldn't do it. The reincarnations had been too numerous already. He had stopped evolving and people were beginning to notice.

Dear Mr Jefferson – Man is born equal. How many seconds does that last? Does the feel of a blanket impinge on such naivety? Do the mannerisms of one's parents choke the optimism imbibed? Finery, it seems, is not widely available. Can't we mix up the babies and have some fun? In an odd way, it might even work – re-seed the world properly (toffs speaking from poverty and scruffs sampling grandeur).

Dear Mr Darwin – I must write again. I have discovered some of your notes and letters which give me cause to cheer you. "It is absurd to talk of one animal being higher than another. Who with the face of the earth covered with the most beautiful savannahs and forests dare say that intellectuality is the only aim in this world?" You do not exalt humans, Homo sapiens, this walking master that believes itself better than the variations before. In fact you implicitly question how long it will be before our turn at the wheel is up. Prokaryote cells, flat worms, pikaia, tetrapods, amphibians, reptiles, synapsids, mammals, primates –

they have all led us to here, this point. But God though – some assert that He stands rampant between man and ape as if we are the final coat of paint on the planet, a providential arrangement. I am not an atheist and you yourself grant that deism, theism and the like is "too profound" a subject, but shall we agree on one thing until a comet hits again or environmental catastrophe subsumes us: that intellectuality is a small, small part of the great plan.

Speed. They loved speed. Didn't stop for a second to consider the atoms around them. Wagenknecht felt the pull into his work colleagues' world, the raging momentum and self-censorship which delighted the stiffs above. He had tried to explain such a predicament to Scotty. There was good bullshit and bad bullshit – both counterweights to the true moral tone. We were all just monkeys still swinging in the trees, amphibians sliding out of the swamps. But what had lungs given us? Were we breathing a poisonous gas or the superior oxygen of civilisation?

Wagenknecht could only think of Ashpound with his high-decibel voice. Unconscious of his separation from mankind, he tumbled around in a kind of backward renaissance, an uncomprehending and illogical noumenon. "Nature's cruelest mistake," is how they described him; a fashionless, gnome-faced man without connections to the zeitgeist. Wagenknecht could read the world, but wanted little of it. Ashpound could not read the world but desired its arm. And yet despite his tangent away from normality and his stuttering logic, Ashpound had moved on.

He had acceded to a wage cut, accepted the humblest of desks and was fearful of eating outside of his lunch hour, however, he now advised clients – was more than an order taker, a dealer, the memoriser of etiquette and procedure. The holy grail of advisory stockbroking had welcomed in – albeit with numerous caveats – the great struggler, Ashpound. Such a state troubled Wagenknecht, who for years had thought about the hop. A change of company, a new gearing of his pride – desperate, desperate especially considering the greats, the giants of integrity who had left (inadvertently abandoned him): Usmann, Nawaaz, Barrow, Thomass, Dawsan, Sullivon, Woode, Thompsen, Khaan, Robshaw, Dunstayie – even Barick.

Who was here now, in the quietude of this Salchester 'tavern', this drunken floor of mediocrity? They were not even worthy of names. The tapering of their opinions suggested a weakness of heart, a barreled sacrifice. Take out of the equation Routcliff and Heselglass – different departments – and you had man not at the apex (as Schelling had deduced) but lingering tentatively with neither grammar nor semantics; fun-seeking hordes prepared to barrack a dreamer, stare incredulously at wishful tenets outside of modern culture.

I'm here, here, toiling with the shit bags, thought Wagenknecht, whilst Ashpound is free. Freer. Weren't the gods meant to be embroiled in a civil war? If so, then who was winning? *Who* exactly? Gods with the iguana-like jaw of Shilp? Gods with a simple, borrowed path ahead of them?

Wagenknecht had luncheoned with Ashpound's new boss, Pony – coincidentally sat next to him on a table of eight brokers and market makers. They had chatted, indulged in finger food (tempura and the like) and agreed that Wagenknecht should contact him –

perhaps embark on his long-awaited redirection. It had been a swanky basement restaurant hidden away beneath the street-level Armani via a long, diagonal staircase – its staff largely clean-faced, crisp-shirted women, its décor slightly Rococo and extravagant. Such gatherings were still an escape for Wagenknecht, a bumming of his staid existence. The beer put him three sentences ahead; his mouth like a kiln messing with the liquid language.

'Where has it taken us – this career? Do you feel vindicated?' were his private words to Pony.

'What do you mean?'

'Looking after money. What does it give you?'

Wagenknecht was racing ahead, asking for more fuel when approached by the waitresses, waving on in the additional mixed plates of food and replenished bottles.

'We protect people's livelihoods. We have an obligation to read to be able to do this – good, meaningful analysis.'

'But *you*. What does it do for you personally?'

The question ricocheted around Pony's head. Such getting to a thing's core generally puzzled him. *Judicious skepticism about the possibility of certain knowledge*. Pony. Pony Chepworth - named that way in his thirties because he always sealed deals with £25. Inflation had made it less attractive over the years, yet Pony was still at it - £25 in a top pocket, £25 down a bra, £25 in the shriveled hand of a needy pensioner. The money didn't necessarily buy him favours or services, but the gesture – the gesture itself – often hypnotised people. There was no suggestion of an order or bullying demand, but rather a game, a 'go on then…business should always be this easy'. Pony was aware of the Bribery Act yet he avoided its tentacles by knowing *when* to sweeten things. And never with clients. Just outside help that had an obviously nihilistic streak.

'I grew up in a children's home. I know the value of money.'

The words were stern. In them, however, he sought Wagenknecht's trust, orbited the retinae of Wagenknecht's gaze.

'You won't catch me playing around with geared products, hedging or trying to find a short cut to profits. I'm a bastard but not that type of bastard. This industry had been consumed by gloss – shiny exteriors which promise Tutankhamun's riches. I'm here to keep it real. What does that do for me? I feel like I sell gravity – traditional, serious solemnity. I feel like I'm honouring something important. Beyond that, I'll leave it to the philosophers.'

He instantly reached for his beer, looked unimpressed by Wagenknecht – how he listened, how his initial unresponsiveness dogged the room.

Say something. Say something then, Pony seemed to be urging. I'm not in the habit of wasting my words, sitting around with too-serious people.

Wagenknecht was still sweating out fragments of his youth – American psychology that had lynched him from the age of fifteen. He had written off for so many things – get-rich-quick schemes – that they had him on saleable mailing lists (SMLs – sucker might like). *The Neo-Tech Man*. Joe Karbo's *Lazy Man's Way to Riches*. He only later realised that the Dyna/Psyc (dynamic concept / psychology / psychic research) caressing his brain was effectively the work of Alan Greenspan's mentor, Ayn Rand. Rand – the wooden bitch – infiltrating his house; chapters seven, eight and nine (Your Unconscious Computer, Where are you Now?, Eliminate the Negative) walking him through decision making: "It is impossible for the human animal to even *exist* without a steady stream of decisions".

And before that, chapter three (Fear as a Factor): "Although few people ever realise it, *fear* plays an overwhelmingly important role in the early-child conditioning...Fear is always a hindering force. Fear is generally a buried force." Such guff, such cod-psychology had quite miraculously sustained him – through the eighties and into the nineties. *How? Why?* he now asked himself. It was the need for a short cut that Pony had spoken of – eluding gravity, taking a quicker track, wishing to avoid a *normal* existence, *proper* training. But look at him now – twenty or so years on. Who had the money? Leonard – Mr Academic. And Douglas, the inveterate heathen; his wardrobes bulging, his warehouse a giant cash register.

'What if you need to speed past the others, aren't particularly patient, have great difficulty with small talk?'

'What are you talking about now?'

'I'm extending the money theorem into earning. Not investing it, but earning it.'

'Listen, William. A couple of the market makers speak highly of you...tell me you're the kingpin of dealing – sharp, quick, a good communicator. You seem to have strayed off that track right here and now. It doesn't concern me greatly, but when you screw your head back on, give me a call.'

Wagenknecht stared into space while Pony made the customary drop. No top pocket for the £25 – only cheap, supermarket shirts had top pockets – and so he wedged it into his palm and closed his fist.

You did not say 'Thank you' after such an exchange. £25 was, after all, a modest visit to the petrol pump. It would take him 150 miles – could get him to Burningham, or a nice part of Wales, or part of the way to Lincolnshire.

Wagenknecht would not be contacting him. He would not run this time as he had with Douglas – embarrass himself, scamper away. What is worse? he remembered. What is worse than making an ass of yourself? Forbearance. Commiseration. *Say them again!* Forbearance. Commiseration. *You sure?* Yes. *Absolutely?* Yes. *Then get over here – line up for a different life.* Jesus – who was in his head? Was it still Rand, Karbo, the other quacks patrolling the psyches of the non-self-made? Tapping in to dreamers' needs?

He tried to shake them off – think of his favourite quotes, whether about himself or the wider, struggling malaise of mankind: "All of them have, so to speak, enforced the career they decreed for themselves by a relentless policing of their beat"; "20th century boulevard entertainment – a 'flashpot-and-sheet metal theatre of noise and exclamation'"; "too intrinsically good for the soulless scramble of life"; "There were people…who believed that in a way [he] was rather simple, that his humane feelings were childish. That he had been spared the destruction of certain sentiments".

Certain sentiments! Was Wagenknecht driving around in his original clothes whilst everyone else had secret pockets, a stash of cynicism and the masterly ability to shut things out? All he desired was a world still full of wonder. And because conversations did not go the way he liked, he created them – wished to push them into ears, wished to sit on the front row in a theatre and watch a beautiful cast of people run through *his* lines.

But then came the barely perceptible whistling – *"self-pres-erv-at-ion soc-i-ety"* – and he had to ask himself how everything around him had come about. The bricks, plaster, spirit bottles, joinery, chairs, clothes, flooring, candles. Taking means you must give something back. The comfort before him had not landed so that Wagenknecht could better relax and laugh harder. It was a statement to him: which bit do you want, because if your plays flop we'll need you – your overalls are out back.

Wagenknecht blinked it away – he would rather crash his car into the supporting concrete pillar of a flyover than cease the exercising of his mind. Something had brought him here to this point – a god, Darwin, Lysette – and so he would cling on, try to prove his worth. *"Humble people seeking to communicate interesting facts to the Royal Society usually found it advisable to cite gentry as referees who would vouch for their trustworthiness: when the Delft draper Antoni van Leeuwenhoek claimed to have seen through his microscope vast numbers of little animals swimming around in pond-water, he invoked eight local worthies to endorse his claim, mainly clergy and lawyers, people lacking any technical expertise themselves but reputable because of their social position."*

What had Wagenknecht seen? Where were his gentry? Was it even possible to articulate the discoveries which poured from him? If he was honest, he knew that he wrote about minds – perhaps a ruse, a stratagem in that no one could disprove the findings over which he had sovereignty.

I make them. They speak some sort of liberating sense. But the audience – does it need them? He didn't know because the little theatres had refused to put on his plays. They had denied Wagenknecht the chance to stretch out his legs on the front row and absorb his life's work through the creased clothes and mannerisms of the actors; even amateurs – someone to frame his words in a molten cast.

And so Wagenknecht had gone looking for an audience in whatever form – taken the opportunity to storm Jasmine's school upon realising that her English lessons had skirted over the importance of the semicolon or point-virgule.

'You would treat this upmarket punctuation mark as François Cavanna did? "A parasite, a timid, fainthearted, insipid thing denoting merely uncertainty"? When setting homework, you *must* do your research, provide a rich background to the thing being learned. What I saw was so naked in its assessment of the semicolon that children cannot hope to care.'

He finished by thumping the desk. 'The strong comma *must* be treated better.'

'Mr Wagenknecht...'

'I've never liked chatting to people this way, but no one listens otherwise...' Strong, but immediately apologetic, Wagenknecht stood facing the Year Five teacher. He was trembling a little – fearful of the consequences, always too many paces ahead, not in the moment.

Jasmine's teacher looked perturbed yet slightly appeased. Her tits were slopped on the desk in her loose-fitting blouse, her light makeup danced across her face in a too-joyful *magna est veritas et praevalebit*. She was a go-getter, a dynamo, but this particular conversation confused her. It was unpatterned, decentrifuged – liquids and solids together. Wagenknecht – where had this man come from? Why had she not seen this spellbinding modesty on parents' evening?

Ah, the woman with him. She ran through the lined list in her head. Lysette – the partner who had him in check slightly. Parts of him had burst out, but not like this. Now, he was acting almost on behalf of the French, a Gallic consortium, the ghost of Proust. "The point-virgule is precious when the subject matter is complex...it can stop a sentence from touching the ground...keep it awake."

She remembered the poet, Volkovitch and his charming defence – a time before the grind of the school had suffocated her. Back then she had read widely – not indulged in the bite-sized excavation of education. People had applauded her thesis on Shelley, understood its necessary blasphemy and sedition ("Breathe out the choral hymn").

Was the matter before her complex? Was Wagenknecht to be threatened for his unorthodox approach concerning something so small? She knew that she could 'boo' such a man. Not from behind a wall or door but in front of him. Startle him – upset his workings. The man unwinding before her, however, pleased her senses, jigged what youthful celebration she had left.

'Mr Wagenknecht – I agree. It is a shame it has taken your visit to rumble that inside me, but yes – the semicolon *should* continue its reign. It is of inviolable importance.'

Wagenknecht sat down. He took in her red cardigan, black blouse, winsome glasses, tied-back dark hair and fresh, fresh face. Probably thirty-five – maybe a good forty, a Chablis, he thought. A woman. No longer part of the needless posing of the young. Sexy. Comfortable. Inviting. Her warmth tucked behind the words that transgressed her lips.

She needn't speak like that, thought Wagenknecht. She simply does it because she's inside these school walls. Trip her into the car park and her smile would forage his eyes, have him elated. A bunkum conversation would ensue.

Allow it. Allow it! For Ms – he thought of his daughter's reference to her – *Tillmann* had not sunk to that womanly level he so despised: condescension (the assumption concerning another's intelligence or discernment; jackbooted women screwing their heels into you).

"Inviolable importance." Let her remove his clothes whilst uttering it, spouting it. Jesus – checks on Jasmine's future work would be necessary; consultations with Ms Tillmann over the quality of language, whether his daughter was ready to see in between syllables, comprehend their grace, understand who they best played with.

Could he do it? Commit such a crime with the shadow of Lysette perhaps only three hundred yards away – through a couple of ginnels, under the street light of their congenial road.

He rubbed his hand against the slight stubble on his face – wondered at fun. How could it be drawn back into his life, safely, securely? Wagenknecht had never made it past half way on Maslow's hierarchy of needs (physiological, safety, love/belonging, esteem, self-actualisation). The lack of a consistent, intimate partner, the banning of certain social groups (or total absence of encouragement) had tortured him, meant he had stuttered, not dared discuss esteem with Lysette. Esteem to her was conditional. She would only value him if he acted like a puppy dog, showed complete devotion and removed the need for satisfaction elsewhere, in whatever form. Thus, he was stuck, not wanting to adjure his children – explain to them the tipping upside down of their world – and coming up short with regard to esteem's battle lines. Perhaps if a play sold it would change everything. On thinking again – no, no it wouldn't. Lysette would have nothing to do with the outside world. Her pushing everything away was partly a manifestation of a lack of interaction with those other upright creatures, but also her past: no father, hypochondriac mother, bullying employers. It was a heavy cocktail – one Wagenknecht had been aware of before falling to one knee, but now, fifteen, twenty years on, he was not sure he had the strength. He had stopped growing – swerved vital unfurling and unfolding. "What a man can be, he must be."

Maslow had studied exemplary people – the healthiest 1%: Albert Einstein, Frederick Douglass, the brains *de profundis*. In them, he had found a path, a simplified order. Without food you cannot have security, without security you cannot have belonging, without belonging there is no respect and finally no accomplishment. Feed the monkey that is humanity. Wrap it up. Show warmth. And then everything will follow. How simple the theory was – the actuality. And yet it regularly fell – bequeathed to tiny, sucker minds both high and low; "Civil society intoxicated with its own power"; *the fear factory of modern work crippling the mind's intended adulthood.* How had society come to be configured at this specific moment? That was the question. Was it down to the ordered activity in our minds?

Wagenknecht had crafted a gig of sorts – that of mute genius. Since leaving school, he spoke less – understood that the tongue embarrassed you. At the right moment: *Fire!* A sparse, release of words – checked and checked again. People's perceptions – he weaved in and around them, took to listening more. The forced questions at school – that place of humiliation – were not present here. There were other fights – political, ideological, those surrounding efficacy – yet the slight pulling away from a mandatory class healed Wagenknecht a little. If not the maker of him, work was at least the waking of his consciousness. *Interactions with the world!* He began to see the befuddled madness. Numbers, gambling, nothing ordered – just the whim of humanity; a deep, arbitrary sickness (money chasing a vanishing target). And so all he could do was form his sanity when away from it, write his plays, use the spurious rascals above him as chess pieces in a much larger game.

The beauty! The beauty of writing about minds. Wagenknecht had a monopoly on certain areas of life.

His experiences, whilst suffocating and stifling, were hooks into the shambolic musings of a quiet elite. *Let them fund his plays but be outwitted by his message!*

Not always an improvement – this progress, this civilisation around him. Wagenknecht wished to call its bluff, lean into the heads of Rousseau and Strauss in order to re-commence the big argument. You like to fuck in a clean, clean house with white walls and a farmhouse kitchen table? Wagenknecht thought, asked the up-and-coming middle classes. You like to part your smart, blonde hair and smile in the company of a strong, triumphant man?

You are taking us nowhere, thought Wagenknecht. I would throw you off the civvy track if I could. "Rational and socially-driven civilisations are not fully in accordance with human nature." Culture is a natural organism, unadorned unity, "a folk spirit". The dangers of this 'other' civilisation which you push are clear: the "vices of social life begin to dominate…guile, hypocrisy, envy, avarice".

Wagenknecht thought of how it had played out so far: the hunter-gatherers, the horticultural societies, the chiefdoms, and now, complex civilisations. Had it ended or was a merging with silicon / artificial intelligence next, "an orderly retreat into highly-managed 'human' environments"?

Give me the simple spring of a pen, he begged. Let trade and conquest go to hell, he thought. But what of the big loss when civilisations fall? Plumbing – the tantalising management of water. Humans were not humans without it, he conceded. Both inside and out. When Rome took its hit due to the Visigoths (who weren't particularly full of folk spirit), plumbing apparently disappeared for ten centuries.

So where did Wagenknecht stand now? Cells, organisms, genes. There was a C.O.G. to life, but yes – he wanted his bath, sink and toilet (the bracing vehicles that Poppy in particular subscribed to). *Let nothing upset their flow!* Lysette he had recently berated for failing to bathe his, *their* children twice a week.

'Humans need to smell good. Not in a perfumed sense, but through cleanliness. Scotty and Jasmine – wherever they go – represent the family. Unwashed hair reflects on us. We become soiled also – our capacity to see out life brought into question.'

'Well, maybe you shouldn't sleep away – delight in the luxury of your parents. Those two evenings rip us apart, William. They do more than you could ever know.'

'You know why. Money. I moved out here for you, explained what would happen. Why do women always add to the list – surreptitiously stuff agreed deals with extras?'

'You work in Salchester, live in Choton and have a family in Fleetpool. Who else does that?'

Always comparing. As if there was a standard in families. Not seeing the weariness in his face, just milking him for more.

'I do not *live* in Choton. It's like a B&B two nights a week. Affordability. Salchester's neighbour. Could I drive home to here every night – do the sixty miles, pay for the petrol? You know I can't. *We* can't.'

'Then get a job here. That was always the plan.'

The plan – with its invisible text, its ignoring the terrain, the hangdog territory. Busting him. *Always busting him!* How ironic that breasts were his god.

Good tit. Bad tit. Lysette – don't you see? Don't you see what I'm becoming? A tired, old wretch – someone who flees reason because it makes me shake. I cannot be too long in its presence anymore because I am not used to it. Diversions from boredom – we all need them. Even Nietzsche and Pascal. The quiet struggle enveloping us.

The three week nights he returned home from the city – Tuesday, Wednesday and Friday – nearly finished him off; his eye lids closing on the motorway, drenched by the outside darkness and spots of light.

And over the River Pibble each time – nothing short of a canyon with a footbridge; his car wheels hugging the tarmac, hoping for few side winds, nothing that would violently alter his path.

Wagenknecht was always conscious though – of what lay below: murky waters and barely escapable mud banks. If he veered off, took a bit of the concrete sidewall with him, then the nearest hospital would not be nursing him. He would simply be a guest at its morgue – a 5-star slab awaiting his beaten bones.

Did Lysette want that? He often wondered. A £400k bounty of sorts was on his head – a multi-salary life assurance plus the policy he'd taken out on the house. £20s and £50s could quite feasibly be walking in his shoes, stuffing Lysette's bank account like an inverse Savings & Loan heist.

He did not quite see such malice in her face but it was the natural step up – from bitch to super bitch; a fleeting evil gripping her insides. Wagenknecht – the money machine, the human gibbon, taking it like a Jewish prisoner, bending at the tip of the pistol.

'Go on then. Go on then! Fuck me over. Have me scrambling around on industrial estates trying to find something, anything! All to appease your cotton wool head.'

A slap across the jaw. 'Don't you – don't you talk to me that way. I'm your *wife!*'

Very little after that. Wagenknecht, the cuffed wrestler, nowhere to go, an impossible fight. In the past he had squeezed her nipples, fended her off in a reasonably delicate way, but such a course of action now was inadvisable, the stirrer of a deep feminist rage.

He was to take a pounding, cover crucial bits of his face, let the fisted queen before him rattle off a few good shots and then run out of breath.

Have a heart attack! God, let her have a heart attack – work herself up too much. A return of the cardiomyopathy. If only toughness was mitigated by one's condition. Then he would be OK, safe. But now – let her clutch her left bosom, fall. He would phone for the ambulance coolly, have her shipped out. Visit? No. But grapes – yes, the colour of her rage.

Dear Mr Ibsen – you once talked of a pristine lake, indicated that such a creation was God's work. He is everywhere, around us, if we're minded to look, you asserted. Well, he isn't here. Is this Beelzebub's work perhaps? Does this crazed woman have horns, a mission from those in the basement? Get me out of it, sir. Get me out of it. And do not say I am to follow Abraham and Job.

Wagenknecht's woman – his *real* woman. *Where was she? What did she do? Had society built her yet?* Just to sit on a bench with her, explore her hands, feel the anti-Lysette ray of her eyes. Wagenknecht, the masked romantic, the crayfish on land, seeking jollification, pleasantness and fun – wanting something simple.

Think back – how many votes had he taken in the Choton constituency? What had the figure been as he'd trampled the school stage? 359 – welded in his head (the turnout 49,774). If there were that many willing to trust their futures to him (albeit 0.72% of the village), then surely one woman – maybe even five trialists – existed now that he was out of his politician's skin. If he could formulate a plan for civil society, then a loving relationship was indubitably not beyond him.

As ever, Scotty and Jasmine's faces proliferated his thinking. The female assumption was that man could cope without his offspring, without the light that filled a corner of his world. *How? Why? Because we're loaded up with testosterone?* Because we display a jocular, non-binding ooze? Don't you know what Salinger said? The only two people to truly know him: his son and his dog. There are no women, no partners in that brief list. So you see, you see it now? You're asking me to go part-time with two people that almost beat inside me. You're asking me not to gaze at them daily – miss portions of their skin that show them to be wiser, taking in the world.

My aim in life has always just been not to have my children pushed around. But with such a thing happening to *me*, it happens to *them*. The likelihood increases. Performance at school dips following separation. *Do you read this stuff, Lysette or is manicuring the blackmail your way, your only way?* Wagenknecht had known she was a smaller dreamer than him for some time, but to kill the vital seeds of his existence also – foreign lands, Asian food, politics, friends, education – was unbearable.

'That's what the prettiest tits do,' Heselglass had warned him.

'What – ignore others' needs? I'd call the whole thing dewiness if I didn't know better. There's plenty in her that indicates signs of life, originality and warmth – and none of that office girl moribundity – but when she snaps, Christ…it's an earthquake. I question the simplest thing: What time is Scotty's parents' evening? *I've already told you*, she says. You haven't – I only have the provisional time, the time we requested. *It's somewhere*. Where? I press her and she explodes. What could have been three or four syllables is now…'

'You want to be organised but women think you're organising them, doubting them.'

'Fuck 'em, Hesel. Fuck them all! Screams digested by the public as proof that a vicious man is about. That's what we're meant to do – come out with our hands up even if innocent. Give in to the psycho warriors, the skirted robots with their ditsy logic and meaningless stares.'

'Women have caused us to build bunkers – man caves away from their blithering asininity. Places we can eat properly, watch boxing matches, discuss the state of the world. Was it better when they didn't have the vote?'

No. But this was certainly an era of angry women. And Wagenknecht had been caught on the blindside – away from their developing fury. To him, many were badly buttered crumpets, troublesome aeons that stood between laughter and sex.

A thousand regrets a day – that's what Wagenknecht had. Regrets over what he'd read, who he'd worked under, who he'd dated, who he'd not dated, what he'd not seen, how he'd raised Scotty and Jasmine. For he had seen it, seen it lately. For over a decade now, Wagenknecht had been taught not to make mistakes. Such clumsiness costs the firm. You get a deal – *don't fuck it up.* Some of that he had taken home, drummed into his kids. Minor errors – the spillage of a drink – prompting a barbed response. But then something in his kids was slipping away – a black and white world seemed to be shaping them, injecting its snide core into their reasoning. He had led them to it without realising – a too-mathematical existence. Cheap judgement ready to pounce, sing patronisingly from the sidelines.

He wished to reverse them away – have a deeper imprint manifest itself on their thinking. Show them the plays – what can be done, what *they* can do. Explore, young Wagenknechts – *explore!* And do not be cowed by the stalkers in suits or the gallows crowd.

Dear Mr Cameron and Mr Osborne – I see you as barely out of the slave house, wishing to maintain a healthy ratio of exhausted grafters to the strutting rich, whips in hand. A double act of small, but self-deceiving intellectual proportions, you trigger the much-heralded words of Charlie Citrine: "If there are only foolish minds and mindless bodies there'll be nothing serious to annihilate. In the highest government positions almost no human beings have been seen for decades now, anywhere in the world..." The man in No.11 is obviously excited by his position in society, yet displays a hollow, mocking sorcery buttressed only by his female lips. As for you, the main man next door – there seems to be an element of McCarthyism in your tracts, your speeches as if still in your baby bouncer associating The Beat Generation with communism; a too-visceral rage, hard on your podgy ears.

Dear Mr Netanyahu – Would you like to gas them all? Nothing in your body language and bellicosity suggests otherwise. You have become a Second World War German – you must know that; slightly Third Reich in your desirable aims. But to inherit the uniforms of your slayers – that is some feat. To swindle the 'labouring cattle' amongst you and next door is a wacky but workable plan. Always wacky. Oh, you Jews, guiding the world.

Wagenknecht sighed – rubbed his eyes like a drunk. Sometimes he didn't know which bed he was in. At 4 or 5am, he would reach around, get his bearings, push his arm out into the cold. In Choton, his mobile with its alarm clock – possibly the most modern thing about him – was set on a wicker basket to the right of the bed. In Fleetpool, similarly everything was to the right but on a smooth, bedside cabinet junked up with his kids' bric-a-brac; Lysette's presence the difference – a noisy morning exit commented on later, dissected by her 8am frame.

You cannot please a woman like this. I am lost, unaware of my very location at times and yet she sends the hounds after me – my ankles nipped, my body sore from racing, always racing. I am a humped piece of human flesh, yet without the sex. Once in four years! Like a bad Masters degree. Why do I stay when I could sleep with a floozy or seek out some clumsy yet lovable thighs? I may be only days away. For this is no life for a man – forever retrenching and pruning one's life, one's interests.

What do you see in her when she's good? thought Wagenknecht. Nakedness. Warmth. A dexterous tongue. The eyes of an angel. Beautiful, beautiful skin. Old thoughts. Laughter. Yes – laughter, that relic, that sometime corpse. They *did* share a quiet resolve, a meaningful blast of rustling with the world, but she wanted too much of him. Compromise was not part of her dictum. She was a hostage taker, which had its ups, but Wagenknecht could not plan or dream under another's rules. *Screw me. Respect me. Know me.* He wasn't asking for a dutiful totty who painted her toe nails in a certain way – just someone that allowed him to breathe. Someone whose mind hadn't been rattled by forces known or unknown. Someone calm, but lingeringly sultry.

Those tits – Christ! You could not recreate them on a pottery wheel. They were *super* tits – dangling sensations that caressed his chest in the manner of two boats sliding out to sea. And the sea was his groin – pulsating, fighting gravity, displaying to her what she meant to him; not an ordinary erection, not a wooden commoner queuing for some soup, but a warrior's spear, an implement that needed careful handling.

Lysette, when she could be bothered, knew exactly how to tend to Wagenknecht. He didn't mind being a prize sucker. It did not concern him that imperfections in her were many. Under the 12-tog cotton roof – fattened up for winter – Lysette began the task of transporting Wagenknecht to a distant planet, of taking and giving with astute synchronisation. A tongue, a hand, a bite, a row of nails – all teasing and threatening him. No woman before Lysette had mastered the basics and more. *Amateurs. Blithering amateurs!* But it had to be the truculent woman with such mastery – a woman you could neither leave nor stay with.

"We *need* purgatory," a debating, religious cleric had said one evening on the radio when Wagenknecht was encased in his car. 'We need purgatory? *We need purgatory?!*' Wagenknecht had mimicked with a different tone and punctuation. 'Who is this protected, jumped-up little shit strolling around his rectory?'

Wagenknecht had punched the soft radio on/off button and sped up. People were no longer people in any sphere. So much had changed since the 1970s. Put me back there! he begged. Away from this built-up world of mock-fear and the real fear of neo-classical pimps. Seeing people shattered on the train upsets me, thought Wagenknecht. And on the way to the train – Christians handing out leaflets on one side of the pavement, on the other a homeless man bagged up, beard and sadness teeming down his face. Would Jesus have dabbled with paperwork, sought recruits, while the very person he professes to care for wept only feet away? *Wash his feet, do something*, Wagenknecht had cursed inside. *You must see him!* Or are the classes divided further?

Even the present was two different worlds: Salchester, the growing powerhouse close to having its own £6bn health budget, yet the poor picked out half-dead tabs from the top of the bins; Fleetpool, Wagenknecht's retreat, old worldly, home to a mere 30,000 – Decimus Burton an ancient visitor now – yet wiggling, speedy turnstones worth 10,000 televisions (the fluff and chunk of their bodies if not graceful then humorous and loving).

Was it a searing clarity? Did Wagenknecht sometimes view the only evidence he needed? He knew when he returned home that hot water *had* to touch his face. The light film of moisturiser – whatever the state of his skin underneath – *had* to come off. A bit of truth, back again, in the mirror. But his face was changing. It hung like a bad pair of curtains. Pleats seemed to be developing. Fear. He was fearful. Of something. Of those around him. Of his bosses. You say 'No' too many times and your star begins to dim. Yesterday, a witty splicer. Today, an outcast – the things around him heavy and disturbing.

Certain types of conversation – if I don't get them, thought Wagenknecht, I fall, chin the floor. They don't understand this. The pickaxed baboons above me survive on lesser brews, but Wagenknechts, Heselglasses, Routcliffs, Boredmans, Dunstayies – Lenovs even – need more. Not the forced merriment of this steel and glass world, but a tangible magnificence – even one which pillories you.

I can't laugh with you, you *bastard. Don't you know?!* rumbled from Wagenknecht. Two breeds. Yes – let's get this clear. There are two breeds of human: the reptiles that still secretly lay eggs and the proconsul, the first ape-like monkeys with better vision and no tail.

I don't even look at the sky. When was the last time I looked at the sky? thought Wagenknecht. They have my face tilted down. Don't you remember the words of Emerson: "The main enterprise of the world…is the upbuilding of a man. The private life of one man shall be a more illustrious monarchy…than any kingdom in history." And what do we have? Who do we get in this far-out century? Pernicious billionaires. Exceptionally large pillocks. The kids buy it though. They don't try to ban it. They buy it. Who schools them? He would chat with Tillmann – Ms Tillmann; see what kind of ethos was rolling around the schools; ask, whilst admiring her grey and beige suits, and short, polka dot – thigh revealing – skirts, whether it was possible to keep a protective screen around the future when industrial man (parent of the future) was fermented by speed, greed, banality and banefulness. Could you take half a dozen kids to an island and raise them properly? Keep them away from the mush of civilisation? Have them eventually rule, not with the de facto poker of a modern James I (outlawing theatre or demoting art) but with an eye on a semi-utopia?

Wagenknecht was certain that dreams were still there to be had, that the juggernaut of humanity could be steered to a better place. If not, either through a loss of his naivety or the noble lie, then the futile race would go on; people messed up; a bourgeois junta breathing for the population; fear on a bigger scale than WWII. When he stopped, he felt the world pushing him. When he soaked things up properly, he felt the compulsion to keep it abridged.

The chip shop suicides – remember the chip shop suicides? The owners of the eatery in his old village of Choton. Two white-attired, perfectly normal, seemingly content people – a husband and wife team. But then they saw themselves in front of the bucket of potatoes one night, wondered at their purposefulness. A steady stream of customers – some pleasant, some demanding, some humorous – was not enough. But then to think it together, lift the gun, decide upon an order of execution. What must that final glance have been like? Meaningful, knowing, Wagenknecht thought. Unlike Kant, he didn't wish to call such an act the degrading of humanity, the supposed "treating themselves as things rather than persons". The engine of the world had already done that – dehumanised man, turned him into a labouring unit with no shared grand plan (the core of which was equality and fascination). We encouraged the boundless prancing of celebrity and hubris, not the wonder and comfort of discernment.

If you wanna shoot, shoot, Wagenknecht decided. In some respects the gun was pointed at the world. Its weakened and distraught inhabitants were merely representatives of a wider shame which was blocked out; the resultant cadavers two more felled lives whose plea had not found an ear.

How many suicides does it take to close down a place? thought Wagenknecht. In this case just two – the disconcerting sign hanging in the window (FAMILY BEREAVEMENT) a PR exercise drenched in understatement. But what of the bigger places? Commercial giants? Five? A gathering of staff, certainty enunciated over the reasons for such calamitous acts. Troubled family upbringing, a history of depression – nothing, absolutely *nothing* to do with the conditions of employment. Let's declare a bank holiday, all retreat for one day and think about this sorrowful moment. But remember to come back tomorrow, fresh from mourning, and let's *hit those monthly targets! Wooooo!*

Ephemeral. The short-lived burst of mock concern. In the past, the people have been first. In the future, the *system* must be first. What a wonderful fellow F W Taylor was. Don't look at the workers' faces. We'll kill the natural patterns inside them, but so what – the law is with us, all paid for and wrapped up.

Wagenknecht remembered the Choton Evening News salesman, newsstand man – call him what you will; his day a varied play on those three words and six syllables. *CHO-TON EVE-NING NEWS. CHO-TON EV-EN-ING NEWS.* The pitch, the muster, the range of notes was dazzling – an outside orchestra. But then the death of the paper's keyword and a change to: The Choton News (some literal wag pointing out that the paper had been available from early morning for a number of years now). And so they had stripped him of his 'Evening' – they had stripped him of a third of his piano. He could hardly inject the same rapture into the redundant article 'The'.

Everywhere, march the spoilers with their 50 pence theses, thought Wagenknecht. Crocks. Wise-ass knowers. Smiling assassins. (His own job given to him by Shilp, the Marabou turd – still jogging, wading, opening his conceited heart to those that looked his way…Buzzards and Vultures for company.)

Dissolution. Wagenknecht had read the word some time ago, but only now did it hold a particular relevance to his life. *I have "risen from humble origins to complete disaster"* he shouted. *I sit with snide compeers who are drawn to procedural drudgery and thus make my old bones look foolish. Disintegration. Destruction. Termination. I feel it all. The kids are coming with their happy-go-lucky grace, pushing us out, making our problems seem whiny and inconvenient. Look at me as a burnt-out wagon! I have put in too many years! I can no longer separate my deeper concerns from daily life. What was it that Popper said? Plato's 'rule of the best' invites disguised tyranny. Yes – I believe that,* thought Wagenknecht. *I uphold such a tract. Intelligence does not equate to ideas.*

Remembering things does not constitute good leadership.

Forget it all and lie down for a moment. Lie down, Ms Tillmann – here in this hotel I have paid cash for; face down in your bra and knicks. Just let me knead your skin, suspend all life for a moment, be in touch with sensations that commercialism has killed. Slow. So slow. As it should be. Nothing outside. No movement. No cars. No people. Just us.

The room is reasonably furnished. Pastel colours on the bed. Clean lines. Lights where they ought to be. Furniture moderately rich. But you there, before me. Not Lysette. Another female. Prodding my guilt. But what is man to do? Exist with nothing? Feel no creativeness? Turn to cinder? I have to have *something*. If just the buttressed flesh from your undergarments.

Jasmine – I'm sorry, but she got me; looked at me and talked to me as if I mattered again. Yes, I am bloody weak, but what did strength ever do for me? We will not discuss your homework and assignments – I promise. What did your mother not do? Well, I felt like an Oxo cube – something to be crumbled in her hand occasionally.

Wagenknecht moved further beneath the cotton of Ms Tillmann's underwear, enjoyed her sighs and obvious pleasure. Christ – the simple things, but so often held up by politics, overwork and minor scuffles. The perfectly generous rump or posterior of Tillmann had him reaching around its curve towards her thighs. Thighs – the last defence before the beautiful crease. How much Lysette had taught him about that area but then locked it away as if chaste.

He did what she wanted him to – removed her briefs and undid the catch on her bra. Wagenknecht then continued the kneading, the massage, looked at the well-proportioned form before him and soaked it in. Keep her vulnerable. Keep her whimpering. Procrastination can be a good thing.

'Go anywhere,' Tillmann softly mouthed, perhaps curated.

Wagenknecht rolled her over, took in her impeachable frame. 'I just want to gaze at you.'

'At least undress.'

If he did it would be the end of him and Lysette. Over a decade of her South American bust, her brilliant smile – but too infrequent, all of it, like something encased in a gallery. How that bust with its deep valley had tormented him! Topless on their honeymoon at the side of the Greek pool and then on a remote beach; a lone cyclist appearing from nowhere, deciding to stop at the side of their blanket and take in the view or views (Wagenknecht seconds from knocking him off his bike: "*Looking out to sea or blatantly taking in my wife's tits?!*").

Regular visits to the heart specialist. "Do you mind if this trainee male doctor also looks at your tits?" Not the exact words, but a postmodern way of gaining access to what was his. "Don't be silly, William. They have to learn." "But not on you. All of them gawping, loving it. I can guarantee that this is a league they've not encountered before. And as such, they'll up your appointments. Increase the frequency. They take more, I take less." "I can't talk to you when you're like this. Do you not see the medical side? Do you not see that they're helping me?"

Wagenknecht couldn't see. At times he was a flailing, jealous boy of a man. When something is being shipped out with regularity, something that lives and breathes next to you – and you yourself no longer know its full beauty – then you are apt to disrupt such transportation. But then Lysette did not always go *out* to be examined, to be stripped from the waist up. Sometimes they came to her – the paramedics, with their electrocardiograms; often when she had mixed up her tablets - Propranolol, Candesartan, Ramipril, Naproxen - or taken one too late. Then the palpitations would start, the skipping of her heart, the rapidity and fluttering.

Stupid to think not of life at that moment but of a familiar scene: other men – strangers – knowing his wife's body better than him, sticking ECG pads liberally over her left breast. One man kneeling, the other watching (fiddling around, feigning disinterest) and Wagenknecht like a TV viewer, elbows on the through-kitchen unit, having to accept this intervention, this ambulance pulling up outside their new beach home; Lysette without a bra (her mature woman protest) to at least delay the inevitable – Mr Paramedic lifting up the two folds of cloth, surprised himself by the ease of this conquest. And then the marvellous tit on show for all to see – in flight almost; scraps for Wagenknecht who was the furthest away. The scene, the context, was not uncomfortable, but disillusioning. He was sadder and wiser. Yes – those. You never really possessed someone. And that is what he'd wanted. Devotion. The old church lines. A true *giver*. And yet here he was pathetically celebrating a stray nipple, somehow ignoring the severity of the scene before him. No, he was not a professional – a cyclist, a specialist, a paramedic (a man given free reign over daily delights). He was a dumb stockbroker – the highest level of charlatan. But need that wreck or plow through his grasp or clear perception of events? Had he let Shilp's standards pull him down?

It could feasibly end like this. Lysette's unerring conviction was that when her heart performed its tricks – not a pleasant show – then she could die right before him. Wagenknecht, suspended by life's perpetual hurry, had the scene locked in his head. Would he wait a while, hold his tempestuous and truculent love? Would he follow the actors in giving out a necessary flow of tears? He suspected it would be shock that first grabbed him – disbelief. Wake up, Lysette – wake up. We have a new plan – compromise on both sides. We finally figured out what each of us wanted. Wake up, darling – when we were good, we nestled together magnificently.

Who to phone? The hospital, the funeral home, her remaining relations? Was there an order to things after such a calamitous happening? Could he really be expected to let the body be taken away, give up on her completely?

It's just a deep sleep. Send the kids to school as normal. Stay with her and talk things through. What was it we came up against? Your affair. My affair. We're past that now. A new start. Too many photos to start again with someone else. This isn't taught. Fucked up at forty. Careering towards fifty. Too many distractions. Nobody watches the sun rising.

Pitted on the bed before him was the woman that might supplant Lysette. Did he dally with her on the side, show his cards or walk out now? Wagenknecht had twenty direct debits on the house, car and other associated assets. They took 85% of his net salary. It was the logistical hell that no one spoke of...facing him and he had no wish to join the messed-up ranks of husbands sagging away in old box rooms, corners of parents' houses that had become derelict and worn.

Comfort or love? Sexiness or kindness? Never both. Only the well-off seemed to revel in such pomp. I want to make you happy, but I want it to be natural. That's the hard bit. Lysette – do you see that?

Tillmann was watching him, beginning to question the hesitating form repeatedly roaming between her breasts and around her thighs with his right hand while fully clothed.

'You think too much. Just attack me.'

Wagenknecht began to kiss around the navel and then lower near the triangle of hair that gave an esoteric and erotic vibrancy to her. His head hung over her revealed, reposeful, reclining frame but something in him was feeble, noncommittal – messing on the outskirts with little intent.

'You look like a doorman. Take something off.'

She sprung up, fastened herself to the back of him and started to remove his outer garments. Wagenknecht started to shiver slightly. It was the same shiver that had caught him, that had permeated him when first sleeping with Lysette. To be desired, wanted – such enormity affected him. And by God's design – the luscious female. You could not draw a better form. Degas. Renoir. De Smet. They had all captured the exponential exquisiteness. Renoir, it was said, painted the aftermath of love – the languid and drowsy. Wagenknecht was far from that – slowly giving in, conceding ground, but not entirely acquiescent to the hinged seduction of Ms Tillmann.

Her still-lithe arms entangled and enmeshed him. Wagenknecht enjoyed the naked form around him but began to think of Lysette. Too much pride. Stubborn. Plenty of flaws. Yet he had sold part of himself to her. It felt like such a transaction could not be reversed. Like a deal in the market. Unless you traded again.

Compare them! he demanded in his head. Ms Tillmann – still those words (inviolable importance). Lysette hated such pretentiousness. She railed against even an aroma of pomp and yet she understood nature's guile and beauty. She photographed seascapes, hillsides, generally non-peopled subjects, a world away from humanity's 'growth' Wagenknecht now realised. Confined, stuck indoors on bad-weather days, unable to hold down a job due to her ailments, Lysette's mind had perhaps followed the half-insane ligature that strangled even the finest intent. Such fission though – a nuclear reactor. The rage in her face made him look away. And it was never easy playing in defence, never easy sitting amidst the often deep disquiet she projected. None of that with Tillmann - the welcoming, buxom queen. Wagenknecht could have her any way he wanted; throw her back on the bed; let her continue undressing him. *Lucky – lucky man!* But with luck comes hell – always in the background. If Lysette could see them now, or if she discovered his indiscretion, then *all* his assets within the house would be destroyed: books, clothes, files. She had done it before. He had been researching Hitler from Kershaw's 600-page tome – getting inside him for his play, *The Accurate Man* – when she had grabbed it from the arm of the chair and proceeded to fling half of it to the floor. *Crazy, crazy woman!* (The accusation: inattentiveness.) And again on his birthday: 'You know the cards are supposed to be on the windowsill by 11am. It's disrespectful not to stand them up.' She had taken Gide's *The Counterfeiters* on this occasion and torn it – as was her trick – in two.

Add them up, Wagenknecht asked of himself. Lay them all down on a surface (her moments of unreasonableness and anger) and tell me you didn't marry a halfwit! Look carefully at everything she has put you through, how she has had you tip-toeing around, and tell me you don't deserve Tillmann for another four hours here in this anonymous room.

Wagenknecht finally saw her, properly, hair around her shoulders – out of its school tie, its formal mode. Still, the fresh face, the slightly plump lips, the beautiful rump. And without clothes – as if blown away, as if caught in a hurricane, an accident. This will be *your* accident, muffled its way around him; words from the altar, from Lysette – here even though she wasn't.

Piss off, Wagenknecht railed in his head, now holding Tillmann's frame under the duvet in only his briefs. Give me this, you bastard, then we'll negotiate – I'll come clean.

'Are you OK?' Tillmann enquired.

'Yes. Yes. Just…nothing – nothing.'

Tillmann slid down him – wished to finally override his obstreperous guilt. Unwrap him and get his dick in your mouth and *then* he'll relax, she thought. Lick him where it matters.

Wagenknecht felt the change of gear, the dynamic burst to another plane. Events filled his head.

Ashpound – always reluctant to get out of the car after ping-pong. Wagenknecht, pulling up outside the station and then having to endure his woe; Ashpound not realising when women were out of his league. *Get out of the car! For Christ's sake, get out of the car.* You can't press on with your interest in this woman. You have to accept, we all have to accept, our romantic station. But no – they'd allow Ashpound to take them to lunch, pump up his dreams. Lunch, a date – they are very different things, my friend. You have to understand that. A man looks for the slightest sign. Women – they're more normal in some respects. Why should lunch mean they wanna jump you? They just want an education. This is part of it. Stop imagining! Stop rolling over such barren ground.

He had talked of a woman maybe 2% beneath him. No tight olive top to bring out her bust, no perky lovability to laugh with, but she's in your bracket. *We all have a bracket, Ashpound.* You have to make your life believable - real in this way. (Maybe miserable sex is what is required.)

The desks – Wagenknecht had put up all the desks in the new house. Four of them. Plus two bookcases. And painted the kitchen. Despite this, Lysette often called him 'lazy'. The neat, little German desk in Scotty's room. The trickier, corner design in Jasmine's hideaway with shelf space underneath for her 'girl things'. And the rest – the back living room and *our* bedroom, albeit it a dresser (the most complicated piece of all). If only you'd seen me, knees aching – pressed against the ground like suspected terrorists. But that pace, always prettying the house up, thinking of the next change – sure, I lapsed. I have plays to write. I don't wish to die and be talked of in a copacetic way. William Wagenknecht – kind to his neighbours, great at DIY, a real domestic chief. *You want someone like that, a chunk of a man, then go and find him!* I won't do an Ashpound. I won't plead or beg – become the tool man. Give me birds at the back of the house – bringing joy in. Let's keep those nuts topped up…that seed. But let's not over-obsess with the interior. Keep it functional – clean lines, full of light, but don't get the decorating bug. You've seen our eighty-year-old neighbour with his great old carpets and classic furniture. That's how it should be. And he was a maths professor, putting mind before matter.

Too many disagreements and the harmony dies. That's when you go nuts, thought Wagenknecht. That's when your path gets crowded – full of other people's junk. Particularly a wife's. That map of the world – it would have helped them all. But despite Wagenknecht concluding the house purchase alone in the dusty office of his Fleetpool solicitor, stumping up *all* the cash, he was to have no wall space.

Lysette's photographs would take centre stage, works of art would hang in the living room, hallway and landing but anything educational or quaint she would overrule. 'We don't want it looking like an office.' Wagenknecht had even tried hiring wall space in Scotty's room – explained to him there would still be plenty of room for his own selection of posters – but he was too young. The concept was beyond him. *Money for what?* No – Messi's going there. Maybe next year, Dad.

But next year wasn't soon enough. He wanted his children to effortlessly be aware of the position of the countries. Luxembourg – wedged between Belgium, Germany and France. The Scandinavian order of

Norway, then Sweden, then Finland (snuggled up to Russia). And South America – you ran down the left trunk through Colombia, Ecuador, Peru and Chile, almost tasted the South Pacific Ocean, heard the Nueva Canción. When the Africans were hacking each other to pieces – *there*, Lake Kivu lies between DR Congo and Rwanda; in it you'll find genocidal victims.

Without visual aids the human race implodes, thought Wagenknecht. Look at Ezekiel and Jerusalem ("For the Jew to have unauthorised contact with the Torah is dangerous"). Look at Cicero and ancient Rome ("…the law courts are mere ciphers…").

Dear Mr Coleridge – You wanted, I believe, the head and heart reconciled. You favoured a new synthesis over originality: human brotherhood of a sort. The mechanistic, reductive principles of 18th century thought killed you as the 21st century extinguishes me. Accountants we have now. And economists (who strangely refer to themselves as scientists). Everyone's an accountant, although I don't know what they're adding up. What can it be? People? Each other? Money? Happiness? You can generally tell by the blouse when you're with one.

Wagenknecht had once thought of buying into someone else's conviction. With his own shorn and depleted, such hooking up, running on someone else's glory seemed sensible. Others did it. And not always with the living. They had paid $25,000 for a lock of Lincoln's hair, £15,200 for Churchill's dentures, $45,000 for X-rays of Marilyn Monroe's chest and £1,250 for a "tiny scrap" of Napoleon's wallpaper. The fluorescent lives of historical characters seemed to excite. The achievements of political men were somehow sufficient.

What could Wagenknecht have? *This*. A woman at his waist. Perhaps Tillmann could carry the torch – be the placid teacher that politicians had once applauded in unison. And behind the model citizen were needs, hunger, an escape Wagenknecht was able to satisfy. *Just don't come home and chat about little Johnny every night.* We can do current affairs before you ride me into oblivion.

Tillmann! What was he getting into with her? A hotel bed for a start. But beyond that – the plan, the scheme, the delineation? It was the married man's error – thinking too far ahead. Little things about her – her clothes hung over the desk chair: silly tights, lime skirt, beige stripper mac, multi-coloured scarf. And at the foot of it, her brown, slinky boots. Such a collection put him at ease; something of the beatnik in her, the hippy; a wild woman needing bliss away from the classroom.

And bliss she was getting or giving. Most likely both. But where were the dints in this motor, the screaming sheets of metal that frustrated and crumpled men? None obvious yet. But what right had Wagenknecht to expect a woman who wasn't tortured by something? Looking at himself and his fleeing certain things, he suspected his claim on perfection was flimsy, tenuous. Good, because such a state carted him too far away from reality.

'This isn't too soon for you?' Ms Tillmann asked, escaping part of the duvet, placing a flat hand on Wagenknecht's chest.

Wagenknecht had warmed to her. She had done too much, too early, but all with sublime diversion in mind.

'I'm married to the biggest albatross that ever lived. Nothing's too soon.'

'Those ten feet wings getting in the way…'

'Flapping, strangling me, wanting to take me over.'

'Mine are only a couple of feet.'

'Good.'

Wagenknecht held her and stared at the ceiling. Strange to have a different body next to his. Sex – the paycheck that never came with Lysette, but Ms Tillmann effortless by comparison. Do they not create a certain type of woman anymore? Wagenknecht had wondered. The type that had hoisted him down off his skateboard as a kid – keen, stable, non-trashy, good lookers? The population of women today were mostly caught up in careers that turned their softness and romantic inclinations into deals. *Don't bring deals into the bedroom!* Stay out unless you're able to take off that daily cloak of bullshit chatter. *I do not want dross and inferior language in here!*

When am I going to leave? That was the line in his head all the time when around Lysette and the family. I wouldn't have that in my head if things were joyful, acceptable, if I still recognised part of myself, Wagenknecht railed. But separating Jasmine and Scotty from the tough, old bones of Lysette – it was not possible. Their faces would vanish as the easy-going tits of his wife had decided to no longer play.

The crazy thing, Wagenknecht thought, is that my relationship with nature is conditional on there being a good woman in my life. I have not looked at a sunset or seascape the same since the pit enveloped me. Creatures too. Squirrels, robins, doves - once tiny offerings of wonder, now largely objects, passing streaks of colour.

Who said man and woman is supposed to work out? Don't you see the sagging faces of the males and the disappointed effulgence of the females? Isn't it the Icelandic people that still share children after an almost compulsory divorce?

'I'll be no good to you, you know,' Wagenknecht negatively eulogized to Tillmann. 'Lysette has my cards and they're not great – probably a bad Tarot hand.'

'Stop thinking about her, William. You're here. Here only.' She sat across his waist, pressed her palms against his cheekbones to get him to focus.

Focus though, he couldn't – not with her radiant tits hanging inches from his face and Lysette still trampling through his mind.

'You, as a woman, need a future. But how the hell can I give you that when I'm working towards a divorce? You'll get caught up in the mess. You'll...'

'Sshhh. Just be a baby for a while. You don't need to be the big man with me.' She offered him her left teat, arched her back so that there was minimal effort from Wagenknecht.

Suck it, or roll her off – that is your choice, you unappreciative dog, thought Wagenknecht. Have her move like this always though – not embroil him in beautiful games only to batten down the hatches later on.

The former, and Tillmann seemed to enjoy it. It wasn't the trick that Lysette had pierced him with: You take but never give; flimsy definitions depending on your appetite. Tillmann – bringing him back to life, virtually wrapping a blanket around him and shoving a bottle in his mouth.

Wagenknecht, a baby monkey, lamb or llama – being tended to, back in his favourite domain of womanly comforts. *Christ – what have I missed?* This relieves a man. Had this been the norm, of pungent regularity, then I could perhaps have stood in a room with members of *Wankers Inc.* scraping my feet on the boardroom floor ready to charge, return to this implausible scene.

Wagenknecht – the mini celebrity, once on *The Choton News* staff as unpaid sportswriter; his columns bounding through local discussion groups and higher-thinking circles like Masaccio entering Florence. But the stolen fan mail – at least seven letters addressed to him over an eighteen month period; all intercepted, all scooped up by the incumbent editor. Two from admiring pensioners, three from doting players and the remaining two from beauties - or so he'd been told. Possible wives. Women who expressed a need to meet him in a stylistic and committed way. Women drowning in the rigor mortis of Choton's provincial and cultural abyss.

'Why are you telling me this now?' Wagenknecht had demanded over a rocking, three-legged table in a grimy part of town.

'We open the post. We're told to run everything by Delly that's unusual or complimentary towards the paper's output.'

'But they were addressed to *me*.'

'He's a frigging oligarch.'

'You assumed they'd get to me?'

'Yes, until the fourth or fifth. Then his secretary caught a half-response on his screen one day. He'd taken your persona.'

'What kind of man stoops to that?' Wagenknecht knew as soon as he'd said it. A man with a red Hitler moustache. A man whose traditional expression had compromised and diluted many of Wagenknecht's early pieces for the paper (the curse of the poor copy editor) – chipping out necessary words such as Bejesus and assuming he didn't know how to begin sentences if without a formal structure. *Delly – you wrecker, you small-time duper and impersonator!* What must the distinguished women have thought when faced with your bean bag frame and ragged pitch? What words did you roll out before them, select for the occasion?

'I heard he lost them both after the first date.'

Wagenknecht nodded silently. This was something other than serendipity. An inverse bit of fortune. A theft. A crime scene. They ought to put tape around Delly's desk, drag his carcass into the local cells.

'The letters? Still about?'

'He shredded them.'

Hustlers! Re-directors! Such correspondence could have saved Wagenknecht earlier – had him breathe in the company of female starlings with their iridescent plumage and fine words. Fewer banging doors – Lysette, an afterthought, pushed out by gifted admirers. Like the ankles under the lorry Wagenknecht had once seen. Sat at the lights. Gazing to his left. A woman about to cross, but little of her to go off. Sufficient though – the black, cropped trousers and flat, homely shoes showing off the beautiful region of skin he would confess to never really knowing before.

Little things. *Just give me the little things!* Wagenknecht cried inside. These blockers though. These invisible quarter backs stealing my ball. *What does man have to do on this rough and sorrowful field?* Forget it, he told himself. Look at what you have now – Tillmann, her saucers drooping before you like a picnic hanging in the air, or on a mattressed bit of countryside; her trim, yet full face exuding, not pseudo pleasure, but genuine feeling and wanderlust.

Forster, thought Wagenknecht – the man held Greek and Italian peasant life in high regard. And this is it – away from routine, nothing complicated, the soft clattering of bodies and amusing duvet tales.

'Buzz Aldrin – he refused to take the photo of Armstrong when they were on the moon together. Something about the late swapping of seats – Aldrin demoted to no.2. Do we let him off?'

Tillmann mulled it over, found Wagenknecht's discursiveness unusual but charming. Not an ordinary man in bed. A serious joker. An enlightener. Someone you could happily be silent with. Chuckles. Often he only needed chuckles to confirm that you were there, present, receptive. He was prepared to clown and clown, moan and curse. But also fall into moroseness and melancholy.

'Do you think it's important that you find *your people* in this life? I don't just mean friends, but a kinship without the blood.'

Tillmann was still above him, on display – a faint rash on her cheek like a safe deposit box concealing her mounds of shyness. 'Something where you admit the need for a bond – yes.'

'Through what?'

'This. Papers. Poetry. Clubs. You know how I work, William.'

'Can we have some music in here?'

'I don't think that was included. Nothing around us.'

'Just you then.'

'So it seems.'

'I can't go back if we mess about.'

'That'll be it?'

'I think it would have to be.'

'Shall I dress then?'

'You know I can't have you doing that. Not until the clock's run down.'

'Three or four hours left…'

'Enough time for a moon walk.'

'A bit of bouncing around.' Tillmann trampolined her bust before him.

'Don't do that. It sends me over the edge. Man is not equipped to handle such…'

'What – this?'

'Tillmann!'

'At least cry my first name.'

'I prefer surnames.'

'Well, I don't. Donna – it's Donna.'

'Donna.' Wagenknecht repeated it. He had nothing further to say. He just marvelled at the lady astride of him. Boss me in a better way than Lysette, he thought. That is all I ask. I carry around weakness for the plays.

Purposely let it hang off me. Why shake off good material?

~~~~~~

'You have your head down when you walk. I've seen it. How can you call yourself a playwright when you don't even see things?' Douglas had asked.

'I suppose I'm thinking. Fewer things to crowd me out.'

'I don't buy it. Relationships. You need client relationships. Instead of prancing along to the library each lunch time to fiddle around with your damn plays, you should be building stuff – looking people in the eye. Dawdling for twenty years you've been. You could have millions under management by now if you'd changed companies, danced the line…the lie. And what do you boys make – 1%?! £500k on £50m. Each year! You took a wrong turn somewhere or didn't bother to turn at all.'

'I can't follow what's not in me.'

'Rubbish! I do. Everyone does. Get the money and *then* dick around.'

'You don't understand.'

'I understand that even the am-dram don't want to put on your plays. You were sat before them on their flimsy, plastic chairs next to the stage, sipping coke, but you didn't market your stuff. A guy who negotiates prices all day long on the stockmarket and you didn't, you couldn't market those lines that you crucify yourself over!'

Wagenknecht couldn't explain art to Douglas. He couldn't unfurl its magnificence, its secret code, its tinged richness. Currency to Douglas was hard, silver-lined papyrus from De La Rue. It was liquor, vintage

Scotch, the calling over of a waiter with the menu prices blanked out. Outside stood his 4x4, his beast of a car. Fit for a race of giants, it warmed its tyres on the mothership, Earth. He would be sickened if he knew of Mother's attempted depositing of photos at the bank, of her slow crisis, her mental decline; their dad vulnerable in the heart, Mum a soon-to-be passenger upstairs.

'I have a theory that the stock exchange is nearing its end days.'

'Theories! That's all you have! Why would you say such a thing? Why? A man goes into broking and becomes a socialist. A man goes into the fire service and commits arson on the side. You obsess with the rich, you become poorer, William.'

Poorer. Was he poor now with Tillmann jacking his penis?

'Failure has constructed you, William. Instead of learning, looking down the alleys for ideas, you've let the game around you subdue you, wreck you as a man.'

'I like to keep a little superstition wrapped up, I suppose.'

'And you're a dwarf because of it. What was it your man Emerson said?'

Wagenknecht crunched through his brain. Such quotes were still there more than the practical stuff. 'Man is the dwarf of himself.'

'There you go. More so when you don't fight it. We all start out as dwarfs. But after that, *you* decide...'

'I don't have a wife that encourages me.'

'And I do?! William. William. *All* women are meant for the scrap yard. They all have maybe three good years. After that they're a fucking pain.'

'But you work well together. She respects your hours.'

'She respects her seven horses. Humans – I don't think so. Nobody sees things behind the front door.'

Feeding those horses – the same outlay as keeping my family afloat, thought Wagenknecht. What people do, he wondered, speculated. How perspective slowly recedes.

'You still see people though. Lysette doesn't even want to see people. Friends. Family. Neighbours. Fellow parents. She has her own island.'

'Then cast her adrift. Chuck her a life float.'

'It comes down to economics, Douglas. I'd be castrated.'

'You know we discussed a job back when. There's a bed half the week as well if you want it.'

Then I'd really be a dwarf, thought Wagenknecht. Such a backward step I cannot bear and so I battle it out with the albatross.

'Fuck. There's no one you can trust. Even Mandela was friends with Suharto.'

'Who?'

'The Indonesian dictator.'

'Why is that relevant?'

'Because I make my way through the world by leaning on others.'

'You shouldn't do that.'

'But what I read…'

'You know me and Leonard don't read. It's no good - sets the bar too high. Perhaps that's why we've accumulated a decent amount of cash.'

Wagenknecht looked up, gazed at Douglas's too-tanned features and largely expressionless face. And they put blokes like this on charitable committees, invite them to balls. You see them shouting from their private boxes at the Cheshire Races. He remembered the story from Douglas – a simple exchange. 'You're lucky, lucky to be invited to places like this,' he had asserted to a friend. Despite the irreverent rhetoric, the half-cavalier insolence, the reaction had been one of wounded indignation – hard-to-come-by money set against easy money. 'You actually think like that? It's crossed your mind but has to dress itself up in jest? Fuck your tickets. You eat them.'

And yet Douglas *was* growing. Faster than Wagenknecht. Having experiences. Even developing a smoother vocabulary. *The money to put yourself in those situations!* thought Wagenknecht. Golfing with Leonard in Portugal, weekend hotels, restaurants, having a private gym built up in the Lancashire hills. Such adventure still had the mind turning, it still imprinted a necessary taste. Wagenknecht's own 'small-scale' experience was at least in his head: little theatre, discussion groups, emailing and writing to anyone and everyone (alive *and* dead), the local driving range, swimming, gymnastics with Jasmine, Fleetpool FC with Scotty. Dull by comparison, not conversational stuff, but then what do you extract from such a list? The vigour was there. He was *interacting*. The regularity though – Lysette stomped on such a wish, bored him into the ground with her preciseness, her timing his minutes with each child.

'Get off my back and just live! Roll with it,' he had screamed one day. 'Stop hunting for excuses, driving nails through my wrists!'

Wagenknecht should have known the higher ground was hers. He should have retreated like a mouse as soon as he heard the purring. Would he have a friend like this? he had lately thought – a strapped-up, wedge of a woman who spoke her mind yet hadn't the inclination for compromise (her inchoate diplomacy unaltered from high school).

'Never fall in love with a set of tits!' Heselglass had made clear.

He had more than likely done just that. Behind the lilac cardigan lay sand dunes, an oasis, the nipples of Aphrodite. Yes, she had a delicious face, plentiful, womanly thighs and smooth, velvety skin, but "Our survey said...70" or even 80. From a poll of 100. If you'd seen them in the Greek pool as I have, wading through the water, singing, flags almost planted on these two new planets (remarkable in their rondure) then you'd understand. You would be the feckless, tormented soul that I am today – dragged here for conversation, there for culture, up for intelligence and down for crooning orgasms.

Don't limp, Wagenknecht often told himself. Life had ravaged him to such a degree that he sometimes staggered into the office. *Walk in proudly! The limp is psychological.* You're letting things consume you. Yes – "Wreck you as a man", as Douglas had said.

But how do you stand? How do you stay upright? Am I like this because I've seen the splendour but realise it's controlled by a tempestuous nutcase? Can a deal be cut? Can we get through this?

It's doubtful. Women are women. For worse or for worse. Sucked dry of fun. Lounging about with their manure magazines.

I am cagey and agitated because I recognise the caginess in others, Wagenknecht harked. Women. Businessmen. Politicians. Even plain old tradesmen. So much 'gummy bear' intelligence – the warped manifesto of a sodden breed.

If I could change one thing, it would be the ethnic mix in professions. I don't wanna see black guys sweeping the streets no more. In Salchester that's all you see. I wanna see Dimon and Blankfein out there earning their corn. *Carlyle – Are these your men? You speak of a divine justice through the medium of great men. You're ribbing us, right? You're in on the act? As for the Grand Old Pillocks...*

Wagenknecht recalled one of the few black men that had climbed, running over his experiences on *Desert Island Discs*. He was typically shown to his table in an empty restaurant – the table next to the toilets or noisy kitchen. "Can I have a *worse* table, please?" was the retort, the riposte.

That's who I wanna be, thought Wagenknecht. A man exuding calm. A man so screwed by the world that his reaction was now one of inverse dysentery. Give me the Afro hair and the effortless moves. I don't belong in this white body. My dick is so full of freckles, so clustered in birth marks, that I feel like a black man anyway.

What about black women? Too hip, too cool; Wagenknecht's stiffness either enticing and laughable or representative of the lair he sought to exit. When you see a white man pulling rank, it's like witnessing a gluttonous buffoon in full regalia. Shilp,

Pony, Leonard even – they were essentially of the same ilk. "These are very important people, William," Shilp had once mouthed down the phone in response to Wagenknecht emailing the top brass with a question. "At the last Town Hall they said 'Our door is always open'." "William, William. Nobody means that. They don't expect *your* hand to be on the handle. You go through the channels."

Two extremes. There were two extremes. The council house mafia who didn't wait for their dogs to cock their legs when out walking. And that around him now – Shilp, almost single-handedly a modern day Stasi; Leonard, his elder brother, hooked to a strange type of oxygen; Pony, the absentee manager and architect of contracts made from putty (Ashpound's daily kicking justified in various clauses).

Was this Medici versus Machiavelli? Wagenknecht accused of "debasing the sacred mysteries of political philosophy"? Even the good ones like Bertrand Russell and Jean-Jacques Rousseau misunderstood Machiavelli's work (*The Prince*): a "handbook for gangsters"; "the book of Republicans". Some of Wagenknecht's plays were like it. Open fights against the elite. Perhaps they would be published posthumously. Perhaps the skullduggery world was not ready. The art of governing – Wagenknecht had opinions on that. He had opinions on women, people, madness, art, the giant struggle around him. How he had served the stockbroking community as Machiavelli had served the Florentine republic for 14 years. But now, yes, he would advocate conflict rather than peace. The foundation of liberty was civil discord. And businesses, families didn't want any of that. Pruned lies were preferable. When I am in your face asking a question don't dress up the answer, don't stutter internally before churning out your staple bluster. Machiavelli "merged with the people". Gramsci understood that. Whether Wagenknecht could do the same was questionable, doubtful. He stood looking at most societal elements with disbelief, shame at people's complicity.

"Citizens should carefully examine the strength of the evil, and if they think themselves strong enough to overcome it, should attack it regardless of the consequences." Such words, alas, let them off. Rather than lift their heads, seek out injustice and stay unified, they crawled away, thought the new laws and bastards too strong, too privileged. But they're *bound to augment* without something from you. You cannot just wait and hope for smashed windows, a modicum of reprisal, redress. Machiavelli wanted national unity. He wanted the scent of the Spanish gone – September 1512 reversed. Don't think he was "whispering in the ear of the tyrants". None of it. He was dissecting the machinery of power, controls over language, the *Agadoo*-ing of culture.

Five hundred years ago! thought Wagenknecht. Why do that? Torture yourself with failed predecessors. You know what Mac said: "All armed prophets have conquered and unarmed ones failed." So unless *you the pacifist* plan on stacking up on guns, you should learn to settle for a little piece of that around you.

Someone had saddled up his weakness. Wagenknecht recalled the birth of the chip on his shoulder. While cowering. It was while cowering – pulling away from his father's hand in his old box room. Nothing too delinquent-like, certainly not reprehensible. Wagenknecht had actually forgotten his crime. But at that moment – after the communique between his parents – his stinging body translated the aggression of his father and vowed within the cranium never to speak to him again.

Four days. That is how long the snub had lasted (over meals and around the house). But because of it, it was now easier to blank people, be unforthcoming and taciturn. He was a practised prince of reticence. The deeper trail of such disquietude, however, was madness – no longer being *with* the Earth, in its rhythms and cadence.

The intonation might not be what you want it to be, but chuck something back, the sensible Wagenknecht mused. You become too introspective and they've got you! And what example is that to Scotty and Jasmine? Stop looking around for trouble (that is Lysette's strategy). Stop going crazy over tiny imperfections. Remember the black man! Remember his cool! "A *worse* table, please. Can I have a *worse* table?" You *can* employ irony, subtle venom. People don't know they've been done over. Not to the degree we recognise. Kindness has a few decent allies – groggy foes to some, words staggering towards them, pissing them off. And that is what you want, don't you? You want to win?

Yes and No, thought Wagenknecht. I want £300k in the bank – enough to avoid breathing in the carbon ratcheting of others, the waspish tomfoolery of lesser souls. But winning? It can't be this if done poorly with a crumpled hand on the canvas, a shyster's eye steering the vision. You cannot be an iconoclastic and eccentric socialist because there will always be one – a wrecker of the dream, a too-insouciant hitter.

Get out there like Steinbeck and work! Understand the soil, timber, dovetail joints. Put your hands between the plants and feel the organisms in your palm. The desk can only take a man so far. Try to understand your natural surroundings – the water down the garage drainpipe, the flutter of the starlings that pass by, the damp braid of grass which exhibits a green unavailable anywhere else. Get those legs used to the elements again – not just propped up under a slab of wood while only the top half of your body is in motion.

"Thoreau's primitivism cannot provide an antidote to the heedless western expansion of the frontier." That is the problem, thought Wagenknecht. Nobody wants the little life. They're all vying for more. His bosses (chatting about discount vouchers and the next mobile phone). Lysette. Peers. Even the church.

~~~~~

Wagenknecht had started going to Sunday mass – either the 9am or 10.30am show depending on his limbs. The duff secular schools around their beach home meant that a quick switch of religions from non-practising Protestantism to leg-dipping Catholicism was necessary. Scotty and Jasmine would thank him when they turned sixteen. Now, there was grumbling; Scotty just months away but not quite getting it; Jasmine, safely sequestered by Donna Tillmann, still a year and a half off the smart blazers and rhythmic timetables of high school.

Wagenknecht had phoned ahead – spoken to the Father of the upturned boat (the impressive beams of the church roof crucially siphoning spiritual notches courtesy of its great architecture).

'I just wish to get the children accustomed to the mores of the church. I read somewhere that taking communion might offend, Father – us being of the other Christian faith.'

'You're all welcome, William. We don't like to turn people away.'

'So you don't mind us accepting the wafer?'

'The body of Christ, William. No.'

The man had a distinctive voice and was bigger because of it. It was a radio voice, an inviting rumble with a carpet of words. Wagenknecht asked him where he was from – got a sense of his history and attitude to life. A nice bloke – not at all pompous; from Preston, under Wagenknecht's old post code.

At first the service had been a discovery, partly enjoyable, like a coat around Wagenknecht's shoulders. Wagenknecht had looked around, mimicked the pros, clasped his hands when required, knelt before Eucharistic prayers and whilst beholding the Lamb of God. But the sins. *Always sins!* Even right from the kick-off with the Penitential Act: 'I confess to almighty God and to you, my brothers and sisters that I have greatly sinned, in my thoughts and in my words, in what I have done and in what I have failed to do…'

What if I haven't? thought Wagenknecht. What if it's been a good week? This is like going to your boss and admitting to insider dealing after dropping your calculator. But something in the Catholic make-up wished to exhume guilt on a regular basis. Did it purify the body, the mind? Wagenknecht ran his eyes down the Jerusalem Mass sheet. There were two glaring opposites: The Gospel and the Homily. The latter Wagenknecht soaked in. It was usually a contemporary story from the Deacon – a sympathetic observation, something judged unfairly then corrected. But then the Gospel – Christ: who was this Jesus they were pushing? A harsh man from Wagenknecht's standpoint – whipping people and ordering destruction (John. 2:13-22).

Wagenknecht gazed at his fellow parishioners. Were they having this? Accepting this supposed man of peace storming around? What could they do – ask for a recount? Perhaps Wagenknecht was getting Him confused with Gandhi – a slightly different look, a slightly different case and country. Consubstantial – the Catholics liked that word (identical in essence though different in aspect). It was in their Nicene Creed, central to their obedience. "Consubstantial with the Father" - did it mean Jesus was "seated at the right hand of the Father (God)" or that Jesus *was/is* God – one and the same?

He could not figure it out but did not have the nerve to ask, could not risk the Pope's children flocking round him and potentially barracking him.

Always a turd near the entrance of the church (on the pavement), Wagenknecht thought. Why did no one clear it up? Was it a test? The lucid points of the morning began to be filtered by his mind. One of the hymns sounded like *Morning has Broken* only with different words. His old stomping ground had found a way in, reversed the Reformation, seen off Henry VIII. This and the Communion Rite, the Lord's Prayer: "Our Father, who art in heaven, hallowed be thy name; thy kingdom come, thy will be done on earth as it is in heaven...' Wagenknecht didn't mind this. It was softer, less pushy than The Gloria ("you Who take away the sins of the world") and The Eucharistic

Prayer ("It is right and just"). He could do joy, a simple, voluntary appreciation of God, but not the heavy stuff, the scraping, lines which seemed to re-enact Puritan savagery.

'You *take away* the sins of the world...have mer-cy on us,' Wagenknecht sang on the way home with Scotty and Jasmine, chiseled it into the fabric of the car. It was light mockery with the mutual understanding that none of them belonged to this world with its ancient scriptures.

Sins? You might somehow lessen the brutality of the world, but you let shysters openly roam around. And I don't see you saving Ashpound with his flat face, prominent nose and round teeth. Had sea air got there before you were able? Deadened the Norfolk man with an anti-swagger?

'William. Pony knows Shilp.'

'No!' You run from dishonesty and a blubber-like asininity gets you.

'They're carving me up.'

'What? How?'

Ashpound – his lack of wrinkles somehow made him more immature. His soft face but hopeless countenance almost demanded regular slaps.

'Hoping I fall. Devising schemes. Blocking any kind of dialogue, yet sniping from the sidelines.'

'Has Shilp been in your office?'

'No. But I picked up Pony's phone. Instantly recognised the bald fart – his oily charm turning into officialdom when he realised it was me.'

That'll be him, thought Wagenknecht. The flick-knife schizophrenia. The ruddy traits of a headmaster's son (bogus upstandingness). The chewed loyalty and mob-like anything-ness of a Nazi.

'I still don't understand why he does that. Switches track. Caste system in a former life?'

'William. One is OK – a kind of face-off. But two!! It's like they're smashing a puck against my shins! What do I do? How do I handle it?'

You get direct, thought Wagenknecht. You grab Pony by the neck, push your thumb against his Adam's Apple, lose your job and get a police caution. The world ought to exempt consequences at times, Wagenknecht deliberated – forgive the little man. Even Ashpound. I imagine he rages but bottles it up.

'They're good mates you think?'

'Met at some function. Yes. A couple of the lads here confirm it. Like our firms are twinned or something.'

'We're certainly not that. Your firm supposedly has thinkers – people who know *where* to invest money. We just have the procedural doers – employees ballet dancing across spreadsheets.'

'I wish I was a doer now. It's become too much. The expectations are different.'

'They must be familiar with each other on a regulatory level. That's all. You speak to Shilp and he sickens you with his flat answers.'

Sanity – find the other piece of it, thought Wagenknecht. We're getting bundled up, sold off like collateral! Always a group of operators ready to do the dirty work as well – their foreheads smooth, de-crimped of emotion.

'I'm not the best employee, William. But, Jesus – every day is torturous. And the man chooses to sit next to me. How can I perform when he's there correcting every sentence and action of mine?'

You elbow him in the face – show him the martial arts. Smash his podgy demeanour with a flurry of home truths.

'I have a similar relationship with the deacon at the church. Not once has he looked at me with any sense of kindness. You're in the wrong line of work I think when I shake his hand. I can't quite make out his face from behind the beard. Is it as unsympathetic with the regulars?'

'Is it?'

'No. I see him smiling. To all of them. Not the toothiest smile, but clearly a greeting or bosom of some kind.'

'Why not you then?'

'He must see me as a fraud. I don't know my Hail Mary, my Ave Maria. It's not on the sheet. They must do that to weed us out.'

'What do you do when it's time to say it?'

'I move my lips but I could be singing *Start Me Up* or anything.'

'*Are* you a fraud?' Ashpound asked with a surprising level of directness.

'Why – of course I am. When Scotty and Jasmine are traipsing into the church, my mind is traipsing with them. But the schooling...what can you do? I don't have Douglas's money. I don't have Leonard's money. It's a simple choice: purple blazer, kids running riot and the next generation of Wagenknechts compromised or black blazer, smaller school and a decent chance.'

Wagenknecht thought of Scotty's recent joke: Where does a frog hang his coat? In the *croak*room. *The croakroom!* It was back to the black – a *worse* table! Black skin. Black blazer. You had to cut it – get them inside the *right* institution. Wagenknecht hated the word, knew the brigade of scammers that usually inhabited such places, but wanted his kids' humour and ambition to be able to breathe. The wrong teachers roaming around – those unable to stand up to Ofsted – and the kids began to see an authoritarian world.

They were slipping away day by day – the growing of a consciousness (and with it bellicosity) largely done through peers and their sudden ability to say 'No' more often, thus throwing Wagenknecht's plans on the scrap heap.

Ideas used to be brought back from the continent by young, privileged men, thought Wagenknecht. Now, they are downloaded, seen instantly. It wasn't a world he felt like protecting. Gratification – its immediacy had wrecked something, mined a large part of this generation's soul. And yet do we all need something, someone lower than ourselves? Wagenknecht pondered. Without Ashpound, am I in trouble, am I swimming at the bottom?

What kind of sleep was it that I used to have? he thought. What kind of life existed before? I seem to smell gas wherever I go these days. The rot of Choton's bypass still haunts me – the spent fuel, the carbon stink; carcinogens at their most ferocious outside the school and dance class. Despair – keen and continuous.

People who look at my house think I have done well. But it could all fall. *It will all fall.* There will be no money because I increasingly get furious with people. One day I will hit someone. *Hard.* I feel it growing. You look at Ashpound and feel sympathetic but at least he's a pacifist. He will piss people off, infuriate them with his Norfolk indecision, but you know he will never strike anyone.

Put a white collar on the brute. That is how you feel when you meet an unsavoury specimen – someone from the Shilp gene pool. Are they encircling you? Do you feel them closing in? Or is it paranoia?

I don't know! Wagenknecht cried. I don't know. Just too many thought processes. I try to keep the plays trim, but always interruptions – fat balls from the garden, problems at home, relationships. It is not the simple track I thought it was.

Georges Debil – that is my play. About a French crack-up artist. You write about one enough, you become one. I have to get a career though. Before Scotty starts asking questions. Before Scotty falls into his own.

Wagenknecht – his shyness had turned into anger. Only the true expression of children seemed to play out in his mind these days; kids giddy-upping along the station platform ("London Bridge is falling down") and muttering easy, sufficiently clear words ("You and me and hotdogs").

The flimflam of adults had slid down the rankings. Why listen? Why even tune in? It was all politicised, broken by this phoney, ramped up world. You see them in TV studios dribbling over insignificant news, up and coming boxing matches, the mannerisms and clothes of celebrities. Too much. It had taken over. Marketing. Grenadine grins. Sheen over brine.

He saw them every day at the brokerage – noosed-up individuals pushing their theories, their cheap observations. Visionless men parachuted in – working within the paradigms handed down. Do not buck the trend even if failure went before. Do not challenge the existing order. Keep saying "equally" as the hors d'oeuvre to your second sentence.

Dear Mr Hayek – Do you still believe that society is a spontaneous order? Even – I should stress – within the dour walls of modern commerce and education? Man has been blunted has he not – told to kneel before the whooping, witless gaze of ice-lollies in suits. Yes – reason can never fully take control, as you assert, but let us not hand the reins to dogs, immoral chargers and the like.

I need to get to know someone again, thought Wagenknecht. I need to feel and sense a brightness that has been absent for so long. Part of my motor has died. The cam belt – 50,000 miles or 50 years. Getting closer if so. Mushing my head with something. Too many words? Too much ideology? *Should have kept it simple.* Hemingway spelt living "liveing". Perhaps he was onto something. Perhaps we're just wriggling around – humanity dangling from between God's fingers.

The consciousness of the masses is not yet ready for the next development, Bellow had said. Looking around, he was right, thought Wagenknecht. A lot of scrambling. A lot of misjudgment. Willing serfs to the higher classes. Get together and become dispassionate and this stops – filthy wealth is replaced.

The risk of losing what they've got though! What they've fought for. Even the peasants are essentially snobs. That's what the grand consumerist model does

– it puts us on edge, has us looking over our shoulder. *Set the alarm! Set both alarms!* Protect the goods because they are like limbs or little babies. Let me rock them, help them to sleep.

Degenerates with gadgets or brethren with freedom? That is the choice, thought Wagenknecht. And they were very clearly choosing the former – fighting it out on Black Fridays or handing Apple their dough for the sake of more speed or dumber apps.

So many suckers delighted by transient thrills. Forget one's duty, forget the bigger dream of placing your hand at the base of mankind's spine and around its shoulder, helping it along. You orgasm in front of your digital screens, exit the world, boast that technology is king.

Damn it – was Emerson that way inclined? wondered Wagenknecht. Some of his words ("With the key of the secret he marches faster / From strength to strength, and for night brings day, / While classes or tribes too weak to master / The flowing conditions of life, give way.") were unmelodious. But then he lacked vitality – capitalism's costume. And don't forget he *had* to be resolute, a single-minded battler, after losing his first wife and a child. Not a peddler, a liar, a quant then. Such a hard formula to refine when considering special cases.

Think when it all began! Wagenknecht insisted. When civilisation first dressed itself. 1440 – do we go with that, when the printing presses started churning out *Aventur und Kunst*? Or later, with the sumptuousness of Shakespeare? Revolution had started its creep in 1603 once the Virgin Queen was gone and *The Tragedy of Hamlet* arose.

And so the quest for human perfection is periodically threatened, choked by self-interest, callous words or necessity. Into the vacuum steps divergence.

Raymond Carver, night janitor – Wagenknecht wished he was him. An eight-hour shift done in sixty minutes. Free time to write with no one *at* him or *on* him, demanding their due; man hidden by the night, his gaze homing in on the stars and through them still dreaming.

Where were the jobs like this now, the Mercy Hospitals of the UK? *Sell those damn horses and give me the feed money and vets bills*, Wagenknecht felt like saying to Douglas. Do a Theodore Van Gogh. *Believe in me!* One day you'll be part of the story. And that's better than having a bulging wardrobe and spoilt wife. Just fix up a standing order, I'll quit and give you 80%. *Some investment!* Yes – let's call it that. Keep it official.

But how could he? Beg. Begging. All but crouched down on the street, near incontinent in his second-rate clothes. If Douglas didn't see that he needed a hand, a breather, a solid collection of moments to re-inflate his confidence, then...what? Doomed? Twenty more years in the chase?

I hate disruption, change, thought Wagenknecht. If I could have a cloud stay where it is, then wonderful – better for mankind. And such a state would help the one homeless man that worried Wagenknecht; a man not in his forties as they all seemed to be, but seventy – easily. Always in the same spot (outside the closed down Chinese with its smoked windows) – Wagenknecht breezing past him on his way home, rushing to Salchester Train Station.

It was possible to see the thinning in this man, the gaunt face and pointed chin. What education he had had no longer resided in his eyes. Reality had taken over – the quest for food. Each day was an update for Wagenknecht – the dabbing of paint on a body closer to death. He was certain he was witnessing a slow deterioration in the man. The sleeping bag, blankets and poor provision of clothes were grimy – no longer fit even for a dog basket or kennel.

Plenty of people kneeled, tried to get some sense from 'Joe', offer him kind words, but he had evidently given up. When Wagenknecht passed now, his eyes were invariably shut. What flesh remained seemed to be fighting against the elements – cowering and concave.

'You do this,' spoke Wagenknecht to no one in particular. 'You do this and think it normal. What have we become?'

'Film his last days and you'll win the Turner Prize,' a passing, unexpected voice pronounced.

Wagenknecht stood still – inconvenienced the swathe of marching bodies around him. '*Stop!* Stop for a moment. Just a moment.'

His words got softer, almost irrelevant. You can't give lectures, he thought. We've passed that point. You can't plead or implore or supplicate. They're simply not there. What you see moving around you is a canister of gas, a wave of blow-up dolls – bouncing but highly coordinated toys.

We have "lived to witness a chaos of spirit, a deafness of ear and a blindness of eye". Yes – many times, thought Wagenknecht – the misfits no longer so sacred though. You don't sign up, you don't take part in the subtle conscription and you're down...slaughtered. Object and be cast aside!

Georges Debil, the crack-up merchant – who was he? Who was Wagenknecht writing about, feeding lines to? Was it himself, a not-so-elaborate cover, the manifestation of his fears and concerns? *You put a Gallic undercoat on the man, that doesn't mean you're free of him. You can't extricate yourself from this*, Wagenknecht told himself. Whatever he *says* is you. Whatever he *does* is you. His *mannerisms*, the whole *caboodle* – it's the life you wanted to express, but couldn't.

Yes. Because I can't live my life as I wish, I've created one. Something of the Oscar Wilde in that. A phantom. An alter ego. But Debil wasn't in Monaco bathing himself in cars, plush hotels and resplendent tits. He was barely around the corner – a veiled shadow, but with the words Wagenknecht could not speak.

These brokerage people (*enter the humourless zombies!*) – money ruling everything, their wives' legs spread. You can't unclip yourself from that if you're not talented. And I'm not, thought Wagenknecht. *My comebacks and ripostes are often one hour too late!* I do enough to remain steady in their world, but behind the eyes I resent their grubbed-up approach, their hard daily dealings.

Each day is the hijacking of my purple go-cart all over again. Something that happened when I was ten but has remained with me. Young Calvinists pushing me aside. Too physical but then I (or rather Debil) didn't put up a fight. A lack of courage. Wishing to avoid the bloodied lip – something I would now gladly accede to if only to do injury to them.

Each decade – always with its quota of bastards, its army of Bormanns. 'Have you ever considered the possibility that you might be a coward?' Leonard had once asked.

'All the time. But what do I do? Is there a Cowards Anonymous?'

Part of it was sincere. But the other part reeling, defensive, shocked by Leonard's indulgent words.

'Everything in you seems panicky, under duress. Somehow you're on a different frequency, in a different land.'

Wagenknecht was on a loop when the depression came – a Scalextric '8' track. Not easy to get off. Round and round. Thinking. Usually small things. He wanted to strip his house down – understand the daft decisions: bath design (the bit in the corner that gathered water); radiators (such a comical, snaking invention); lintels (did they really support doors and windows?); gutters (vulnerable to falling tile mortar). He should have been stoical, accepting, but instead - as with Herzog - "he let the entire world press upon him". Where do I go when this happens? Where do I take myself? Into a darkened room? Under the duvet? *You shouldn't have died and left me with these contemporary narcissists!* he demanded of Miller, Pinter, Mailer and Bellow. All of them gazing into mirrors, seeing nothing but their own shrunken minds.

Wagenknecht had a hunch – he knew why Leonard and Douglas had gotten ahead. *Born at home!* I was born at home to some drunken mid-wife who went easy on the oxygen yet heavy on the pethidine. Something in me doesn't shift from left to right. My mind feels disjointed. I think there is jelly between the grey matter and white matter. I get the permanent sense of a dumb lining, something blocking out the signals from my brain. And yet because of this (I think) I weigh matters up more - I have what is known in the trade as triple *compos mentis*.

'You try to get too much detail on a woman,' Routcliff assured him, corrected him.

'Yes. Yes – I do. But only after Lysette and that feral woman, Serena. Both infiltrated me – made me jump back, look in astonishment at the gallery of females left.'

'Eusebio wouldn't agree.'

'The footballer?'

'Yes. They asked him in the hospital "Does your heart hurt?"'

'And?'

'"Only from the women I have lost,"' he replied.

'Then the man is naïve. And I'm surprised at you, Routcliff – pushing such romantic propaganda.'

'I'm not pushing it. I'm just telling you.'

'So what am I to think? That every loss kills me? Because they don't. Some of them, quite frankly, have me re-born.'

'But I don't think he's saying that.'

'It's a bald enough statement.'

'"Only from the women I have *lost*," William. To rivals. To fear of the unknown. Those that fled or stumbled away whom he regarded highly.'

'If he's saying that then fine. A brief taste and wonder at what could have been, I can understand. I think it's more sweeping though, as if he's a Don Juan.'

'Maybe.'

'I struggle to flatter her, Routcliff – I really do. That's got to hint at some kind of finality.'

'Lysette?'

'Yes.'

Wagenknecht stood there in his old clothes on one of the many Salchester bridges that traversed the city's ship canal. His fleet of dated attire was almost symbolic of the calamity central to his marriage. His tired skin took in the occasional potato stench from these parts.

Routcliff gave him one of his quizzical stares – a stare he had clearly never studied in the mirror, for it was a cocktail of doubt, accusation and booshit.

'You can't flatter her at all?'

'I can't get past the sourness in her.'

'You have Donna now though?'

'Sometimes in a hotel. But not fully.'

'Flattering two women is dangerous. Stick with the affair and don't ask for too many extra portions.'

Useless, thought Wagenknecht. Useless advice. Not one of their better lunchtime strolls. Sometimes it was like this though. Within minutes of leaving the office and tramping the streets with Routcliff, he wished to shake him off – be alone. The man's vertebrae seemed to click as they walked, his sharp nose condescend to Wagenknecht's rubbery, negro-esque nostrils.

Always the ironing-board torso as well, thought Wagenknecht. Routcliff had wandered over every hill and mountain in the north-west with compass and flask to hand. What is it, what is it about people that have better direction than me? Wagenknecht mused. A bit of me grows to resent them – the steady crowd, the marching, practical types; coffee annoyingly poured with the flask-lid still half screwed on.

'Why do you continue to strap Lysette to you?' Routcliff asked after a baleful silence.

'Why? Why?' Wagenknecht responded, more to himself in a trance, through the filaments of a dream. 'Because the boat might rock more without her.' He was tempted to accentuate *more*, but no – it wasn't needed.

'I understand,' Routcliff replied, perhaps witnessing the embezzlement of Wagenknecht's brain, showing the single-layered oft-sensitivity that Wagenknecht mostly missed.

How did he build this current life? Wagenknecht sometimes pondered. Ridiculous, incredible to think that ownership of these bricks has come about through what seems like a pretend world – numbers on screens, me buying and selling, having none of the face-to-face direct interaction that Douglas has. Do we all take stock when we first pull the duvet over us at ten, eleven, twelve at night? Do we realise that this is so far away from what was described in the careers office at school that it almost feels like a lie?

Think. *Think of anything!* Just get away from this gloom, Wagenknecht prescribed. What have I done with Leonard in the past? he thought. What have I done that is good? We have walked through galleries together – the great ones: Guggenheim; Museum of Modern Art; Phillips Collection. We have shared an appreciation of Picasso, Miro, Renoir and Rothko. And the tennis balls – we'd throw them hard into each other's iron hands; one stood on the patio, one at the bottom of our parents' garden. That was fun – little to think of, just a moment. Now, Wagenknecht somehow wanted things finished before they'd begun. Little moments were hard to conjure. The rush of his job had carried through to the important side of his life. Lysette was always saying it. But how to grab the handbrake?

Listening to the radio whilst driving. Daydreaming. Reading. Swimming underwater – goggles on. 'Solitary pursuits – that's all you have!' Lysette had wailed.

But through them he was saving himself – just a bit of himself. That's what she couldn't grasp.

'Is it all for everyone else? Are my actions and deeds not my own? Can't I keep a little?'

'No! Not when you have a family.'

'But a plan. Let's make a plan – please everyone. A bit of sugar for us all.'

'You're not listening...'

'The thing I've just said – respond to it. Don't veer off into another lane.'

'Stop interrupting!'

Like that. Always like that. Not even tempestuous – just deficient, inane, senseless. Wagenknecht watched her hand movements, her steamed-up face, the bewildering plasma that seemed to suspend a more truthful expression.

What the fuck have I married? he thought. Who is this? What kind of person doesn't like to organise life? Nothing in the handbook. There was nothing in the handbook. And the instruction leaflet was blank; an army of feminists rubbing out crucial assistance.

If only Lysette *was* a feminist – such a narrow cascade would be easier. But, no – Wagenknecht had chosen a bushman's fire; the raw, slow-burning of !Kung coals.

Dear Dougie – I left my gloves at your house. They are a special pair – warm, but also capable of keeping out the rain. Thinsulate, I believe they're called – little felt pads on the fingers for extra grip. If you would kindly put them to one side in readiness for my next visit.

Wagenknecht was splintering – interrogating the simple bits of his life that he had somehow lost the key to.

Dear Mr Richardson – You didn't prime me for this. You said that maths would be enough. It isn't. The whole thing is a charade, a power struggle between illiberal bigots. I don't think I have met a more unnatural crowd than resides in the office world. Indirectly you put me here and I'm bloody angry.

Dear Father – I would like to come into church on my own, take advantage of the confession chamber and ask you some fundamental questions. I feel that I would be abusing the system however – not confessing but rather asking how I get rid of a duff wife. You, of course, could not hope to assist with such barbed catechizing. I will write to the papers or ring the Samaritans instead.

P.S. I like the fact that you have broken the crucifixion down into twelve plaques (six on each wall) – it reminds me a little of the flick-books I had as a child.

Wagenknecht – sometimes he woke up and the skin on his dick felt too slack, not tight enough. *Insufficient erections!* he thought; Lysette, his home gym, pushing him off the equipment. Was manhood somehow judged in such a frame? Did the increasingly pathetic penis barely swinging from his groin now represent who he was, his status and kudos within the firm?

'Twelve years and still not seen at the urinals!' Shilp ribbed him with one day.

He was right. There could be no denying it; Wagenknecht slipping into one of the cubicles – preferring to sit down, but yes, anxious over what his award-winning dick had become.

Sometimes he shook it about like a puppet – his forefinger and thumb gripping the skin and hoisting it up and down. Exercise. He was giving it exercise – breathing life back into it for when his next woman came along.

At least a new band of Nazis would never come after him. Plenty of skin here, Jerries – you can keep your Star of David.

Saturday morning. Minimal chance of Lysette wishing to hunt down his jewels. He sometimes stayed under the covers – feigned a lie-in, waited for her to hobble down the stairs to breakfast. And then the faces in his head – harder to isolate or pinpoint one these days. A sexy woman with ethics…not you, you, you, you, you. Mostly a wasteland and so his emergency women (actresses), Violante Placido and Marisa Tomei allowed to skim his thighs and slowly consume him.

Wagenknecht got up with a smile after that, a tired approbation. Shuffling across the landing, past Scotty and Jasmine's rooms, he locked himself in the bathroom – engaged with the man staring back at him in the ruler-length mirror.

You're a dud, relying on this. *A dud!* Too scared to ship out your things. Trembling instead of making a go of it with Tillmann. Will Lysette give you a break, ever treat you like a man again? Wagenknecht knew the answer, just as he knew that their wedding ring sizes put side by side cruelly spelt NO. No! *Even the poltergeists knew that you weren't right!*

The bust-ups were many. A woman that doesn't *get you* or get her own way does that. She fights – slugs it out with no consequences. The landscape was a free run for her fists, her hard palms, her ridiculous kicks (as if starting a moped). *What a joke!* But not to Wagenknecht who somehow had to catch all this, spring it back in an orderly manner or absorb it, thus suppressing the words queuing up in his larynx.

Wuh-mann! he sometimes bowled at her in a Caribbean voice as all his other ideas, his solutions, had run dry. It hinted at a pre-franchise era, a simpler time. And of course, she pilloried him and lashed him for it. Always lashing him.

'Don't speak to me that way, you *bastard*! Little woman am I?'

Bastard – never a big word with Lysette. Introduced somehow to a table of new peers including bugger, contemptible, unpleasant and unfair. When said in the vicinity of little ears it seemed to tear the fabric of the family.

Too hard to interpret the damage when someone is loose with their words. Lysette, if witnessed by teachers, the police or judges, would be put in the stocks, shackled for her own good. The holder of a preposterous objectiveness, she had not said 'Sorry' in eight years. A full eight years.

You can't map this, thought Wagenknecht. There can be no warnings for a person in their mid-twenties.

Sometimes you land the wrong fish – have to hurl it back. But when you shift position, ready to throw, you realise the regalia has changed. Scales have become the heavy, 'jewelled dress' of Robert Walser. The high maintenance weighs you down. You tip back – end up crawling around the mud-edged lake with a strange, evolutionary bird.

All of us on the floor if we're not careful, thought Wagenknecht – doomed by others' piffling standards. *Be strong!* Take the blows. But come out swimming, sane, and finally…upright. From *Pierolapithecus* to *Australopithicus Afarensis*. Make sure you walk on two feet!

Wagenknecht recalled the madness which had visited his parents' neighbour. Unlike his quieter hall-to-hall semi, his parents occupied a living room-to-living room dwelling and so televisions were effectively conjoined. The thud and stamp of the old tube-dominated device flew through the wall along with the associated gaiety from the neighbour plonked on the couch (drinks trolley at her side). Did they serve her up Laurel and Hardy DVDs from 6-9pm? It felt like it.

'I wish they'd take her out with a tranquillizer gun at seven whatever it is,' Wagenknecht's father moaned. 'I didn't retire to suffer this.'

A short man with large hands, he cosseted the remote controls – shuffling them almost while hunched and bound up in his blue dressing gown. 'I'd set us up in the back – rejig the household – but then she retires at nine, laughs in her bedroom next to the portable until 11pm. And that's at the back!'

'How do you know that?'

'How do I know it, William? I speak to people. I see the lights go on and off. You think I'm a schmuck?'

Wagenknecht didn't mind the directness of his father. He was unlikely to receive a slap during the course of their dialogue. There was little chance of a personal assault. Things were confined – limited to the matter at hand. Recriminations and vindictiveness were purely Lysette's domain, the warped ammo of a life gone wrong.

The only thing keeping Wagenknecht sane in light of this – and some doubted he was that – was not yet imagining his children as totally conscious. Not believing that they were able to absorb the severity of that around them or form opinions. In some ways Wagenknecht spoke to them as if in a play – a nine and ten-year-old with himself as Peter Pan.

'Let's put it off. Let's put the day of reckoning off,' he muttered to himself. Christ, they were growing – Scotty developing a taste for hard rap music and Jasmine tumbling her body on the home gym mat when not at Saturday class. Some days it seemed too late to influence them – his playful words discredited, decrepit and irrelevant. Wagenknecht thought back. Lysette had been the one to show them technology – a world that now completely enveloped them. Music videos. Chat. Sport. And the speed at which those little fingers flicked between the screens! That is how Wagenknecht knew he was half ready for the scrap heap. Even if he tried, he could not keep up with those precocious princes and princesses. He had been dead to any kind of advancement for ten years. *Ten years!* Hanging on somehow, watching the new troop of anthropoids.

Atten-tion! Wagenknecht generally looked the other way – had no wish to be rounded up and cajoled, prodded, steered down a bullshit path. '*You're* the nihilist,' he said to himself. 'Not Scotty – Scotty will find his way, but you...you...'

It was all closing in. His mother at the bank no longer understanding cash. His wife, the bruiser. His employer paying him, but boring him – sinking his mind to a functional level.

Let me out! Part those damn clouds. Open the door, God! And not the one to the church. There are no beans in there. Reciting old scriptures, penitential acts, Cenacolo, organ recitals, the Gloria, "Die that we might live". Formalising things. *Strapping the congregation into the wooden pews!*

Always on the front of the newsletter in a bold box:

Attendance last Sunday: 387

Church Collection: £934.62 received with thanks

There to give an average but not state it explicitly. *Do the sums!* £2.41. And what did Wagenknecht put in, what did he place in the little hands of his tribe? £1 in Scotty's palm. And £1 in Jasmine's. 'You're short, you measly, pathetic man,' Wagenknecht heard a commanding voice pronounce. 'I have magazine subscriptions to keep up. My family – it's growing, consuming more. I thought you understood such matters?' 'Listen here, chump. We've got robes to pay for. Ongoing church repairs. The body of Christ. You think we can just drive down to the local cash and carry and purchase such things?'

Money – they all wanted it. Wagenknecht had seen the extra, appreciative smile when a well-dressed woman in the congregation had put in £10. Go on, give her status, Wagenknecht dryly demanded. *Elevate her!* Have her removed from the stalls into a special area.

Even the Pope dabbled – woke up to his multi-billion pound portfolio. What to do today? Sell angels and drill in the arctic? Melt down the Pearly Gates and use it in 5G? Where was the "new man hailed by Rousseau...purportedly brought into being by the French Revolution"? Wagenknecht couldn't see him, but the by-product and residue was all around him: "Stresses on the self-fashioning individual". Murat and Pinel had called it correctly – "insanity...a disease of sensitivity, whose causes were to be found in the torments of life".

Think deeply and you're a goner. Let in or begin to think that civilisation is the standard and you falsify life – expect too much. So which road to take? Obama's and his mock-MLK marching? (Crooked ears fighting the wind.) The noble lie. *Remember the noble lie?* The hordes can only face up to so much. When you're inside government, sat at the desks of the civil servants, you suddenly see the whole shit-storm: the Chinese slowly becoming our masters; the importing of energy and food; the population expanding too quickly and infrastructure creaking.

That didn't bother Bob Marley – thirteen children by nine women. Charles Dickens ("his villains were...himself") naming all ten of his offspring. And let's not exclude BB King – fifteen juniors running around.

Rousseau or Ruskin – Wagenknecht never remembered who it was that had all five of his children adopted. Must be Ruskin. You don't come up with a clever chains quote which precedes Jefferson and then ship out your own blood.

NO MAN IS GOOD ENOUGH TO BE ANOTHER MAN'S MASTER. Wagenknecht had in his head the old slogans and words on three-stick banners. Yes, he believed such sentiment. He sympathised with what now seemed like quaint concerns. They've got in your head. Did you ever march with the radicals? Did you ever feel the brotherhood, the kinship? No, but I walked alongside them on the pavement. I went to a socialist workers gathering at Salchester Town Hall – listened to the speeches, witnessed Paul Mackintosh Foot, heard their talk about shares.

And yet you still became a stockbroker? I did, but money – it was only ever about the money. I didn't alter my convictions. I didn't salute capitalism. *But you didn't lie down in the road against it?* No, but I wrote, I write plays. *You write plays?* Yes. *What about?* Crackup merchants. Melancholy. Pensiveness. *Saving the world from afar – too scared to get up close.* Perhaps. *There's no perhaps about it, William. You're the worst kind of shyster – not a blatant one like Shilp who bulldozes his shitty mannerisms at people, but rather a sneak thief. Too much observing and not enough action. A man who likes to hoover and then look at the plush carpet but not pull it up.* I buy a lot of that. *Well – you better buy it* all.

OK. OK. Go easy. This is a sensitive time. I approach people like you, William – do you know why? Why? Because you dither, weigh up everything. You can't move one fucking inch without a risk assessment. You're an apostate! A pavement socialist! You stand for nothing! You've done nothing!

Wagenknecht couldn't bear it. Where were these damn voices coming from? Shrieking a little. Insistent. No bloody rest. He was driving and so pulled in to the nearest lay-by. Your keys – put them on the dashboard. That's what they taught you on the driving course. The police have got to see them otherwise they'll stop you. You can't use your phone without them there.

He did it – killed the engine and flung the big set of keys onto the dash. History on that key ring – there was history. His wedding band, as if anticipating this day – too painful to wear now, shooting pains up his finger, the Dupuytren's contracture like a real ailment (bigger than the asthma and the geographic tongue). The old penny piece his grandfather had illegally drilled through. "Go your way in safety" – the fob his grandma had bought him for his 21st. A Fleetpool mascot which symbolized his time together with Scotty. And Jasmine, precious Jasmine – a colourful running man, made from loom bands and the ultimate skill of his daughter's fingers.

Who was running now, or rather not returning? Wagenknecht, sat hunched in this truckers' resting place, peering out at the archetypal black litter bin, burger van across the road and petrol-stained hedgerows. This is who I am now – a cheap nomad. All the warmth has gone. It will be like a blizzard when I make the call. Lysette will shoot me, cut me out of their lives for months. Where does the strength come from for this? Who is equipped to stem the blood, the emotional massacre?

Wagenknecht's cousin, Waldot was a pro at such things. He had ditched *two* fiancees, had sold his share in *two* houses. A mess was a mess. Give it a month, maybe three, and they'd thank you. Brave, knowing his mind, Wagenknecht thought. But no children and only ever *half* marriages. Pointless seeking his advice. He was a straightforward man – a little like Douglas. You argue ten times, you leave; the big, ball-busting arguments. Just get out – find a different pair of tits.

Another woman – that is what eased things. And lately Wagenknecht had been getting heavier signs from the gods that it was time to go, time to walk away. Only so much. I can only take so much. *Enjoy the fruits out there!* Find some other fruits. Pick the lot. Go on a frenzy. Bed hop for a bit. Turn off that damn guilt every now and then. Who had loaded him up with so much culpability? It was, at times, like cartilage damage, a limping brain, the dutiful doziness of an anaesthetized patient.

This is *not* a mid-life crisis, thought Wagenknecht. It is reality – an array of fleecing marshals crucifying me; the trick being no nails. He gazed out of the car window and still held his phone. A grim place with its speeding cars and architectural relics. A sheltered monstrosity occasionally lit up by the high, streaming sun wishing to remind God of His nooks and crannies.

Look at that man, thought Wagenknecht – holding his cheeseburger as if it's *Les Rougon-Macquart*. That's all he needs. Right now, that's all he needs. I wish I was like that, wandering around with moist lips, shortening and breaking up the day.

Instead, it's always the big one with you! When the reptiles first crawled out of the water, do you think they had projects in mind? Did they hitch their happiness to some kind of lizard utopia?

Sharpen up, you bum, you worrisome gadfly. *Stop being Georges Debil!* Separate yourself from your art.

Jesus – if you can't do that then you're writing your own downfall. Your wife, Lysette – she doesn't take you seriously, therefore end it. Man doesn't need incredulity, censorship, being harangued from close quarters. You know a number of ways to end it, so do it now! *Phone her!*

Remember the bloke who took his wife away for the weekend – seventy miles from home. Woke up the next morning, looked at her and just left. Time to return and clear out his things without the emotional debris. Time to calmly exit – leave a note. Perhaps a chicken shit way, but a clean break. Better for both sides. No one wants it ugly.

But isn't she entitled to a little ruck? *Listen to yourself!* She's brainwashed you. This has become the norm. Think back to when you were free. Do it, William! No more half life.

It felt as if a force was gripping Wagenknecht's shoulders. He was slowly becoming conscious of his old life, what he'd expected. Half way through the marriage he had thought: Yes, it is true. I wish to go back to dating her, seeing her in the evenings only. Much simpler that way. Oh, to have Saturday and Sunday free for sport, documentaries, politics, quiet lunches, swimming and long walks. *Women are evening things.* During the day they'll mess you up, fuck up the most basic schedule; have you swap one piece of grass for another, miles away. Always chauffeuring them, stroking their illogical ways!

Wagenknecht continued to sit in his old car – a royal blue, 1.6L Ford Focus or *Communist* as Heselglass liked to say. Nothing fancy about it. Tough, a good amount of acceleration, but dust everywhere and bird shit outside – Wagenknecht, an immaculate house type person, but automobiles, cars, just there for A to B.

Ever seen a council house with a slick, expensive car outside? Yes, many times, thought Wagenknecht. And I don't understand it. Who wants to travel well but return to a box? Give me the damn space anytime. So I can't show off on the motorway, smile at a few bimbos – so what! You accept the *Communist*, you accept me. And then I show you what I've built, the home I've become a near-ascetic for, frugal, not out on the lash. Far from Dougie and Leonard (*glamorous* Tories) – who managed to have it all – but not regretful.

Except, with this call, Wagenknecht was signing over the last fifteen years of his life. *You call me a ditherer for thinking things through, being risk averse?!* Let me see you give up your satanic double bedroom, the very bricks around you! *Wherever, whoever* you are, there's a stake, something that needs putting on the roulette table for a spin. And your penguin suit doesn't mean a damn thing afterwards. Just like the car.

'You can't sleep in a car,' Wagenknecht had told Scotty, forewarned him due to his son's youthful obsession.

'How much was your Affordable, Dad?'

'Three thousand. I've never gone over that amount for a car.'

'How much is a Mercedes, an Alfa Romeo, a Ferrari?'

'Too much. Maybe forty thousand. Who spends that on a car...'

'I will.'

Wagenknecht just laughed. *The perspective of the young!* Just skidding around, posing, jostling amongst themselves to be the coolest. It's soon over. And then you just look feeble, anachronistic. Unless you're big enough to know what it was, look back on the photos and not be embarrassed. Leonard consigned such history to the attic, deep within wooden chests. He had once worn lipstick, trilbies and white pants – strutted around to Duran Duran videos and maybe dreamt of a less orthodox life. You spoke of it now and he switched subjects – had to be serious, didn't wish to be weighed down by the inane past.

Wagenknecht remembered that they'd lived on the poshest street on the estate – often had girls wandering down from the 'Bronx' fascinated by their so-called ways and less messed-up mannerisms. If you lived on Wagenknecht's road, you apparently surveyed things, didn't rush in and knew an awful lot more about how to get on. Perhaps your dad was an engineer instead of a bin man, a teacher instead of a labourer.

Did that experience turn you into a prince? thought Wagenknecht - feeling above a certain class of people. Leonard just wanted out – for *his* street to be the surrounding streets also. Douglas, never a toff, simply liked what money could do for him.

You, William, you did the dangerous thing – hung around too late, right into your late twenties. Let it imprint itself on you. Your paper round – they'd swarm around you, one here, two there. It was like being in a laboratory for them. Douglas and Leonard never saw the true deprivation, never had five-year-old girls coming up to them with cuttings from *Playboy*. 'Ever seen a snatch?' Wagenknecht talked back to them in a hard manner, lectured them, but he could see they were goners already. Probably only twelve himself with a fancy bit of beige leather across the back of his jeans, but serving the community – the only Wagenknecht or Forrest to do so. Taking home his £5.20, understanding money from an early age like Pony, but probably valuing himself without inflation. A killer that – open to exploitation, too hooked up to the past.

'No history, no fears,' Leonard often said. 'Wipe the slate every twelve months.'

'I don't work that way,' Wagenknecht had responded, still with the girl's disturbing face in his head.

He was a posh dick to the eleven, twelve and thirteen-year-old Bronx females. He had an appendage wrapped up in finer cotton, he smelled a little sweeter, washed his hair more often. Maybe such elevation had sealed up his pride, compounded it. He had begun to believe their projections.

They weren't awe struck, but you could see them clambering, re-arranging their inferior clothes, conscious of grassier surroundings, thicker window frames, longer drive ways. This was Wagenknecht's patch. But when on *their* territory opening letter boxes, fearful of dangerous mutts, the standards dropped.

'Get dick out!' Not all of them clamouring for a sweep of his fly, a zipped entrance to his groin, but sufficient to give him cause to think: Is this what dead, uninspiring estates do? Wagenknecht looked around at the partially-curtained windows, the uncut grass, the broken toys, the peeling paint.

154 | Jeff Weston

Some amongst them will be pissed off, fried by the twisted laughs and junk personalities that roam around. The *adults* I'm referring to now, stressed Wagenknecht in his head. But there's no way out. That address on the CV (Kentless Road) – notorious. The well-meaning and pleasant mind – deserving of something higher but not ruthless or quick enough. *Those Humboldt days are gone!* Language – "a mental exhalation, a spiritual mission, a creative outburst". *No more!* Not when mocked and derided.

'A lot of people have been shot down, William – thinking they can get through life with humour or beauty when only brains will do.' His older brother liked to give him snippets from his own ascent – the proven but bent track which stoked inequality.

'There's certainly beauty on the gnarled estates. But what does that become? Modelling? A short catalogue career? The wife to someone of means?'

'It doesn't become anything.'

'What do you mean?'

Leonard's hair fluffed out more five weeks after having it cut. That and his stolid face gave him the look of a scientist pouring over reams of data. 'What do I mean? Well, they're not super models, so it's a scrap using what they've got. Not knowing whether to take their blouse off, maybe their bra, for an amateur camera. Didn't one of them move into our parents' street?'

'Yes – just one.'

'Wanting to get in just as we got out. How peculiar.'

'She was a little bit different I think.'

'How so?'

'Softer edges. Not as brash. Probably well brought up.'

'On the top street?! Is that possible?' The millionaire curse – generalisation, thought Wagenknecht; a prick of a brother, reads the *Daily Mail* in waiting rooms. More on the sandwich: 'A few of them asked you out, I seem to recall...'

'The whole area pretty much, but then I had the paper round. You were being fattened up for college.'

Perhaps that's what weighed on me, Wagenknecht pondered – convinced me I was one of them.

'And the girl that lives on Mum and Dad's street now?'

'Yes, she asked me.'

'But you said no. To them all I believe.'

'Because through you and my friends at the time, I was a snob.'

'You're putting this on *me*? A Forrest. We're back to *that*?'

No more. There could be no more. Leonard – the trainee millionaire made real; his Irish immigrant wife somehow above the area he had fled. Leonard – his former favourite artist, Kandinsky more of a draughtsman than purveyor of art "as the great expression of the human spirit".

A stiff! A damn stiff. But Wagenknecht still somehow needed him. Foolishly gauged his life against him. You can't even go where he goes, William. You can't catch the same planes, eat the same food, sit on the same balconies. Your account would be wiped out after a week. Just a week with one of his road trips through California.

You'd have to beep the damn horn on your jalopy, hope that he'd hear you, turn around, drop a few dollars through the desperately wound-down window. And what example is that to Scotty and Jasmine anyway?

Scotty knew about the Maserati parked up in Leonard's garage. A car his uncle never drove but it represented an investment – its purple skin a layer of fumigation that the masses were not meant to penetrate.

'I think I'll have five garages, Dad.'

'Scotty, Scotty – have I lost you?'

Anything that shines and moves quickly, thought Wagenknecht. Pointless preaching now. Somehow he'd ridden up front in Douglas's Audi as well – seen the splendour, felt the comfort.

'You can't drive a book, Dad. That's what Uncle Douglas said.'

'He did, did he. Well, tell him, you *can*. You *can* bloody drive a book. Better than an Audi B1.'

'It's an *A*1, Dad.'

'Accelerate through the pages, Scotty. Go on. Take this…'

A faded lump. Wagenknecht was becoming one again, in front of his son. Technology – the seducer; hard, sleek lines fibbing around in young minds. But pages – actual pages – not even recognised as anything of wonder anymore.

Dear Mr Hus – Jan Hus – I'm reaching your age, the age at which you were executed and it feels like they're slowly taking my son. It is like a scene-by-scene stuttering execution – his uncles throwing large steaks in his direction. What do I do? I do not wish to curb his curiosity, but it's back to the flies in many ways, the shit-orbiters. He sees a very narrow strip of the world and I find it impossible to widen his view through the kaleidoscope. Perhaps if I could obtain a documentary produced by the school on him? That way I'd know his playground patter, get a better understanding of where his morals sit. Without a level, I cannot begin to take him through the sinister highway of his teens.

Do you have children yourself? You seem to be one of the most overlooked men of history and yet you castigated the fiscalisation and bureaucratisation of the papacy when heresy was fatal. Six hundred years apart we are – almost to the day (which makes me think that reincarnation is considered every hundred). I think you would identify with Adorno who discussed the twin dilemmas of modernity: injustice and nihilism. Although, I don't know that nihilism is a doctrine of destruction for its own sake – surely a softer working than that, a readiness to refuse the doped-up pills given out. How much slack do we honour humanity with – I suppose that is the question, always the legislative nail. Does injustice eke out a living in the lower quarters only or is it also seen romping around – quite unchecked – behind toughened glass? Abuses, I think we call them – very similar to your day.

The unintelligent are not entitled to comfort. That is how it is, thought Wagenknecht. And because of that we have not shifted from the primitive definition of man as a warrior. The charge, the spear, the con is all in the brain now, less so in the physique. Inequality makes second helpings look like a transiently-dipped little finger.

Phone her, you chicken shit. *Phone her!* Yes, I should, computed Wagenknecht. Do it here in this grotty fold because it reflects a little of what you'll become. No Accrington brick. No generous vestibule. No sweet, meadow-edged front garden. No castle, even if the Lord was never in charge. This is it – the slayer of many a man. The infantilisation of a former adult life. But think of the sweets you'll now get to taste. Think of that ivory skin - even a cocoa brown – underneath the sheets.

Yes. I may have outgrown English women, Wagenknecht assured his demons, the voices that increasingly flew in. Perhaps the indigenous English maid has had her day. Certainly, refinement seems to inhabit the bones of subcontinent Indians over and above the laddish vehicles that traipse the precincts. The snarl has become an almost compulsory greeting from the high-heeled donks that purport to represent femininity. Something occurred. A wrong turn was taken. Even Lysette's sadness eclipses that.

But the Indian women half-Westernised (that statistic perfectly sufficient) – crowned in the arena of seductive gazes, Wagenknecht thought; built to last, not submissive but respectful, just bloody well hot at a time when the locals had hollowed out, become narcissistic. Puff your bloody lips elsewhere, Wagenknecht demanded. Have something other than the extended nails and laugh of a faker.

I can't phone her, thought Wagenknecht. Not when my 2010 manifesto planned to gut the 1st-class carriage of every train and have it replaced with a 'Pregnant women & Over-60s' zone. What kind of hypocrisy would that be? You help the needy but walk out on your family. You have things to settle first.

Always conversations in your head before meeting people, phoning them. But nothing this time. Nothing for Lysette. That can't be right. Don't go in cold. Don't humiliate yourself. The church – you sometimes stare at the great hips on the pew in front of you. You're chanting or singing but drifting like a sand storm. Why do you do that? Understand it before you leave her. Try to map it. Slow down, man. Think it through. And the girl – maybe twenty-two – in the ice-cream shop or café, the special window for people walking by. The way she handed you those 99ers, waited for you to pocket your change. Didn't simply plonk it all on you. That's what you miss – courtesy, manners, everything that's squeezed out of you. She slowed the world down and you loved it. That was strength. She had it in droves. Think of that in an older model. Can Lysette be that? Can she be reset?

I don't think of it enough – not like that, Wagenknecht realised. I'm in a damn cauldron all the time. Work. People demanding things. Decisions. Quick decisions. Constantly. Always. I need to wander through the *Louvre*. Not listen to people telling me that the latest sacked man will be OK. We picture him as OK – away from the money chamber. When...when there's heartache. I know there's heartache. You're flat after such a kick. Flat for a while. Not even able to re-draft your CV. Those that remain laugh again – carry on. *You have to fucking carry on!*

'Find one thousand idiots.' That's what Leonard used to say. 'One thousand idiots will make you rich.' At times, I've looked for them – I have. Did they want my raincoats, my old master replica paintings? I still have two raincoats (navy I think) and a Corot and Constable (*The Cornfield*) rolled up in a US-style brown grocery bag. He'd advise me to ditch them. Leonard. Say I'm hanging on to the past. No history – remember. Keep the mind free. Don't clog it up with failure.

Mr Bellow – "Never the principal – only on loan to myself". Oh, you don't get that now. Honesty. Sharpness. Nobody wants that kind of sharpness. If it's not earning, it's blunted. Culture has become pork scratchings.

Other things. There were other things you said. Maybe not you, but your cast – those people that spoke for you, in and out of the novels. "What makes [the] project singularly difficult is the disheartening expansion of trained ignorance and bad thought. For, to put the matter at its baldest, we live in a thought-world, and thinking has gone very bad indeed". You can't think – not down here. Not amongst the flashing numbers.

You know what I see when I go out to lunch, enter the convenience store? The security guy – his eyes on the casually dressed, never the suits. And it's the suits slipping Lion Bars into their back pocket. He should take a sociology course. I've been in dressed up and dressed down. He doesn't look at faces – only the garb. I'm guilty in jeans, respectable in pinstripes. I tried speaking to the manager, asked about the training. He thought I was joking – chuckled, broke up his day. But then you persist and people get angry. Their faces alter. Humans – such two-sided coins. So you see, I'm concerned like you and Lukács with "resistance to the 'weakening of reality'", the deep dilution around us.

My friend, Routcliff doesn't believe in charities. You say that to a wider crowd and the mini-minds attack you. Robots? They're already here. I'm inclined to cross to the other side. "Hatred is self-respect," you said. Or was it Nietzsche? "If you want to hold your head up among people..." Yes – that sentence can never end. What would we be admitting? That we want to slaughter the chokers, the feckless, the non-union types, the bounders, the obscenely rich? Christ – there'd only be me left (or am I a choker?). And Boredman. Don't forget Boredman. His former too-steep driveway doubtlessly occupied by a struggling man. Because that kind of luck can't come around again so soon. Still a mecca. But only for what, who it held.

Tillmann tonight. That's what Wagenknecht needed. But in something other than a hotel. He'd need her to nurse him, talk of the future in a settled fashion, assure him that walking out on Lysette was not apocalyptic. Marriage took over one's blood – impaled itself on the chromosomes. Loyalty become more than loyalty. It dressed each morning out of duty and fondness. You have a right to be mixed up, Wagenknecht pondered. This isn't the cool lemonade of a relationship, a steady 'affair' – it's a marriage; *rum*; *hard liquor*; a bovine circus flashing from trapeze act to troubled clown. Its magnitude isn't even measurable. Words potter around but never quite describe the event.

Marriage. To Lysette. Christ – those lilac cardigans she used to wear; the zip leading straight to the bra. They had all been girls before Lysette – a mere training camp. Nothing substantial when you really thought about it. No living together. No hiking up hills. Few trips and home-made sandwiches. She had laughed like a woman – introduced him to *real* privacy, intimacy, a sense of them being above the world. They were locked in a moment, a bubble, the ratcheted splendour of bed sheets and candles. It came to a stop – the *whole fucking* planet. And that was the aim – surely. To mock the guinea pig existence, the experimentation that coated most lives. Sex meant you escaped. Being next to nakedness ran down the concerns of the brain.

You might think with your dick, Wagenknecht pondered, but it probably keeps senility at bay. Let the brain park up at times – look out to sea and over those wonderful hills and dunes.

He phoned her. If, through the pleasure of the past, he owed her at least this then that seemed fair. They had both discussed being apart several times. When the anger quelled they sometimes spoke with honesty, a flat percipience.

'Lysette.'

'Where are you? We expected you back. It's your night back.'

'Lysette.'

'What is it?'

Wagenknecht shifted in his pathetic roadside seat. To do it here – fuck. This is a mistake. She'll tell everyone you didn't even look her in the eye. You'll be more of a bastard than you already are.

'Us. We can't go on.'

'I've made fish. I'm just about to put the asparagus in…'

'Give it to the birds.'

'Jasmine's making the drinks. Four glasses, William. There are four glasses.'

Crucify me, why don't you. Talk of my children's faces next – their disappointment, how they're struggling, hitting lower notes than when we lived in Choton and I was full-time. Fleetpool – *your* choice, but it's killed us off, somehow extinguished the simple life.

'Put one glass back, Lysette, Now. Before it gets harder.'

'What are you saying?'

'I'll be at my parents. I'll pick the kids up at weekends. Wednesday – I'd like Wednesday as well.'

'You would?'

'Yes.'

'Jasmine. Your father's glass. Drop it on the floor.'

'It's full, Mummy. His blackcurrant...'

'Do as I say, Jasmine.'

Wagenknecht heard the crash, the performance, Scotty's exuberant cry of 'Fairground!' as it met the floor.

'Ex-communicated. Goodbye, William.'

She had to include them. It had to be theatre. Always theatre before truth. Using the kids like pawns. Irrational. Mongrel-like. Mercurial. Crazed. But he couldn't do what the Icelanders did and pretend this was normal – families being apart. This isn't a vase. The crack has consequences.

"People no longer seem to know why they are alive," Miller had said. Wagenknecht, if not before, knew now. *Why? Why?* To prompt smiles. To make people glad. And what had he just done? (It only takes a few wild seconds.) Brought suffering, a deep fracture to his own family.

Plan B though. Lysette had always referred to it as 'Plan B' in a threatening way. The *bastard* got in first though. Enacted it. The *real* bastard. Rhetoric had become the spit and polish of a new start.

Wagenknecht had meant to mention Scotty's progress or stuttering moves of late. Cutlery. Scotty hasn't been using his cutlery right. Can you keep an eye on that? And football – the coach has his tactics wrong. He needs to play Scotty deeper. The lad needs more touches of the ball. Finally, his algebra – keep testing him. Keep his interest awakened.

'Even now you're not really talking about us,' Lysette would have said. No, because the kids' problems should be addressed first. *Then* it's us. *Then* we fly.

'First? First?! A spare cake at the dinner table and what did you make them do? Roll a die. The highest number gets it.'

Somebody has to lose. God knows I lose enough travelling into Salchester every day – its stench like a giant dog biscuit. I sit amongst automatons, make enough to run the household, but I'm dead behind the eyes. They may as well put ARBEIT MACHT FREI above the entrance.

Further away from Jasmine and Scotty the more he pressed his right foot down. Wagenknecht was losing a chunk of his sun. What burrowed into his eyes now was a biting nothingness. No warmth, gaiety or balance – just the feeling that he was driving away from everything that kept him respectable and sane. You pass a certain point and you need something else to believe in. When the narcissism and solipsism die, you have to have something.

That became Jasmine and Scotty. How could it not? Those meaningful eyes of Jasmine so full of damn hope and expectation. And Scotty – he'd been saying of late that I was not as hard on his sister and therefore I loved him less. If only he knew how much promise I had in him beyond the stupid, stupid names that befell my lips out of frustration. I don't get pissed and angry on beer these days – more on disappointment in myself. The names Scotty, only at low, low moments ("dickhead, bugger, little shit") – self-directed really. Appalled at myself for struggling, not finding a way like your uncles who could feasibly retire now.

I hope to God you're not relieved that I've gone. The truth is I could never handle being in someone else's grip – an employer, the wrong partner, poor friends. Recalcitrant. That is the big word, Scotty if you wish to use it in an essay. Not susceptible to control. Rudeness, it should be explained, compensates for my shyness. I'm going off people just like your mum. There has been no Premium Bond win, no lottery, no inheritance, no large transfer of funds from Nigeria. And so I chug on – ordered to do so by the now deceased Thatcher.

I can't tell you how long your working life might last. You'd be mad at me. Forty, possibly fifty years. Who can possibly do that without some crack ups along the way? How many are we permitted without finding uncomfortableness? It's the unspoken stranglehold that bucks us, slowly ferries our dreams out of town.

Wagenknecht – here at your service, Scotty to at least provide food and shelter. For as long as you like, son. Don't – whatever you do – dive into a job at twenty and get mortgaged up. That's when they own you, when the chess board becomes loaded. These steely bankers – taught hardness *after* the charm. Unforgiving. Just a line on their spreadsheet. Your circumstances nothing to them. And the more you need to keep that property, the more you beg at work. Sickeningly so.

I've said things I'm not comfortable with, but never fawned before the chiefs that like to mug you off. Your cousin, Garrett – I expect he'll be present at jelly-wrestling competitions with bikini-clad women in the near future; a Cambridge man perhaps.

Part 3: *THE CRAWL*

Wagenknecht trundled towards his new home, his old home – the Dodderers HQ which housed his parents. They ate in the gazebo during the summer months, the wigwam at the bottom of the gooseberry bush garden. Not one to join the crowded palash, he sat stiff at the rectangular, mahogany table indoors. Mats – his mother was big on mats. His place was covered in rolled-out fabric, stiff corkboard plate and drink mats, and a wool base. Wagenknecht looked around. Back. He was back in a part of Choton – the town that had given him life, his first sight of the world. But forty-three – he was a 43-year-old baby still suckled to the tit; roast chicken, lightly peppered fish and chillies instead of milk.

Sit at a table on your own *after* you've had a family and tell me it doesn't stink, thought Wagenknecht. Tell me you don't think about the meaning of life and what people advocate. *Suicide. Defiance. Irony.* Which category was he? Most were choosing irony these days. The thinner life got, the easier such a selection was. But didn't you beat up the electrons in your head with that flimsy option? Wasn't it an admittance that you'd fallen lower than suicide? Everything a joke. Everything a damn joke, thought Wagenknecht. Look up the word. Reach for your seven dictionaries. "1.Mildly sarcastic use of words to imply the opposite of what they normally mean. 2.Used to draw attention to some incongruity or irrationality."

Was Wagenknecht in the game? He could be. At times he held such a crown aloft – perpetuated it without realising. But he preferred defiance. If only they knew at the brokerage house that his password was Trotsky! ("In a serious struggle there is no worse cruelty than to be magnanimous at an inopportune time.") Oh, the uncompromising liberal idealist. And, later, the "unthinking naïve joy" of 1989. A quarter of a century into this new world and what had it given him? A revolution betrayed? The salted minds of a speeding public? Leonard and Douglas didn't mind. They embraced the hammering juxtaposition of politeness and evil. There was an odd respect for the fury and banality of businessmen. Wagenknecht had seen too many cheap faces to take them seriously. Yes – they probably had a knack for generating money, but what else were they?

They were more than him. They were accoutrements of the environment around them. "You must live with your time, but do not be a product of it," Routcliff insisted Wagenknecht heed. Use the world around you, but don't fall in. In his parental, slightly stooping way, Routcliff redressed Wagenknecht's stumbling, sometimes astoundingly simple view of life. 'It is this. It is that. You have not factored in people's machinations, their schemes, the apparatus by which they operate. "Economics is an alibi for capitalism" – surely you know that...'

Wagenknecht had built a board, a sign. Within days of arriving at his old home he had dived in the garage and used his father's tools in a limited but necessary way. Saw, chisel, sandpaper, gloves, vice, paint, hat. Wagenknecht blew the sawdust off his work half way through and stared at the chiseled verbs: READ, PLAY, LISTEN, EAT, WATCH, LOVE. Sometimes the most basic functions escaped him and so this, hung in his room, was a reminder. It was also a counterweight to the heart-shaped carving hanging with crass intent from his parent's kitchen wall: *Live the life you love!*

Such expression was like a boastful thud from the retirees. Wagenknecht still had a vague idea of what he loved, but the insistence from others with time on their hands and a sufficient pot of money – it was brutal!

Live the life indeed, thought Wagenknecht. *If only I wasn't too busy croaking it!* If only something dribbled down from the gods. Wagenknecht looked at the state of his clothes. Out of shape. Old. Their classic sheen long gone. Both inside and out he was becoming ragged, frayed, tatty, broken. Leonard had looked at him the last time they had met and exhaled. Was this really his brother? Why the ten-year-old cardigans, the shirts with worn cuffs, and those brown boots you've had since the Russian ruble crisis?

They still keep me warm, thought Wagenknecht – upright. I see no need for a change. I used to shop every two years. Now, I suppose it's once a decade.

Routcliff and Heselglass were similarly dressed – musty concoctions, colour clashes, untailored sacks that showed they were thinkers. 'So long as my penis isn't flapping in the wind, then you should be pleased,' Heselglass offered as a rebuttal when drawn on the matter.

The three of them – antiquated amigos from a lost age, but ahead of Ashpound; still ahead of the backward Renaissance man. Grumbling had its benefits, its ups, its lustre.

Walk around the house while they're out, thought Wagenknecht. Look around. Observe. Can you get used to this? The peacefulness during the day. The swathe of photos – smiles and glumness beaming out at you. The potpourri. The cushions printed with LIVE, LAUGH, LOVE. The tabloid papers piled around like rat infestations. The cooker that vibrated slightly even when off. The long cup rails and reams of plates as if twenty guests could descend at any moment. The coats hung glibly under the stairs. The tall twigs in pots – a flash of fashion that Wagenknecht's mother bought into. The baskets congregated at the bottom of the stairs. More LOVE plaques – this time in the bathroom. The endless cushions and blankets – his own bed smothered like Cleopatra's. The selection of small, useless drawers. The bedding box on the landing. And the numerous, numerous figurines and ornaments. Did his mother speak Yiddish?

All of it, at times, seemed to be coming at him, closing in. He could not see one clean surface. Minimalism had been firmly chased from the house. Wagenknecht had to get outside. To breathe. To re-evaluate. To get a handle on his stuttering existence. He leant forward – rested his palms on his knees. This. This drive that I played cricket at the end of when I was a boy. This copper beech tree now partially cut down because the mad woman next door complained of a lack of light. This street that he had chased around with a water gun in his hand – laughing, yes *laughing*.

It all seemed borrowed – no longer real. He had shot up to 5'10" and with such height came handicaps. Wagenknecht. He knew he knew something. But what? *What?!* Was his wisdom inside the plays? Did he have to look at a script every time he needed direction? Even then, it was *little* theatre. Did little theatre ever guide a man? Minuscule. Petite. Small. Baseball with no crowd.

'Have you tried to make money recently?' Douglas had asked. '*Real* money? You do that and the art follows.'

Time was giving both his brothers' words legitimacy, logic. They were edging him, bounding forward. Wagenknecht was in a slower game. Outside of the brokerage house it was one careful word at a time and then the fastidious scrutiny of theatre directors and readers.

Possibly all for nothing, Wagenknecht thought. There will be a few of us out there – failures, relics, men behind the curve.

He listened again to the mass of words swooping into his ears – conversations from the past that now had resonance.

'There is no pattern – don't you see! Cash is the closest we get to control, slowing down.' Douglas again – the man he had told people was an inveterate heathen wading around in wealth. But growing faster now – yes, growing faster. Back to Maslow and his Hierarchy of Needs.

You can't join them at this late stage, insisted Wagenknecht. What would you do? Lock up? Make the tea? The cloth has been cut. Trundle on. Get back to broking. Show Shilp you're serious now.

End my days alongside the Marabou Turd? *Never!* I'd rather stick tights on my head and hold up the office. He phoned Routcliff, wished for some sensible input – words not infected by the seasoned pioneers of modernity.

'What have we got, Routcliff? What have we got that's still alive? We've tried politics, art, humanism. Where does man go after that?'

'I heard someone say "You can't resent the era you live in without being severely punished by it". That doesn't help, I know. But it's a starting point.'

Wagenknecht could make out his authoritative face over the phone, the spindly fingers that had once brought his keyboard crashing down on his desk. Something in Routcliff stepped over sacks of garbage. Something in him was heading for the same finishing line as Wagenknecht.

'Our conversations have been running for years now. But I'm beginning to feel – as with a lot of things – that we've not made much ground.'

'Ah, but that's the thing. We're airing modern man's predicament. We're not industrialists though. Two thousand years of bluff, William. The little man mostly tied to his fate.'

'So why talk then?'

'I thought you knew…'

Wagenknecht thought of the city he worked in with its catwalk of meat – nothing more, just bodies with coloured garments on trying to attract. Popular music – "it resolves things easily". He had heard that on the radio recently and it made more and more sense.

His mind turned to the place the removal men had shipped his family to. Fleetpool – good in parts. Lovely. Beaches dotted along its edge. But further south and the hotels were burning down. Arson. More and more common. A slow destruction of Fleetpool's former glory; cratered roofs visible from the promenade. And at the back of the tower – no grass like in Paris, but the hard pavements of cheap commerce. A breed of person walking on the strip with one eye lower than the other. Depravity screaming from their bones. God – keep Scotty and Jasmine away from this now I am not here. Don't let their teenage years be consumed by miscellany and confusion.

Wagenknecht sensed that wishing such a thing was like a Chinese man re-arranging his hair. It always ended up the same whatever he did. Life now would pull Scotty and Jasmine along – throw them in amongst the stragglers and crooks. That is why Wednesday was important, he thought. It could act like a conference, a mid-week tête-à-tête. And if he started taking Tillmann along, then a new balance would be there. They would be an example to the kids. Not a wreck. No longer a wreck. But harmony. A pocket of steadfastness enjoying the world. Yes – that's what he needed. Don't just lecture them, thought Wagenknecht. *Show* them happiness. *How a man and woman ought to be.*

He marched upstairs, resolved to organise his life – even here in Choton, away from the coastal vortex. The toilet – he needed to stand in front of it and hang his appendage over its 20th century pot. You think when you pass water. Your mind takes a different track as if meditating for a moment.

Make a grab at Tillmann's tits. Know that she likes the raw approach – something that Lysette came to detest, vilify him for.

'It's all you want. Not me. You go straight for them.'

'Maybe because you used to drape them over the bannister. You used to entice me.'

'Well, you've not earned it. And I've grown out of that.'

'Grown out of fun? Titillation? How?'

'The menopause, William. The menopause. Man's boulder. His step too far.'

Wagenknecht looked down. Easy to slump. Fall back into boredom. Marriage – the killer. A long piece of rope. An empty contract.

Piss. There was piss on the basin. From his father undoubtedly. This was it – his new world. Stray trajectories. Failing eyesight. Bellow again. He thought of Bellow. "Man is free whose condition is simple, truthful, real." It was certainly real. But simple, truthful? No. And he could not forgive such an act. He had no wish to wipe the front of the basin every time he relieved himself here in this corner of the 1930s build.

The origin of work? Wagenknecht wondered. The origin of public opinion? Bismarck most likely. And Herzen. Amazing what ran through your mind as you became lighter. Both areas now dominated the landscape. Work had become everything. It filleted a man. And public opinion – a construct, bogus outrage, the kind of lower stench that recruited bigots.

At times there was no place for Wagenknecht. No seat. No menu. He was adrift – surviving only because of Boredman. *Throw back the lesser brew!* Be clever and well-off enough not to care.

Everything has a bearing on life, thought Wagenknecht. Where you park, where you walk, your parents' friends. Some of this stuff, I wasn't shown. The altruistic mother cosseting me, protecting me – even from girls. Now, I walk down an unfamiliar road in Choton and half panic. I see the shattered glass on the floor – mankind's crime scene. Distasteful. It's distasteful, ruinous. It plucks the feathers from my mind.

Dear Garrett – Soon you'll very likely see me as a mad uncle. That label might even be encouraged by your mother, Poppy whereas your father thinks I took a wrong turn in the road. Your recent awards (Latin and mathematics – everything but literacy) – well done! I was only doing big multiplications at such an age. I noticed the back of your T-shirt when we were last down there walking in the sun on the common – a collection of words or qualities apparently (clever, ambitious, creative, faithful, disciplined, diligent, considerate, patient). Most of them are OK, but go easy on the 'disciplined' once in a while. It can sap a young mind – have it explode later. You're welcome to visit. Uncle Wag (WW).

Wagenknecht felt like a hemlock-threatened Socrates talking about a different set of gods – a more realistic set of affairs. He was sure Leonard and Poppy would see the letter because they inspected everything. They were a bomb disposal team, a couple of paranoid cranks worried about their son becoming normal. All the best sons had surpassed normal. It was Nietzsche and his *Uberman*. Capes – they just needed the capes.

It had all become so different and Wagenknecht could not have envisaged this. How the dynamics change. How people drift. How brothers love you less. *Why give me the rich siblings?!* he yelled. The comparison is too much at times. I'm a bum – every morning. I climb out of bed and think of them. See their cuff links, their en-suite bathrooms, their silk dressing gowns. Possibly a wink in the mirror to themselves. Meanwhile I'm here – relegated further; our parents shuffling small portions of food into their mouths in the gazebo.

Dear Companies House – Please can you carry out a thorough search of my little brother's accounts? His name is Douglas Forrest of D.F.X. It would be unfair of me to assume his operation is not legitimate, but the bunce, the dough that it generates. It just doesn't seem in keeping with his academic record. This may seem snide, but I need to know. If I can fail just a little less, then...

He slumped into a rotating leather chair. No voices. Jasmine. Scotty. Lysette. Nothing. The emptiness was beating him down, trampling on his finer side. Bitter – I've opened the door, met with its CEO, Wagenknecht thought. And you don't just wash your face after such an encounter or pull out the smelling salts. I am changing, becoming routinely angry. There is a perfunctory menace to me. I am in the body of a disappointed, crazed individual.

He wanted to meet up with Tillmann but such a move risked his aces under the table. Tillmann could only care about the man of conviction, the grammar-obsessed oddball that had wandered in one evening and wrestled her from kids' books and crayons. *Women did not want weakness!* That is the one thing he had learnt after a quarter of a century on the circuit. You were to tend to *their* weaknesses and gripes and not always have the answers. Just be a good ear.

He got in his car. Drove. Anywhere. Familiarised himself with the area once more. The Bronx to the right. An old-worldly village setting to the left. He took the full tour, looked at the houses where his friends had once lived. If they could see him now in his bruised and beaten-up car. Back, or in a mess like Austoff. "Depressives cannot surrender their childhood". Remember! Ha – it was true. *And why should they?!* Boardrooms did not giggle. They did not understand that hanging on was sometimes needed. Godledge as well – lost his dad early, so was playing out the missing years.

Look at that basketball net, Wagenknecht observed. Drilled to the side of the house, but its hoop hanging at 120 degrees (never to be straightened). Where is the father that should be climbing up his proud ladders to put it right? Were they all missing, AWOL, no more? It will be a higher percentage – a higher percentage round here. This is the *top road and beyond* that Leonard had disparagingly referred to. A black market in many ways.

The coal bunkers Wagenknecht had hidden in as a child. Their game of hide and seek stretched far and wide – an agreed 400-yard radius. *Find me in here, you suckers!* They hadn't, but Wagenknecht had found this other world, the sadder faces that marched by. Leonard and Douglas had only ever hidden near the posh houses – smelt a different kind of shrub, felt the adjunct therapy of well-ordered gardens.

Wagenknecht made his second call of the night.

'Hello.'

'Leonard.'

'William?'

'Yes.'

'Christ – I've only just got in. Does it have to be now? This is family time. Family time.'

'I am family.'

'You know what I mean. Poppy. Garrett. The bigger stuff.'

'It's important, Leonard.'

'Go on then. Go on.'

'I know why.'

'Know why? State the facts, William. Finish the sentence.'

'You didn't look in the open coffin – when Grandpa died. It was only me.'

'And? William – dinner is burning. Speak clearly.'

'I looked in. Saw that unrecognisable face. It changed me. I'm sure it did.'

'I've never liked doing that. I have no fascination for that.'

'Neither do I. But I felt like I owed Grandpa a farewell, a final look.'

'It must have been hard then. I'm sorry you had to see what you saw.'

'But something in me has fallen. Since that day. I thought I'd got over it, laughing a little at the memories with Uncle Ba at the wake. But…it's not there. The old me is frazzled, spent.'

'You try again, William. You get on with things. That's all you can do.'

Wagenknecht felt like dropping the phone. His energy was sapped. His direction skewed. Truth in that box, that coffin, he thought. There was truth. The harshness of one's final hours on earth. Dumped. We're all just dumped – eventually given over to rampaging insects or grilled at high temperatures into powder. How about sailing me off, he mused. Another ending. Something better than the staple British farewell.

'I still see him – the gaunt face, nothing like the big man that entertained us, showed us things.'

'We all fall, William. Become weaker. You *have* to accept it.'

'Remember when he used to park in the treasurer's spot at the golf club?'

'I don't. I think I'd left by then.'

'Are you sure?'

'Yes. Yes, I am. I only played golf with you once. And that was at the municipal.'

Speaking to a stranger. *I am speaking to a stranger*, Wagenknecht thought. Leonard was being hurried along by something – contorted, controlled. Or maybe he was fearful of finding his old self – the trilby hats, the lipstick, the glint of dangerous nihilism.

He could see him behind the phone – muting him, swearing, rolling his eyes, tipping his head, signalling to Poppy that the deserter, Wagenknecht (no longer of family name) just wouldn't hang up.

And yet Wagenknecht had many things on him – the night Leonard had spent in the police cells (mistaken identity), a photo of him as an irascible and dour teenager (arms shooting out of his school blazer) and failed manoeuvres for women.

Little bro' William was a risk – a risk in a drunken room or in front of a freighter of executives who knew only the exam-toting and sensible Leonard. *Don't come to London!* I have a new life down here and you – quite frankly – are a hick.

Movement became the thing, thought Wagenknecht – the new sacredness (even packed up in its rattlesnake grace). If you're not moving, seen to be speeding along the track, then you're screwed, ill-thought of, ill-treated, mishandled.

'You can't keep fucking believing,' Leonard had once shouted at Wagenknecht – the inference that naivety still had him against its bosom, or worse that William refused to enter the real world.

A buffer – there will always be a buffer, something to push back the pain or a director/producer to edit the strip of film. You're in a movie. We're all in a movie, but some cuts better prepare you. At some point you have to face life's bastards. *Do it now* – get it over with. Better to settle in early.

Now, back with his parents, the studio was in full swing. He could feasibly avoid certain nasties – have his food dished out by his mother, ask his father to take his car for its MOT, have chunks of his life warded or fenced off (charity callers, neighbours, odd-job men, Jehovah's Witnesses, postmen).

This is why I have to cut a deal, thought Wagenknecht – get *some* independence back, not fall into a momsy existence. Have my own key. My own building. Start again, but not like before – because Lysette had not wanted him to live alone. She had shackled him early – puppeteered them all: partner; parents-in-law; solicitor; estate agent. A more northern part of Choton beckoned; Lysette finally escaping, no longer "working as a waitress in a cocktail bar". The gravy train had arrived – part Bisto, part Wagenknecht testicles. And Lysette was choo-chooing.

Now, separation in the bag, she was perhaps quietly celebrating its privatisation. Bonuses for the bitch. A fat income – no questions asked. Because Wagenknecht had his children to tend to. He had little bird mouths that needed wriggling worms and regurgitated food.

"I grew up overnight into an old man." Who said that? thought Wagenknecht. One bad day with a woman and you're stuffed, pickled – taxidermists approaching from all sides. I can't seem to breathe properly now. Full breaths are beyond me. Decisions have become harder. I see too much. Think of every angle...which paralyses me.

The pock-marked garage. Just get in there. Start your new life. Look at what your small investment has brought.

The trips to Fleetpool had been few. To retrieve his belongings, to see the questioning faces of Scotty and Jasmine, to stop off at Donna Tillmann's; her small, yellow car parked up outside.

'Are you seeing someone else?' Lysette had asked, disinterestedly.

'No, of course not,' Wagenknecht had lied. A 'Yes' and she would go to the governors, the headmistress, anyone that thrived on normal human faults. Tillmann would be slung in a room – kids' desks pushed together, serious-looking individuals corralled for an impromptu session.

Wagenknecht found some of himself again at Tillmann's. She was less emotional than Lysette, fewer frowns tortured her face. There seemed to be a strong, benevolent family behind that mien.

'It might be best if I use your car port when I come around. I don't wish to risk your career. If she knew it started before the split...'

'That's sensible. OK. And leave under the cover of darkness?'

Wagenknecht liked how she put things, how there was excitement in every word, a not-too-serious tease spread across each syllable.

'Yes - if I'm worthy of such a stint.'

'I like bumming around with you, William. I like shutting out the world.'

What could exceed "bumming around"? thought Wagenknecht. Christ – how she framed things, how she diluted the trickier elements of life.

Just invent. *Invent what you want*. Put some bricks around it and all is good. He had probably spent a dozen nights with her now, seen most things in her wardrobe and got used to her curvaceous spec. She liked to catwalk for him at the end of the bed, try outfits on, combinations, dresses.

Wagenknecht liked the bit in between when she was in her underwear. He liked to see her full, womanly plump. He would contribute – name an occasion for each set of clothes: theatre; local pub; country pub; Ascot!; miniature railway; boating lake. He would mess with her, throw in 'Recycling Centre' and 'Newsagent' and where Lysette would have fumed, Donna took it in, thought it amusing, engaging, admired him for it.

Damn – this is better than I imagined, thought Wagenknecht. Lysette may as well have had a burqa over her such was the concealment, the rare glimpse of skin. But Tillmann's mind, Donna's thought patterns – more than he'd expected given that most females were stuffed with gossip and tripe from an early age (never to recover).

The feminists would thank him for saying it. They would herald him a modern man or rather a much-needed classic in this duff age. Wagenknecht had a couple of de Beauvoirs, five Virginia Woolfs, a George Eliot and an Edith Wharton cluttering his shelves back in Fleetpool. They were there for Scotty and Jasmine, never to be retrieved, never to be re-housed.

Wagenknecht would start again, gaze at critical and reference works instead. *An Age of Enormity* (Isaac Rosenfield). *The Red Hot Vacuum* (Solotaroff). *Feminist Literary Theory* (Eagleton). *The Invention of Ethnicity* (Sollors). *Freedom for Sale* (Kampfner). *The Selling of the President* (McGinniss). *The Uses of Literacy* (Hoggart). *America* (Alfred Kazin). *The Culture of Cities* (Mumford). Stout books. In leaving behind most of his fiction, he was trying to make it real for Donna. That was his commitment. When she stood there in her lacy bra, hands on hips, and waited for him to sweep her up, Wagenknecht needed weighty sentences.

'Do you know that Nixon could talk for one minute and know it to the second...'

'I know now.'

The conversation didn't have to flourish. It just had to have bits of piquant beauty. And she was soaking it up. Wagenknecht would run out of lines eventually like he always did with women, but why not spade in the aggregate while he could. He liked to see a woman smile. This woman. He liked to suspend her radiance.

In here, Donna's getaway, her modest residence, everything worked. Wagenknecht worked. He was less broken – his socks and pants peeled off him when she liked to rush. Wagenknecht sometimes looked at the unmarked books stacked up in the living room. Children's lives including his very own Jasmine. The scribblings of an as-of-yet unwounded generation. It was all to come – the disappointment, the realisation, the fifty year slog. But in between there *could* be magic. He believed it now. Bumming around! Watching her face. Inside though – it was all inside, a curtained-off haven. But then he was a home bird – his driving instructor had said so in the 1980s. He sometimes hated to go out. Just wished to lounge around. Had to meet a woman who liked to stay near the perch.

'There is no single adjudicator,' Leonard liked to remind him.

'But I have to conform?'

'Yes.'

'To who?'

'To everyone in part.'

'No wonder I don't go out. No wonder I lie on my bed and dream.'

Papers, magazines and music had been Wagenknecht's upbringing. Not much companionship to speak of, but enough. He was not Ashpound. That story was of a social urchin. *And there had been news.*

Sat inside his converted garage which Tillmann had not yet visited, Wagenknecht had taken a fidgety call from the man himself. Summoned to their usual pub, he ventured out.

Ashpound was still vociferous without realising it – an incredible state of affairs. He looked across at Wagenknecht with eyes that were somehow independent.

'He's sacked me. Pony's finally done it.'

Wagenknecht had to do the forensics, had to dig below such a thin statement. Still the journalist's mind,

William thought. Despite the shafting. Despite the provincial fraud.

'How did this come about?'

'He left the main office. Went down to the boardroom and then phoned me.'

'The *chicken shit*. He could have walked down with you.'

'Listen though. I'd never heard his voice on the phone before. Couldn't be sure it was him. I didn't anticipate what it was about. Presumed it was the client base I'd asked for. I looked at my jacket, put it on, but then thought of the tie. Do I wear it? Do I leave it up here?'

I'm not sure it would have made a difference, Wagenknecht thought.

'You left it?'

'No.'

'So you went down to the big boardroom togged up…'

'"Insufficient progress". Those were his words. I asked for more but "No comment".'

'Who was in there?'

'Pony and some other guy.'

'And did he say anything?'

'Yes – "We're terminating your contract".'

'How did you feel?'

'Extinct.'

'I'd have shaken the table.'

'Well. I had to think of the reference.'

'Did you stay long?'

'It felt like I was sat there for minutes, absorbing the scene. It was like some theatre production. They'd got a crew in...except it wasn't.'

Ashpound was eloquent but some high-grade material was missing, some slate or rock.

'You weren't happy...You have to see this split from Pony as...'

'A good thing – yes.'

'You'll contest the sacking though? Get the conciliatory boys in?'

'I can't.'

'What do you mean?'

'Six weeks short of two years. Cable, who I effectively voted for in 2010, reduced my legal rights. Used to be a year.'

'You should have voted for me.'

'You weren't country wide.'

'Pony knew what he was doing then.'

'A shit head thing to do.'

'We never doubted he was that.'

Wagenknecht wondered how such decisions came about. "A bastard but not that type of bastard" he recalled Pony spouting off. This had to come down to volume. Pony, in his feeble wisdom, had sat Ashpound next to himself. The new boy next to the boss. Unprepared for his awkward way with clients and his booming voice, twenty-two months had been enough.

Do it after eighteen or even twelve months in future, Pony! Don't take them to the wire and then use the law. *And sat with your fellow board member as well!* Did you think that Ashpound was gonna get violent or was this the witness thing? I bet you never advised Ashpound he was entitled to have someone in there with *him*.

I'd know who to call, thought Wagenknecht. Routcliff, with his sporran face – and he'd maul them. Hustle them up. Heselglass would perhaps show himself to be a lachrymose king. The occasion would get to him. But Routcliff – Christ, he'd have a damn go.

You pull away from this. You pull away from this suffering when you've got it good. Look at how Ashpound's lips smack together. And he isn't even eating a chop. Isn't that just cause, a butterfly theory of sorts? Wouldn't you have done the same? He pisses both men and women off for different reasons. There are perhaps only Icadyptes penguins that haven't been undone by his arcane presence.

Such a plummet helps you, Wagenknecht. There have to be some that you crawl over, some that you hurdle, if not in merriment then out of need and necessity.

Growing up – the slow realisation of how unremarkable you are, thought Wagenknecht. The busted, fighting with the busted, waiting for that ride – someone to pick you up, show that they care, toss you a few pounds. You cannot climb without the requisite optimism though, Wagenknecht insisted. People just don't want you around. Ashpound may only be rung three. But I am rung four. Angles, I give the brokerage angles and original thoughts but they turn them into sawdust, stick with their frigid plans. Many a duff executive I have wanted to open up to, but they have displayed before my third sentence their absolute incompetence and slavish fawning and brownnosing to the upper ranks.

There is not enough grievance. It is off the table in the pious belief that positivity calms the work force and bestows greatness within the field. *The colossal problem is that I do not do lightheartedness.* I cannot be lighthearted. And yet that is what they desire – their puerile functioning bloody and worn.

Wagenknecht had sought other vocations, but the job specs, the wording – such hideous language (enthusiastic, confident, dynamic, flexible, adaptable, energized by opportunities, vibrant, outstanding). *You upbeat bastards!* Even when I am at the height of ecstasy, I am not dynamic. I never will be and so you are squeezing me out... a good man. *Work. Women. Madness.* We are back to that. *Tell me something the three do not rule!*

Give me knockers pushed out slightly, a bag strap in-between a 38-year-old breast. Give me a sip of Merrydown *Schloer* (Red Grape) or the thin Ben Shaw cans that I can no longer find. Give me a jazz parade that leads my eventual coffin to the church. Give me sweat and banter in the table tennis halls. Anything but your stiffed-up ways, your light rye flour.

Dear Chernyshevskii – I think it is you I should be writing to. What is to be done? you once asked. The question has come up again but I am not sure if rational egoists are sufficient anymore. Progress has become a dirty word hijacked by supercilious men. The still-existent raznochintsy may be the answer but even some of them have floated over – joined the whiphands. It is not Siberia as punishment today, but rather a drip; they forcibly put a drip to one's clemency.

Wagenknecht hoovered up a few biscuit crumbs from his fingers. He was on his modest leather couch, in the garage – his new abode – thinking. Work had fallen off. He had missed a few days, played the crazy fool in the surgery, looked at people in the waiting room for too long.

Build and expand and the brain whittles down, Wagenknecht pondered. It had come into his head. He felt like a mini-philosopher these days. All manner of theories washed around inside him. What were they for? What purpose did they serve? Was this a slow counting down to his final hours? If you weren't in the race, if you were burnt out before your time, then people came calling, cerebral entrepreneurs took their slice.

Wagenknecht had £16,000 tucked away – enough for 14 months. £16k – that is who I am, he thought; the only statistic or brief that matters. Is the news my gear, my speed? he wondered. Are people like me? I don't see many. But then I don't gamble anymore – talk to strangers, neighbours even. I'm apprehensive at times – always afraid of something going wrong.

Tillmann. Think of Tillmann. Use her face to settle you. You missed the surviving group of freckles on her nose. Bits of her still unravelling! And much more than the sum of her physicalities. You damn well love her warmth and outspokenness. Not many women have both qualities. And to land her after just one affair or one fling. *Exquisite! Lucky!*

William Wagenknecht – you might be mad but if madness brings with it the skin of an original woman then you are better off than most.

~~~~~

It was morning. Wagenknecht could hear the chirps from the birdhouse screwed to the side of his residence. Each flotilla of noise delighted him –

reminded him of a world beyond the absurd marching of traded stocks, of people believing they were engaging with the world but hopelessly miscuing. Give me this every day, he thought – a slow getting to my feet, the assimilation of sounds, the sun in my eyes, the gentleness of radio with its warm voices.

Why have I chased what I've chased? Wagenknecht questioned – the procedural mutt of a city job, the bigots stalking the floor, the narrowing of life through numbers. You shut your eyes, re-open them and suddenly you're old, forty, hooked up to a multitude of direct debits with nowhere to go. The people around you have shamefully become your kinfolk. They have more of an interest in the role and so they eventually look better.

People are noticing your disinterestedness. You're beginning to tune out. Updates, evolution, new ways – they all mess with your fixed ideas, your knowledge from five years ago. And you can only renew your understanding so many times, do the dance that they require. This translates into 'losing it' because you resist. And resisting means you are no longer a company man. I doubt staff can even resist at the top these days, Wagenknecht thought. They all seem to nod in harmony. There's a synchronisation, a smiling glee, the buffed-up faces of business people without innovation.

He shook his head in order to rid himself of such tepid concerns. Think of this around you – the field leading down to the fairway, the birds in flight, the building that you have prepared for your chicks, Scotty and Jasmine (their first weekend with you only four days away).

I can't wait though, Wagenknecht grieved. Man should not have to bypass fatherly customs, needs, the scampering of his offspring. And this was just the initial negotiation with Lysette, the first bit of his old life she had reluctantly agreed to re-fit. Everything after it still promised to be hard, a battle, the cursed dealings with an emotional blunderbuss.

All this stuff that I got to know, thought Wagenknecht – did it make me happy, did it stop the crude meanderings of life, did it transform things as it ought? No, but then you chose to seek out the bigger questions that certain disciplines provoke. You wanted meaning, academic inquiry, a correction to the "structural defects" of the Enlightenment. *Social progress, not scientific progress!* Wagenknecht quietly hailed. I can only lament what I see.

I have to brush my eyes over them today, Wagenknecht vowed. I have to see their green sweaters bobbing around in the playground, the excitement plastered across their frames. He had a tiny bit of cereal – stared down as he ate it. This was the mode that often led to foreboding, the current in his head off its track, firmly at the front of his skull. It acted as a dark, zipping cloud, the blocker of anything good.

My mind – why does it fumble around? thought Wagenknecht. Has something outside of my personal life hurt it, decided that sufferance is necessary? *Get your pants on and go, you old crock!* It takes an hour – one hour. That is the length of your sanity, stretched from Choton to Fleetpool like a band.

He walked down the side of the main house through the scuffed gate. His car awaited him on the drive. *A banger!* He drove a banger. It hadn't bothered him before, but now...everything was aging. *He* was aging. Rust seemed to fall from him. Christ – too old to keep your head upright. Too old to confidently chat with your children. What was that about hunting for their future, working on their miniature CVs, gliding into places of work with a letter of recommendation? *You don't know anybody, Wagenknecht!* he chastised. You have two estranged brothers, faltering parents, friends you stopped taking phone calls from years ago and colleagues who offer your own frazzled industry and nothing else.

Where to lead them? he wondered. *Somewhere.* I'll think of somewhere. He got in, started the engine, belted up and selected a station other than politics and current affairs. Music, he needed music – soul tunes or addictive pop. *Keep it light, you menace!* Stop taking the heavy route. Quit thinking you have to sort society before yourself, *before your children!*

His hands become steadier. He fixed his gaze ahead at the tarmac and the backs and sides of the other cars. Get there and just look at them. Don't act foolish or suspicious like you're not a father. Remember you've laughed with them, sat in the cinema with them, eaten out, told stories at night. *Lock onto their faces in your head and don't weep, don't bloody weep.* It'll come together. You'll start to see them regularly.

He turned the wheel suddenly towards the curb. Horns blasted behind him. Inconvenience – one of the worst crimes or hands you could deal the human race. Two or three cars moved out from behind him, sped into the middle section of the carriageway and gave malodorous stares.

Wagenknecht waited for a few seconds. The handbrake was still off but his foot was firmly against the brake pedal. 'Glory equals history. History means you had a pretty good life,' he muttered. Something in him couldn't get going, like the passenger-side wheel was tied to the curb. Come on – you've only gone five miles. And you know their morning break is 10.30. Miss this and you'll struggle even more. *Move your leg – clutch in! Come on, William.*

Who was talking? Where is this voice? Wagenknecht asked. It's not in me – it's somewhere else. It had to be Godledge or Austoff – a capable mind. He was living *something* for them – half a career, a more elevated path. Cheap, but high up. A killer of good cells but deemed the best course.

He resumed his trip, what would be his surprise appearance at the school gates. Steady – he was steady these days. Stuck to the speeds, indicated correctly, moved through the gears smoothly. From the inside, it's half OK, he thought. Outside, the car was dented and damaged, unwashed and without shine but inside, it just about passed. The seats were firm, the upholstery and dash were solid. The heat lines in the windscreen bewitched him a little with their jaggedness.

Wagenknecht trundled along, had the necessary punch when required but generally refrained from racing. There was enough of a race at work, in shops, on building sites. He had no wish to add to that, generate a burn or buy into haste.

'I don't concentrate as well,' he brooded. 'Speed has broken some of me. It's always "Next, next" instead of "Reflect". Driving here pulls me further away from Salchester, from the pit, and so something lifts. We have better suns on the coast. The brightness, I notice.'

He felt a little freer. The spruced up garage could never be home, even with the stuff on the walls – the art, the education, the sneaked envoy of propaganda (to Scotty and Jasmine). *Pull up soon*, he told himself. *Don't park too close or outside the school.* You can see them from the pavement. Just walk around and beyond, stand near the sea, and then back again – small looks across. Nothing to unsettle. You unsettle one and suddenly it's a mob; unthinking and grizzled hordes assuming the worst.

Wagenknecht parked his Ford on a wide expanse of road with grassy buffers and good-sized pavements. Apart from the screams in the playground it was calm. The area seemed tranquil with little bustle or activity. Just a few more days like this, he thought – absorbing things and finding who I am again.

A convenience store with a yellow band around its brick top stood on the corner. Next to it was a cheap Italian takeaway and two hair salons. Scotty and Jasmine had taken to roaming inside the shop after school, inspecting its bargains and sugary bottled drinks. First lesson: money. Kids respect money, Wagenknecht realised. £1.50 per week for Scotty. £1.30 for Jasmine. They were bloody disorganised before I left – money scattered across their desks – but somehow they're aware. Of the total pounds in play, of minor thefts or their great ability to lie.

Whatever We Do, We Do It Well was their school's maxim. And after that, if they go Catholic: *Be All You Can Be.* Wagenknecht had a fondness for such mottos and the badges or coats of arms that came with them. We all need a bit of Latin, he thought. We all need direction ground down to simplicity. Within both there seemed to be a licence – a reference point for Scotty and Jasmine to throw back at their seniors if met with horseshit. *We Do It Well* – we take our time. *All You Can Be* – even if outside the governance and stipulations of the school. *Free up there*...flying, Wagenknecht thought – a place I've not been for some time.

And the school before Fleetpool's Sawbreck – Choton's Randers Primary: *A Good Start for a Better Future*. Not as good, but stirring nonetheless.

Wagenknecht tripped along the concrete slabs, his legs a little heavy from the drive. He felt like he should have on a pork pie hat. He felt like a door had been shut and he would never be young again.

He knew his pace. He felt the cancer keen to bloom if he dared race past what he was now capable of. It would be pancreatic cancer from all the hassle at work. His stomach had troubled him for some time now – on and off, off and on depending on his food intake. The Canadians with their strange wheat or canola – he was sure it was them; covertly prevalent in cereal bars, cordial, chocolate.

If I don't eat properly, I can't operate, Wagenknecht whined. Sometimes I stagger around. My solar plexus feels vulnerable. There's a wind inside me which leaves me doubled up. No coconut, no French bread with its often suspect flour, no carrot cakes, no apples and no wafer.

The kids in the playground made him feel happy. Happy, but old. Such gaiety, such small thoughts unhindered and unhampered by the joke ideas of adults. What would they be given when they got out? War. Intellectual prostitution. Dwarf politicians.

Wagenknecht leant his arms on the rails and bars around the school. He seemed to fall into a small coma. Other lands – where are they? Does it take a space mission to re-inject hope? Or can we give *these* something else? *If not, how do we tell them? How do we tell them?*

'You lay that on him and you break his childhood,' Leonard had once minaciously said – the reference to too much disclosure. Scotty was not to see the world. Not before turning eighteen. Not before a sound dose of *imperial evangelism*.

There, playing now. Wagenknecht spotted him coolly laughing and chatting – his hair longer, his face buttoned up with young exuberance. And Jasmine, just six feet away – her olive complexion making her stand out, making her beautiful to the tiny, winsome kids. Always close – the sixteen months between them nothing really for they sniggered at the same things, shared stories and would only ever be one school year apart.

Wagenknecht was content to watch, see them converse. He would know them more this way, come to see facial gizmos and twitches often buried in adult company. Look at them, he thought – getting on with things, somehow buoyant. That's good. I mean it. That's good. *Independence – a great thing!*

He had not always seen it way. Age four at Randers, they had each been given extraordinary access to scissors and other implements – stuff that put eyes out if you had one crazy kid in the pack. Those days were not comfortable, Wagenknecht recalled. I did look at you both in the evenings, however and think: *How* did such wonder, such brilliant vulnerability come about.

A fast few years though and now here, looking at you, under different circumstances. Yes – a terrible husband. I've admitted as much. I didn't read your mother; women, such enigmatic and exotic creatures. Her ailments – the part of me as an adult that was supposed to step forth never did. If I'm honest, I wanted to stay in the pocket, the safe zone – never stray. I was anti-risk and my job in terms of fuck-ups reinforced that. *The king pin! The best dealer they had!* But scrutinised – so intensely that the numbers dimmed my senses. Phlegmatic, a stolid disposition, not easily excited – I think I became that.

But you try it. *I knew how they'd graded me for the last ten years.* I knew they were aware of my output, my errors (even my charisma, my alignment). I thought – would a court let me fall if they decided at whim to oust me? Always thinking of the money as you grew up, the pressure, the possibility of a conspiracy, attrition, the way they had operated with others.

People fuck you over, Scotty. Too hot for Jasmine's ears, but one day I will tell you. I will draw the curtain back. I used the word 'phlegmatic' with the counsellor, Scotty – in one of my middle cognitive behavioural sessions. I'd stored it up, thought it the perfect description of how I felt. Wasted though. I don't think she knew what it meant. She was thirty – how could she. Just a professional pause (silence) and me the little man, the struggler – I wasn't about to turn the tables...interrogate her. Still that beauty spot on the incline of her breast although she'd taken to covering it up, had stopped wearing brown linen dresses and the like. Probably sickened beneath the veneer by my petty fall. Maybe riding a brute every night – *a brute that didn't cry!* And I thought I could leave your mother for her after that first session. So many first sessions with women – solicitors, shop keepers, market makers even. But all blown away within days.

God – I'm naïve. *The Wagenknechts were made naïve!* Seeking what – service and smiles? Theatre and Radio 4? The masses don't need that. The grubs don't need that. The toffs don't need that. We're out on our own with our fully-functioning organism – language. Humboldt knew it – our "formative organ of thought"; perpetual flux that you have to back away from occasionally – particularly now with not even short hand but an ugly mess of exchanges. "Mental exhalation" though – the best was this. Even the raw expressions and yawns. Language fits things together. But keep linguistics metaphysical and poetic otherwise, as Hofstadter pointed out, man becomes a "brute or automata".

'Can I ask who you are? EXCUSE ME. Can I ask who you are?'

Wagenknecht blinked, turned to the woman looking down from the playground and panicked a little. He had been thinking too much. He had been elevated by the improvement to transcendental reason. Kant – you were wrong! The formation of thought is through language. We have control so long as too many people don't wish to kill it.

'I'm a father,' replied Wagenknecht. 'A father,' he finished, doubling up, mimicking her slightly.

'Your name though? What is your business here?'

Business. Always business. Even in schools. Why not craft, or métier or topic? He looked beyond her. Scotty and Jasmine had not noticed him and that is how he wished it to remain. He would see them at the weekend.

'Nothing.' He walked off, thought the woman brash, a long-nosed, sour-faced kvetch; *another Modigliani!*

'Don't just walk away. You can't...You have some explaining.'

Wagenknecht hobbled off – slowly. But then the whistle – an alert to others. Like a gunshot! A damn beast of a gunshot. Not a thud though – a shriek. Six more of them seemed to be immediately in attendance and taking instructions or rather following the accusatory finger of the whistler.

Had they been reading Nabokov, filling their minds with wacky scenarios? I'm looking at *my* kids. Is that now a crime? thought Wagenknecht. And even if I weren't, even if I were looking at other blood lines – their joy, interaction, gaiety (the qualities that lifted old crocks whose dreams had perished) – since when did such an act become illegal? Is it in the unwritten constitution? Does it no longer embody Britishness?

You're looking *inside* the school, Wagenknecht's serious side counselled. Although there was no bluff in him, no ability to lie (that mechanism mostly dead), he still just about understood why general etiquette might resent such behaviour.

'You need to come back, sir. *Stop* please!' Wagenknecht – what could he do? What options did he really have? None, he conceded. Seven is too many. And then other people milling round – they would inevitably join in the hunt, assume their bloodhound status. *A mini-jury!* A jury of protectors, of straight, catechizing didacts on his trail.

He stopped. 'What is it? I was passing. My kids attend. Do you often do this – vilify parents?'

'What you were doing – it arouses suspicion. You cannot watch children anymore.'

I cannot watch children? In all walks of life? Wagenknecht wanted to challenge it, desperately turn back the clock to a pre-bullshit era. Men had become killers, smotherers of innocence. The brain had become an instrument of how *not* to act rather than a scooper of all the sensory stuff before it.

'Do you not have a job? Why did you walk off?'

Harder questions. Completely inappropriate and byzantine words which sought to make irrelevant facts relevant.

'A job? Does that implicate me if not? Have you changed profession to that of a lawyer or prosecutor?' Wagenknecht was irritated. He had to give *something* back, stop the cynical rotation of the world.

'We are within our rights to question you.'

'Was I *inside* the school? Was I consorting with the children?' He was representing a body of people that he no longer came across. Wagenknecht had to believe that. He had to stand up and be forceful in the face of this apparatchik avalanche.

'You were infringing and we have a duty to protect the young ones.'

Wagenknecht gazed at her. Such self-belief in that face – a fatuous ball of skin. This is how they build them these days – in the lab with coldness and no valour.

It was then that she stepped forward. Wagenknecht had been too perturbed to notice her in the group.

Tillmann. His very own Tillmann; her expression unrecognisable, stern almost.

'This is Jasmine's dad,' she reassured the crowd. Walking a little further on with him, she lowered her pitch. 'There are screams in the playground. Do you not hear them?'

'*After* the whistle?'

'Screams, William. Just go home, yes...I'll tell them about the separation.'

Ignominy. He would have to accept it. You could not bait seven bears. The cosmic melody, Wagenknecht thought – Herder opening up the epistemological horizon (new understandings of the world). "Language provides the organising principles for our experience". Subjective perceptions conceptualised, not just taken from on high (transcendentally)!

But this now – cornered by an impervious flock. It was Heidegger country, a blackness, something "intimately bound" even with wrongness. Shovel the mis-users away, thought Wagenknecht. Christ – have these sanctimonious fascists tied up while they listen to stories which highlight grey. Neither good nor bad, neither wrong nor right. There are things in the middle, but little teachers know not how to comprehend.

'Did you see those beautiful kiddies?' Wagenknecht's mother asked after he'd trundled onto the driveway.

'I did. Briefly. Yes.'

'I was thinking, William. I have a few photos – rare ones. You can deposit them. Catch Douglas and Leonard up. I know their wealth bothers you. This way you all become equal again. That's what sons should be.'

It had continued – his mother's seeing photos as a currency, special stamps. Bits of her were closing down, linking sentimentality to value. Not in this modern world! Wagenknecht felt like shouting. Certainly not here. The more you wonder about the past, the more it corrodes you. The speedsters will trample all over you, knacker a few ribs, tell you to believe everything they put up on the big board.

Wagenknecht put his arm around her. 'Whatever you think best. Shall we look later? Pick the best ones out?'

'Yes, William. Eight o'clock – once we've settled. Once I've got tea out of the way.'

Losing more, he thought. I am losing what I know, but I don't wish to build again. The kids, the youngsters, don't get that. How *could* they? They haven't got the rings around their stomach, they haven't pounded the earth like we have. At some point you stop – stop absorbing the bile, the misbegotten and bastard words around you. *Shut your damn mouth! Just seal it up. Don't come at me with that crap, you translucent pettifogger! Dump the excrement elsewhere! You think I'm a sucker? You think I'm Ashpound?*

Wagenknecht dabbed at his play for a while. There was still the stage – the stage away from real life. But none of the pros wanted him. And the amateurs doubted his skills. 'Playwright? More like *Carpet*right.' 'It's too thick. The wood of the stage disappears the more I read it…' 'Call this dialogue? Who have you read? Who have you seen?'

'Miller, O'Neill, Lawrence.'

'Well this reads like O'Mule.'

Always the haunting words from past interactions. They trotted around inside Wagenknecht like a latent master or vicious guide. Yes, I went to more than one little theatre. I never told my brothers though. It was a spree – one night I developed the courage and just drove around the north west. I forced my best script, my best words under the noses of six directors.

'O'Mule.' 'It stinks.' 'A reasonable first effort.' 'Not polished enough.' 'Come back when you're Coward.' 'Choppy – this is too choppy...treacherous.'

The past smirks at you, thought Wagenknecht. Life is not as simple as I once thought. The over-complicators have taken hold. Magazines – I dip in them because of the moribundity around me. *And yet moribundity rules!* It has been allowed to harness humanity.

I need to chat with both brothers – Douglas first.

Wagenknecht was flighty – either ruffled by his mother's worsening plight or unsettled by the colour of the future. 'You only get real conversation at the bottom,' he muttered. Aloud – a lot of his thoughts were now with the volume turned up. He was unmuted, contemptuous of criticism even if still sometimes afraid. Had paranoia opened the door? He just about felt with it – maybe perched on top of a slide. *You stay sane though – for what?* Administration? The grim modern world behind that thick office glass?

'Show me what you know,' Wagenknecht had told his father a few years back. 'Half a profession – some *real* knowledge. Anything but this...'

He had gone into his room. Circuit boards, soldering wire, the naked backs of radios and old TVs all shone out at him. No order. There is no order to this, Wagenknecht thought. And I need that just to start. It is like taking the scraped remains off someone else's plate.

'Take a seat.'

From the original crack-up man? Wagenknecht thought. What is to say my heart won't twinge like yours? (Sat in your workshop – seeing little of the world, but fixing...fixing relentlessly.) Did they up the pace in the later years or was it that you were getting slower?

"Men and morals corrupted by advances in higher learning" – that is the problem, Wagenknecht reasoned. The whip has got longer; his father – pushed off the treadmill, busting his head against the wall.

'I respect your profession. We should leave it at that though. I'm sorry I asked to see this, but I know...I just know...'

He knew that he didn't have 'the button'. He could not autopilot the world. Wagenknecht was a measured man. He needed context, history, opinions, deliberation and intrigue – the last bit especially.

Intrigue was looking at Douglas's 19-room house (a former farm) and wondering how, *how* this had come about. *His face didn't change when people offended him* – remember! That helps. Whereas *you* – over and over Douglas says to his wife: 'If only he didn't have shame.'

Shame – that god damn heavy anchor! Not so much dishonour as mortification. Embarrassment wrapping its fur around him. *Collared by the great morality in the sky!* And yet Wagenknecht was learning to dislike Ashpound – his high-decibel voice taking over pubs, his champion naivety, the sticking of his eyes to women's breasts. The man was doomed and you had no wish to save him. *Figure it out, figure it out, Ashpound!* Talk to yourself in the mirror. Tone it down. Find a degree of respectability. You should have strangled Pony. Regional papers (circulations in decline) would have appreciated that. They need fury, men willing to do a stretch in the name of frustration regarding modern life. You were that man but you missed it. You could always go back – ride your bicycle into him one evening as he's exiting, descending those lead steps.

Did people look at Wagenknecht as he looked at Ashpound? We all need a sucker below us, but no, *surely not!* Wagenknecht revved up at the double gated entrance to Douglas's palatial beat. Crazy to think of the stocky man inside with the crisp tan - his movements similar to Johnny Weissmuller permanently holding a spring chest expander. Crazy to be asking for his time, but Wagenknecht needed his gloves back and a brief talk about life. He needed a reassuring glance he supposed from the Forrest family's *second* millionaire.

'Don't think I've got a million in the bank, William. It's all tied up – in hard goods, physical commodities. You office people get wild ideas. You love the sound of "million" as if we've reached the finishing line.'

Wagenknecht looked at him in sweater no.42. That damn wardrobe – bigger than an abattoir. And the underfloor heated porch they'd extended out in order to accommodate their six dogs. Nice dogs – Cocker Spaniels and an Alsatian but yappers and howlers with giant paws. Wagenknecht enjoyed coming really. It seemed that they were all on the payroll, but some got to lounge around and bark – others had to strive.

'I see that in you again. You're the guy with his hand out helping the last man into the boat when you probably need to just grab the oars and speed away.'

'Maybe I've passed that point, Douglas. We've established I'm no good at commerce. I don't mind an entrepreneurial household – I really don't – but bending corners, I never knew when to cheat.'

'*Cutting* corners. Taking short cuts. You do it. Little businesses survive that way. Ignore the government! You know I didn't even fill in their census and look what happened – nothing. This damn fear perpetuated inside big organisations. You do your little CPD online courses and believe this horse shit!'

'It's regulation though. You're lightly regulated – import/export with its fake certificates and hand squeezes. Finance – everyone's after us…the man walking his dog, the governor of the Bank of England.'

'I still believe there's room. You just didn't hawk yourself around. There are compliance mugs that do that for you. I've seen your old articles in the paper, Will. Sport. Money. You could adapt. You should be pitching your quirkiness to *The Economist*.'

'No.'

'What do you mean "No"?'

'I said no.'

'You never realised *who* you were, did you…'

'*Who?*'

'Yes – *who*.'

'Give me a beer please, Doug.'

'You know where they are.'

Wagenknecht walked past the hearth and into the stone kitchen. It was a step down – a step which wobbled him, distorted his centre of gravity. 'Oh…'

'You OK?'

'Yes. There's no Peroni!'

'Too gassy. Try the other stuff.'

'Stella. What sort of chump drinks Stella?' Wagenknecht grumbled. 'A peasant's beer. For the under 20s. Do I look twenty?'

Douglas heard him. 'It's free! Take it while you can.'

'Only because I'm thirsty.'

Douglas eyed him up as he returned. Two older brothers – this one broken. Look what he drives. It should be lifted up by a scrapyard crane – a bloody big magnet on its roof. Even Scotty has moaned to me about it. Speculate to accumulate – he never understood that and yet look at his brain; pushing his skull out, talking about shit I could never comprehend.

'When are you going to do what you need to do? If only for Scotty…Jasmine.'

'What does that mean? I don't know what that means.' The Asperger's came out at times. Wagenknecht knew he had it, but couldn't get it diagnosed. It only hit him periodically – at times when normal people misunderstood his life.

'Accept a career. No longer rage.'

'Rage is a young man's word, Doug.'

'OK, but avoiding that…speaking about your career.'

'The things I like I'm a failure at.'

'You once got fan mail you said?'

'I did, at The Choton News, but it doesn't build a man. It's a fleeting sensation.'

'More than most have tasted.'

'That may well be the case.'

Douglas felt like cranking him up – providing a jolt of some kind. 'Move your life along, Will. Shift your skills into an area that pays. Wasn't Salman Rushdie a copywriter?'

'You want me to write ads?'

'If it harnesses your talent in exchange for money, then yes.'

'Have you got my gloves? I better be going.'

'You've only just arrived.'

'Still…'

'Will. William. Sit down. Come on – stop pacing.'

'Where are they, Doug? Where are my gloves?'

'That's not important right now. We need to get a fix on your direction.'

'Direction?'

'Yes.'

Wagenknecht started to hear dripping taps, clocks and their shifting second hands, the low rumble of gas circulating throughout the house. I'm never quite here, he thought. Always pulled away. Always distracted. Can drink do this – take you away? Or is it the genes or the wiring?

Dear Lysette – It's my brain that will go – pack up, you know. In case we don't speak again, I thought you ought to know.

Wagenknecht could not imagine Douglas in the boardrooms of London. He didn't have to be. There was dirt up north which polished up nicely. Leonard, on the other hand, was a class apart. Somehow he had infiltrated England's nucleus. He walked across floors William and Douglas would never see. The floors of tax cheats and people much bigger than Shilp. He led his army of accountants and management consultants into dens that needed restructuring. *The great adaptor!* Leonard was carrying them all really.

'You gonna keep me here?'

'Until we've talked properly – yes.'

'I could just walk.'

'And I could just snap my fingers and have the dogs block you.'

'Cocker Spaniels?'

'Led by an Alsation, Will. You're forgetting the Alsation.'

'Jesus Christ! I have things to do.'

'You have *nothing* to do. You've walked out on your job. You're estranged from your family. Time to settle this. Get a new route for you.'

The low hit Wagenknecht. His position described by a younger man! You either deny it all or let bits come out, he thought. This isn't Routcliff or Heselglass, but it's blood. And blood mostly tugged at one's sensibilities. It confounded the pretty outer layer built up over months and years.

'I...I don't know. I don't know anymore. The years sap you. Retirement still twenty years off. I can't bow to younger men. I can't bow to this generation coming through. But I never rose the ranks so that I'm above them...'

'I wouldn't like that either.'

'You don't have to.'

'I guess not. Humanity wouldn't pity you though. It'd be stark, frank. We're in a meritocracy.'

'Yes.' The word was a weight – something Wagenknecht could no longer fight. *Admit defeat. Admit it all!* Cower in Douglas's nineteen room farmhouse – hold out here for a while.

But...documented. It would all be documented. Maybe not in his medical records, but by the wider family. William Forrest, sorry *Wagenknecht* – the crack-up, the disgrace, the man found pairing socks in the gutter; mud and tears quick to dent his thirty loyal years of Darwinism.

Humiliation is everywhere, Wagenknecht thought. And it is Heidegger who has brought us here – radicalising Humboldt's position, cutting up language and giving it the world. Brute or automata – remember! A nothingness darker than nihilism; the compensatory line: more of us will know who we are. Am I getting this wrong? Wagenknecht asked himself. Or is Heidegger's consecration of language an invitation to the manipulators – those with the dominant narrative? "Language is the house of being... perpetually preceding man, it possesses the unique ability to attune him to the voice of Being, to ground him – bring him into dwelling."

Bullshit! thought Wagenknecht. Did you not think that they'd commandeer it? Even Kant beat this with his esoteric transcendentalism. Does language institute truth? Wagenknecht asked. If it does, then I do not consist of matter. At least Adorno saw what was coming and what is here again. A different fascism, Wagenknecht thought. But real nonetheless. Real in the non-patterned voices of office colonels and the legitimisers of a voiceless culture. Derivatives riding high. Suckers believing the economists!

But you don't have a skill, Wagenknecht told himself. You've tobogganed through three decades without a damn skill. Not a skill that they'll pay you for, not a skill that you love.

'You wanna be one of those old princes, someone given a free pension, a st...'

'Stipend. One of the clergy or something.'

'Would that be fair to say? Didn't you once ask me for a non-economical job, something to keep the "maulers" away...Who do you see the maulers as, Will?'

Wagenknecht stared into space. A hard question. His answer changed from day to day. 'Everyone, I think. It depends where I am. I look at their glee and it hurts me.'

'Because you haven't got your own?'

'Probably.'

Wagenknecht's eyes wetted up. *Stop it, you soft dunderhead,* he told himself. *Stop it.*

Douglas stared at the floor. He didn't wish to corner the man or frame his tears.

Wagenknecht got up. 'Grit. Grit in my eye. Where's the sink?'

'Just use the kitchen.'

Douglas listened. To the water hitting his butler sink. To the slow movements of his brother. There was no evident whimper or sob – just the leaden trail of the old stockbroker.

After two minutes of nothing, Douglas followed him in.

Wagenknecht's arms were pressed like girders against either side of the clay and kaolin sink. The man was staring out of the low window, soaking in the fields around him or giving himself up to a meditative gaze.

'You OK?'

'I am.'

'Stay the damn night.'

Wagenknecht nodded a few times.

'The red room is free. You know where that is?'

Another nod.

'OK.' Douglas left him alone – went to his office which occupied the centre of the house.

Wagenknecht hated it already. The red room – *what kind of highfalutin*…He couldn't finish his thoughts – they were pushing him towards ungratefulness, damning everyone for tiny things.

He hurried to his room – hoped not to bump into anyone on the vast landing (a sister-in-law, a niece, a nephew). *Nobody wants a weak uncle!* Nobody wants to make conversation with a faller. Wagenknecht – the Grand National jockey but without a whip, thrown by numerous nags. Is the going soft, hard or firm?

He looked at the carpet beneath his feet. A good weave, he thought. But then it was all good. Douglas had a wife who liked change – a blonde marionette. She was always getting people in, filling her hours, spending the export man's money.

Thank God this room – the red room – is relatively bare, thought Wagenknecht. He hated kitsch, fuss, efforts at popularity. The colour of the walls peeved him from Douglas's pseudo-interior designer wife, but he could at last settle, take this corner of the world and do what he had done in his teens – stretch out, dream, ignore the bad stuff.

There was an en-suite, a small window overlooking the moors and little else. I am back with nature, Wagenknecht thought (albeit in a castle!). Did any of this feel like his? No.

OK to think about nothing, Wagenknecht mimed. OK to pull yourself away. They want you on the damn treadmill – Cameron and his shitbags. They want you to get better at going from nought to sixty while they smoke cigars. This is the world. Still a class thing. Except Douglas and Leonard had broken through. The sons of a poorly paid TV engineer had found the swag – come out the other side with Mediterranean breaks, toughness and clichéd poses on bridges ("Live for today as you never know what's round the corner").

Wagenknecht hated the *carpe diem* crowd. How the hell could you seize it when you were strapped up, bollocks on the table being hammered by a mallet? Wagenknecht cracked his first smile – *happiness at the lips of the abyss!* This is how it would end – in maniacal circumstances. Understanding the world turned by Callicles but no longer fettered by its food and drink.

Come and get me! Come and chase a mad, old goose! Yes – prison would break me, but I'll be long gone before then. Just lie me in a meadow, give me a cloudless sky and throw in a few butterflies and rare birds.

A big enough house not to hear the murmurs, thought Wagenknecht. And thank God for that. If there was pitying talk, he'd rather not listen to it. Concern had two faces – the duplicitous dab, dab 'Are you OK?' and the medium term rumblings of 'He'll have to do *something.*'

Wagenknecht pulled the goose-feather duvet over his body, adopted his usual sleeping pose of right arm under the pillow (support for the side of his face) and shut his eyes. Give me twenty hours. Something longer. I have a lot to figure out in my dreams. And please – no interruptions in the morning, no polite facial cadence.

Dear Douglas – I'm afraid I've fallen out with the world, Wagenknecht wrote when he woke up. *Women are an unnecessary risk, work is boring into me, and my plays are not selling. I should step aside for a while. When I see the heavy doors of jewellers, I wonder what we have become. If you could forward on my gloves. I saw no evidence of them last night.*

Wagenknecht dressed and fled. Better be quick before the others rise. He knew they'd laugh at him, railroad him into taking pills if he hung around. Fruit and exercise was not a quick fix.

What do we tolerate for the fuck, the great fuck? he thought, as his car rolled down the hillside track. Everything: the ripping up of dignity, character, humanity, playfulness.

A frown enveloped his lips. He stared ahead with the veracity of a Jersey cow. 'Money – money is everything,' Douglas had once said. 'You don't have to be packed on the cattle train when you have it.' Maybe so, Wagenknecht admitted, but getting there...

His shoulders virtually hung around the steering wheel. He joined the motorway and did a pathetic 55mph on the inside lane cursing the drivers around him. *Why should I? Why should I speed up?* he shouted through the glass. Where are you rushing to? Some needless social engagement? Try unfolding your mind! We're all stripped down at the end the same, Wagenknecht asserted. There might be posher funerals but we're all just lumps of flesh – misguided, misgiving, disoriented.

Tillmann. Tillmann came into his head. But with that firm stare from the playground. What had he done? Pushed her away? Had her wonder over his sanity? Donna – so different from the others with their phallic heels. Women – wanting to have a dick, or butch up, but not Donna. The faint rash levelled her. Her voice still had damsel in it rather than androgynous blare.

He owed her a break. Nobody wanted a floundering collaborator on their arm. And once the deed was done, Wagenknecht would go into lockdown mode, hibernate, shut out the world from his converted garage. Suffering – rarely done "on anything so distinguished as a cross" he reminded himself (using Herzog's cogitation). A private affliction, an unbloody wound that required dressing of a different kind.

When you start to read every tick, every inch of a person's face and manner, you are in trouble, thought Wagenknecht. But that is what I have done – with my bosses, my wife, my friends. And they resent it. They want the superficial to dominate. Sometimes I fall into childhood again and look out at the mess. Maybe the old folk have rediscovered truth, but the rest...What I am looking at is a massacre, rude human bullets fresh out of the barrel of a gun.

I will drop a note off in Donna's cubbyhole, Wagenknecht persuaded himself. She cannot be allowed to see me like this. I cannot carry a beauty when I am in this state. I cannot sit next to her and clap. And yet, I want to remove her lime skirt. I want to have her begging and heedful at the bottom of the bed.

Good citizen, bad citizen, Wagenknecht thought. You let the elderly or infirm cross a zebra or side road – indicate with your open palm that *they* are priority, that you care and feel good about the act, only for the next zebra to arrive and you cannot safely brake. 'Bastard,' some mutter. How do you please them all? How do you please humanity? *That is what you are doing wrong*, he thought. Do you see Douglas and Leonard unduly halting their good-looking metal boxes? Do the strugglers matter to them?

I don't know. I rarely travel with them. I hear that Douglas goes to charity functions though – empties his pockets for good causes. *After* the masked raid – yes. After his daily business has ended. He has CCTV now. He watches his employees. Why does that bother you? Wagenknecht asked himself. Why think of the contentious points all the time?

Because man is not above man. I can never accept that. But it thins my skin. Some days I want to fight them all. I see them all around me. I feel like a musketeer. But good with the sword – are you good with the sword? It doesn't matter because the braggarts and cynics have the stage. Sceptics are lepers.

He drove on. At least he was thinking it out – here amongst the East Lancashire hills. Better to be barren, undeveloped, pleasant on the eye. No cranes in sight. No machinery.

I don't know who I am when I get dressed up, Wagenknecht thought – put on that awful suit for the carpeted kingdom. *Having to be an ox – Christ! I can no longer do it.* Weakness. It just seems to be weakness now. Running out of me like sap from a maple tree.

It started to rain. Wagenknecht put his wipers on. You walk in that and you're either defeated or brought back, he thought; dragged down by heavy clothes or cleansed. Sometimes when it hits my face, I feel enormous – like I've won back nature. The water feels purer. I connect – am somehow plugged back in.

We used to walk a lot – Lysette and I, me and Lysette. She showed me Choton's high-up paths, historic towers, half castles. All on the outskirts – away from the grime. It goes though. You become a damn prisoner – an urban psychopath.

Just a road with rain beating on it. Surely this was the way to God. If ever there was a talk to be had then it was here – now.

'What is the big plan?' Wagenknecht demanded. 'Do I expect too much? Have people exaggerated your powers?'

Silence was a killer or karma. Fortunately, Wagenknecht seemed to be coming out the other side. Little glimmers. Something seemed to be picking off the pupils in his eyes. Not enough to resurrect his relationship with Tillmann, but sufficient to hobble along himself.

Don't be too ambitious! That has been your error. You've jerked around and kicked yourself when failure strikes. Go back to the sportswriting. The plays are killing you – they're taking too much. Thinking, thinking up vexatious lines all the time – no one can do that without stewing the jelly in their head. An entertainer or a literary flop – they are your choices. But I warn you – the latter, they generally go mad. Figuring out the impossible is like repeatedly cutting yourself with a razor blade. Why do it? The scientists are screwed. The economists are screwed. And you – literary man – are, in reality, no better. It is just that silky perception, that harmonic gathering of words - it sometimes makes you think you're close.

Wagenknecht nestled in his seat more – less of a cloak over the wheel. *The smaller pieces, when I am not juggling too much,* do *provide satisfaction. They do not hang from me daily, overnight, plague my thoughts. And yet they* can *be intriguing, enough to survive on. A smaller diet – that is what you need.*

His head remained up for some time. Wagenknecht was somehow at ease given the momentum of the car. At some point I have to stop though, he thought. Either the petrol runs out or I reach a destination. Where am I going? he asked himself. I'm not sure, he replied. What do I need to do? Donna, Leonard, then lockdown. And then it's over. Or is it in a different order?

He drove to Tillmann's work place and started on a letter in the car outside. *Dear Donna – I can't wait for your judgement. I can't wait for your school's judgement. I merely leaned on a fence and stared unwittingly into the playground. That some choose to hyperventilate in such circumstances is unfortunate. Perhaps I was not responsive enough to the woman with the whistle, but as soon as she severed what trust was there I have to admit to gravely disliking her.*

Such a cause or stance these days is frowned upon (we should all be dutifully mature) but I am afraid I hold grudges. Daft fights with the world, some would say. Others would point to 20th century reverence.

Wagenknecht scampered into the school. It was a good hour – a sensible hour; just the cleaner about. He knocked on the automatic door and waved the sealed envelope at her. She looked back, thought him respectable, and pressed the grey button to release the door.

'For Donna Tillmann. She has a pigeon hole, a cubby hole.'

'OK – I find it.'

Hispanic, Wagenknecht thought and with human features that were slowly being killed off. Such a simple exchange, yet it held him. Kindness. Warmth. Simplicity. He wondered if Donna exchanged pleasantries with her, if she looked up from the bacon fat that the school imposed. *Panjandrums leading the conga!* Bitches and bastards peering over the tops of their glasses whether actually there or not.

Catch the train now. Turn up at Leonard's. Have a conversation in the capital. It seems only right – like a form of parliament deciding Wagenknecht's future. But three of them against you – even Garrett (perhaps a bit of vaudeville piano thrown in to undermine Wagenknecht's serious proposal).

Are we them? Are we our children? wondered Wagenknecht. Do they at age ten represent the sum total of our parenting? If so, then I am in trouble, he thought. 'Touch the ceiling, Jas? Do you want to touch the ceiling?' Sometimes that's all he had – lifting her up and having her stretch one arm out in order to feel big, like a conqueror; touch the impossible. He could not give her a pure academic route like Leonard with Garrett and so a literal height somehow sufficed. But the joy, the innocent joy, had recently turned into a groaning exasperation. 'Daaaad!' Is that all you've got now, she was saying. I'm grown up. Stop lifting me.

Wagenknecht had somehow strayed when they were each about seven. He had thrived on the daft artillery of magnified talk, but now the real chips were down he offered neither a great memory nor technical proficiency. He seemed, instead, to skittle all before him – come bounding in like an overweight clown.

He bought the ticket – a return to Euston, that rough introduction to London. From there it was a taxi to Waterloo with its extra smooth floor (courtesy of a solid union of cleaners with mops) and finally a train to Bimbledon. Wagenknecht climbed inside the Virgin carriage, felt a little nervous but knew a showdown was necessary. £300k. How many of the other passengers were on a mission similar to his? A wealth extraction exercise. A bridging of the north and south. Three hundred thousand pounds. Surely it was like a trip to the cashpoint for Leonard. Surely such a sum wouldn't trouble him too much.

Begging. Was this begging? Wagenknecht asked himself. Is there a moral pale that you do not walk beyond? 'I feel that I would do the same,' he lightly muttered, arousing the attention of those around him. 'I feel that…if there was any other way…'

He flashed his eyes dartingly at the other passengers. The assertion from them was that they knew him already. Disturbed. He must be disturbed. To mutter random words. It explained why Wagenknecht was in the habit of sitting next to the perceived misfits on a train. It lessened his rickety irreverence. It placed a cape over his dubious dalliances. Also, he felt comfort in their old normality.

Today, his seat number was on the ticket, however – the imprecation of a long haul. And he was sat amongst the screws – unofficial prison staff, look-outs for odd mannerisms and those that struggled with the high diplomacy of modern life.

'Suit or suicide,' Wagenknecht despaired. 'Damn the bastards. Is that our choice now?'

He fell silent for a while. Thinking. Watching. Eking out a path in his head. If I come back empty handed then…what, what do I do? The weights are everywhere – wife, children, lover, parents, friends, acquaintances, relations, colleagues. Pushed down by dialectical laws, "struggling along on bended knee". Will Leonard see that the lesser brew – as with Boredman – cannot sustain me or will he have fancy shoes on his mind?

'Yes, I'm aware of the hypocrisy - tax cheats' money giving me an early retirement. But my time will be spent…'

He wasn't entirely sure, but journalism – it would include journalism. 'Funding my execution?' he could hear Leonard retorting.

'Well, no, maybe – not you personally…'

'But my *clan*, my profession?'

He was there. Wagenknecht was there. In Leonard's scoffing house – Poppy and Garrett in their peregrine striped chairs, studying him, disbelieving the scene before them.

'What do you think Garrett? Do we conclude this deal of the century? Do we wire the money?'

Don't defer to the kid, Wagenknecht thought - anything but that. Part of my life is already controlled by a 30-year-old, but a 10-year-old - King Oyo deep into his reign, tinkling a piano instead of the Chwezi drum! Slaughtered blood dripping from him!

Wagenknecht linked his fingers together, attempted to calm the tremors rocking him slightly. Words. Interactions. The arbitrary cruelness of humans. Make it clear my proposal is ridiculous, but don't pad it out, salt the meat, flick on the oven.

Garrett didn't speak - his long arms and graceless legs marauding the chair, but his mouth dutifully still; sectioned by his mother.

Not been naughty since the age of three, Wagenknecht thought. Driven at *his* age, but ready to have the last laugh once sat in his corner office (the concierge fetching his car each evening at seven).

'All those letters you've written to Garrett, *Uncle Wag* and you want our money?!' Poppy suddenly fired.

'They were efforts at broadening his horizon,' Wagenknecht offered, his answers initially floured in meekness.

'Chatting about Guy Fawkes and his *heroic* deeds?'

'I thought you were Catholic? He was fighting a cause for you.'

'But the blowing up! The gunpowder.'

'"Sooner or later the confrontation has got to turn deadly",' Wagenknecht recalled.

'Leonard. Did you hear that?! Easy violence. I cannot reason with this man.'

'William. William. How best to address this. Have you ever walked past a short man?

'I expect so.'

'And how did it make you feel?'

'I don't un...'

'Better off? More elegant? Superior even?'

'I...'

'If you're honest.'

'I suppose. Height does *something* physiognomically.'

'Well...Garrett – can you leave the room...Poppy, the door please...'

'Well?'

'Well, with money it feels five times better. You're suddenly walking with fewer burdens.'

'I get that.'

'But the fight. The fight must be your own within the laws of the land. People are given things and the whole system collapses. Nevertheless – Poppy, the cheque book please...'

'What?'

'The cheque book. *Please.*'

Wagenknecht sat there like a death row inmate, with Leonard as priest or governor. He noticed him pull a suave ink pen from his pocket and then begin scribbling against the wad of cheques.'

'You've come here seeking help. It's a long way. Here...'

Wagenknecht reached forward with his begging bowl hand and immediately examined the oblong piece of paper.

'Ten thousand?'

'Yes. Enough for a new car, a suit and some self-respect.'

'But...it won't get me through a year.'

'There has to be compromise on both sides, William. And I can't have you living off capital interest. It wouldn't be good for you. Listen – I heard that there's a spider housed in your car wing mirror. No more of that then.'

'I don't mind the spider.'

'What do you mean?'

'If it wants a home there then fine.'

'But it's effectively squatting. You'd want to clean up such a state of affairs, right?'

Wagenknecht was quiet. Is this my fall to the lowest common denominator? he thought. Cars – why do people worship them? I no longer want this man as speaker at my funeral. Douglas – just about, and Heselglass and Routcliff but not Leonard. He no longer makes me feel good.

'What do you fear, Will? What do you truly fear?'

Wagenknecht looked at Poppy. An ounce of pity seemed to be creeping in. She had only previously seen her husband's brother in a more dogmatic mode. 'The ambulance.'

'Ambulance?'

'Dad with his heart. Mum with her memory.'

'I think his heart attacks come in cycles. He'll be OK for a few years now. Mum though – what do you mean?'

Wagenknecht didn't know quite how to start. If you don't witness something, see the empirical...

'She's started to put the asparagus on top of the cabbage.'

'Is that it?'

'You don't understand. I know how she presents food. And it's not like that. She's losing her finesse. She's making a lot of mistakes. She enters rooms and just stands there wondering why she's come in.'

'We all do that.'

'But not like this. There's panic in her face. And the photos...'

'What about them?'

'She's been into the bank trying to deposit family snaps.'

'A safety deposit box?'

'No. Into her current account.'

'What?'

'She thinks they're worth something, that they've become a currency.'

Wagenknecht didn't wish to mention the levelling out, his catching up with Douglas and Leonard in their mother's world. Keep it from the toad.

'You must be mistaken. That's all I can conclude.'

'You don't "conclude" when it comes to your family, Leonard.'

'No. No. She's sharp. Worked as a bar maid - did the numbers before the introduction of electronic tills. Latterly a house wife, but always with it.'

'And numbers fend off senility?'

'Yes. Yes, they do. Don't ham this up, William. Don't turn this into one of your god awful plays. I've seen her recently and she's fine.'

We all have a certain amount of tears – Leonard fewer than others, Wagenknecht thought.

'Just let me make one thing clear, William. You don't suggest this or encourage it with Mum. If need be, you smile until she dies.'

'This is just like the theatre,' Wagenknecht stressed. 'I told you where to go, what to see (*A Doll's House*, *The Iceman Cometh*, *After the Fall*, *Humble Boy*) but no, you watched Nicole Kidman strip off in *The Blue Room*. You suffocated my insights. Always the rich…'

'Whose house are you in, William?'

'What is this – the deep south?'

'No, but I expect manners…'

Something had gone, disappeared within Leonard. In order to maintain this Bimbledon blue print, language had to be narrowed, a blow torch taken to it.

"You think history is the history of loving hearts, you fool!" That is all Wagenknecht could see in his mind – a *real* lesson in history and its savage modes of production.

'Leonard…' Poppy's slight intervention tempered her husband's outburst.

'Just one more thing, Poppy. I've got to get this man out of his shorts. Look around, William – look around. It's murky, isn't it. The world is hard. Stop saving others and just find your track. I'll be honest – some people need tossing in the river at twenty, maybe thirty. You know it's all over for them. Industry is a great judge. But you…some would consider you successful, William. House, kids, qualifications.'

Wagenknecht looked at him, his older brother with his too-short sideburns and plump cheeks. Yoga was losing out to the business meals. His hair was a little fuzzy – short and disciplined, but sprouting in parts. Douglas had fluked his way to wealth, but with Leonard it was meticulous, a five or ten year plan in the manner of the Chinese Communist Party. *The damn irony!*

'Who do you open up to, Leonard?'

'I don't get you.'

'I mean what I say.'

'Emotionally? Christ – he *is* the mad uncle, Pops…'

'Who then?'

The brief chuckle turned into lampoonery.

'Why did you cut yourself adrift from the bourgeoisie, Will?'

'I didn't. We were never part of that, in that class.'

'But the potential. The Forrests. You could have followed me and Dougie in. Instead, you changed your name. Bloody *Wagen*knecht. You may as well have called yourself Ho Chi Minh!'

'Here's the cheque, Leonard.'

'What? No! Come on – stay. Let's do business.'

Just as gone as me? wondered Wagenknecht. Needing something to fill the hole, cement those damn emotions.

'We used to get on, Leonard. We once drove through America together. But I'm not sure why I'm here…'

'For the 300k!' Leonard shouted glibly.

'A mistake for which I apologise. A huge assumption.'

'That's 3% of our wealth, Will.'

Wagenknecht got up, looked around the room. Peaceful here, but chaste, he thought. I couldn't do it – the Starbucks run, the "Yah, yah – surely ought", the rarely seeing poverty. In one sense you're inside a giant condom – protected, amongst a bell-wielding ever-so-polite bike fraternity. But I see what these people do when off their bikes, thought Wagenknecht – they tear things down, they disrupt, play havoc.

'I know you stole that handbag.'

'*What?!*' Leonard tantrumed. 'Still talking about that? Get him out of here, Poppy. Get him out…'

'The crooks always win. Is it the Lords next?'

Leonard shook his head. Biting the hand – was that bit not printed in your rule book, because it was certainly in mine.

Wagenknecht was bundled onto the driveway – both of them pushing at him. No time to say goodbye to Garrett. No time to dip into the fridge for a snack.

'I'm fragile,' Wagenknecht propounded. 'Brittle. Don't do this just because I investigate.'

'He's Columbo, Poppy. I knew he was something, but finally the news has broken of his vocation.'

Plato, Wagenknecht ruminated. He made Socrates a pretentious bore. I refer to passage 66b of *Phaedo*: "So long as we keep to the body and our soul is contaminated with this imperfection, there is no chance of our ever attaining satisfactorily to our object, which we assert to be the Truth." People do that to you. They warp the board, deviate, let in the alluvium. He couldn't talk to these London genteels. They had monopolised civility and breeding in the wrong way. Leave something raw, Wagenknecht thought. Let them hang their arm out of the window.

'Some of us have to be vigilant, Leonard.'

'Neighbourhood Watch?'

He doesn't get it, Wagenknecht lamented. He doesn't get it. Either that or he's overridden the circuitry. But me as didact kills it and so I cannot excessively trump the cause, the softer machine which breaks through "menstrual ice", Ashpound's seniors and senescence.

Art must remain immune to censorship, Wagenknecht *breathed* inside. That is why I love the plays, he thought. No matter how badly perceived they are.

'Do you remember the white dress, Leonard? Mum in that white dress all those years ago – when we lived in Sarwood?'

You do not ask such a question on the drive, but in comfort, Wagenknecht told himself.

'Sorry? Here, now, you ask that? You really have no sense of place, do you…'

'Tell me though.'

'Yes. Yes – I remember. She looked very elegant. Why?'

'I just wanted to see if the past was in you at all.'

'It beats, William. It beats. Don't try the clever stuff on me.'

'Where were they going that night? I was too small to remember.'

'You really want to know as I'm kicking you out?'

'Yes.'

'Very well then. Elton View I believe it was called. Tables, big bands. It was Grandad's 65th. You would have been five. I was nine. I remember everything from around that age.'

'You do?'

'Yes. But eras change. Things change. You do realise that, William?'

'I suppose.'

'That's hardly conclusive.'

Wagenknecht felt trapped. He had assumed that art held the past and business the future. But for Leonard to recall such an event so easily…What did he have? What did Wagenknecht now have that was just his?

'I'll be going.'

'Hey! You spent a night at Douglas's, so spend one here.'

'Thanks, but I'm a northern man, Leonard. It's too hot down here.'

'You sure?'

Wagenknecht nodded and then turned away. At least I'm doing something different, he thought. At least I'm seeing things – new faces, buildings, lawns. But how many were rushing past him, making him tune out? 'Thousands,' he whispered. And that's not only the Asians and Americans, but the damn Europeans. Was there now no continent which held his type?

If there are no fuckers reading the same stuff as me, if there's no one to laugh with, then…where do I go? What's the point? Old friends? People you parked away from? Even Scotty was on fast forward. He had seen it in him. "Just finishing this," his staple line – technology gagging him, motoring his senses.

The crook-necked pillocks on the trading floors with their concern over descending indices. He could not blame them. They were just operatives. *The Wizard of Oz* – where was he? *Who* was he? Ready to W.O.O., solicit, court, chase, pursue and importune; most of his subjects suckers. Back to Chomsky – clever chap, but you know the masses are corrupt and deplorable. Surely you have thought that at least once?

'Police, police,' Lysette had shouted years ago upon Wagenknecht wrestling her to the kitchen floor in self defence. Such an overreaction did not sit with the normal flow of events. It was a blip, a seismic interruption and it illustrated perfectly the vulnerability of men.

We cannot be judicious, or if we are humanity piles in wielding its tabloid paper folded up like a fly swatter. I think I have largely been a good man – done my best, but the world skins you, thought Wagenknecht – its heavy bits dismantle you.

'Will!' It was Leonard calling him, still watching the departing lump.

Wagenknecht merely slowed down – waited for his brother to catch up (slippers a rare sight on the streets of Bimbledon). His mind seemed to be fixed elsewhere already.

'Why have you got yesterday's paper under your arm?' Leonard asked.

'What? Can't I hold on to a day? Is the past so bad…'

'We all have forty eight hours in which to fall down, Will but I fear that you're seeking a con-trick larger than a weekend. And society won't have it.'

'It'll have to have it.'

'The play – is everything riding on your play?'

Wagenknecht looked at Leonard. It's the first time you've asked. I may as well have been making macaroni.

'A good portion of my future – yes.'

'But what about fiduciary responsibilities?'

'What about them?'

'You're effectively a trustee to your family. They need to benefit from your manoeuvres.'

'One day they will. I keep them afloat. I don't neglect them, Leonard.'

'But now, Will. They might want more now.'

Wagenknecht gazed at his unsmiling brother. You can do it, he thought. You can be with people and somehow exit healthily. I seem to see people as dangerous these days. Some kind of schism has taken place.

Even Jasmine, even his daughter, had recently claimed in a fit of junior invective: 'You don't know anything.' It was true. He couldn't even remember what colour socks he had furnished his ankles with this morning.

'I try to push this old body, but…I'm like a wind-up Lada at times, Leonard. Honestly.'

'Just know that women only want to shag cool and comfort, Will. Over-emotional doesn't cut it. Let's break this bread now before you wreck things for good.'

'I'm with Donna now.' He didn't know if he absolutely was, but Leonard was haranguing, beating him up in a way that only brothers could and so Wagenknecht threw in his best card.

'Another woman?'

'Yes.'

'I knew you were in the garage, but I thought you'd retreated from it all, like a monk.'

Lockdown – yes, Wagenknecht thought. Sometimes he pressed his organs and groaned in pain. I would not have got on with Dewey, he realised. Consternations bombard me. The urgencies of common life are all well and good but man's head…it disintegrates, pulls at his every limb.

'Lysette roughed up my heart. You know that.'

'You have a history of bad women, Will. Pin the donkey would have brought more success.'

The Forrest oxygen, Wagenknecht thought – so keenly altered by Leonard, his face a mass of gastro delights, his eyes unartistic and mechanical.

'I've got it right this time.'

'I hope you have.'

Wagenknecht looked back at the house. Poppy was still there – grazing at the door. Why didn't she take to me? he thought. Why did she always jump in with that female battering ram? Risk. Because you're high risk. That again. Your form is bad with this particular household. Sometimes you have to ask more, be graceful, laugh and be bitchy about the right things.

I can't shift my face though. I can't shift my face. It's not in me. And so I offend. Not many will like me.

Neighbours. I can't have kindly neighbours. Because I have off days, growl, despise humanity...its trinkets and baubles.

A garage – that is probably where I belong, with the snails parked up against the cold brick. Near the tomato plants. That was my first job, he remembered – watering them. Fifty pence per week. The smell – it stuck with me. Such an easy, natural fragrance. And the pubescent vines, like my own growing arms. I used to produce, cultivate, make things, *carry a watering can!* Only food, but it meant life was within me. Green to red. Then stop and examine the wonder. *You won't con me with anything off the vine!*

He raced away from Leonard suddenly and with a smart turn of heel. The tarmac – like a damn race track. Especially brought in for the residents of Bimbledon. *There are to be no pot holes here!* Possibly pot, but no holes.

'I need to speak to someone,' Wagenknecht muttered, loosely navigating his way to the station. He pulled out his phone – an old model, a kamikaze bit of plastic and turned it on. Two messages flashed up. *Don't run out on me. Donna. xx* And then Leonard – already, before he'd even made a street: *You need to tell me more about Mum. Just be sensible. Leonard.*

Sensible? Ha. That's what he didn't want. I may as well have concrete feet, thought Wagenknecht.

Who? Who can I speak to? Routcliff? No. He had a habit of rationalising everything and he had heard him describe his fallen brother-in-law ("Lunatic"); a not-so-secret detestation of the mad, whereas Wagenknecht actually warmed to them – saw the holes, the pinches in the curtains.

It was the counsellors who sometimes took this track also – especially the cognitive behavioural therapists with their flowchart prescriptions and set answers.

You don't go home with me, Mr Counsellor! If you did, you'd see it – the shapes at the window, the fear of getting out of bed. Tell me what it's about. Tell me what this dance is about.

Wagenknecht phoned Douglas, marched up and down the station concourse awaiting his train out to Waterloo.

'Hello.'

'Douglas. Did you find them?'

'*Will*? What?'

'The gloves. My gloves.'

'I'm afraid Cindy threw them out.'

'Christ!'

'She said they looked old.'

'Yes. Four months old.'

'I'm sorry. We'll replace them.'

'No. You know how things move on. You can't get that type. They no longer sell that type.'

'Will. We'll pull out all the stops.'

'What else does she throw, Douglas?' Shoes, puppies, babies in prams? The spoilt…'

'Now, Will…'

'They didn't look old. What kind of crazy judgement had them as old…'

'You phone back when you're calm.'

Wagenknecht dumped his rucksack on the floor and put his head down into his hands. *They keep doing it*, he thought. Madcap things. Those gloves were perfectly visible on the kitchen table. Adult gloves as well. Not yours. Not Douglas's. And so you ask. *You damn well ask.* Don't open a hotel, have the guests go ballistic!

A new car at twenty-one, Wagenknecht recalled. One dangerous act from Daddy and the girl is set on a piffy path. *Everything free!* Nothing with a hard-earned value against it! And now Douglas starring as Daddy II.

This is the kind of case courts need. *Bigger than murder!* Like ripping away Gandhi's loincloth. "We'll pull out all the stops"! You're a metal man...scrap metal. This is refuse – seagulls or pterodactyls flying over them now, ready for landfill or incinerated already.

Hunting. Still hunting for Scotty's future. How?

He got on the yellow box train – found a neat corner he could rest up against. Do I have a heart? he wondered, staring out onto the track. Was it poisoned in the big encampment that is England?

There is no answer, he decided. You choose your truth. Choose your tits, choose your truth, choose your virtue. Conviction, but not enough arrogance – that was his error; hauled back by the shuntering multitudes.

"Man is the dwarf of himself". On the button, Ralph. Yes. "Few real moments in [one's] life." Except now. I think I know what to do.

He took out his diary. Looked at the entries scattered before the month of January. Recycling times. School term times. Library times. Big annual costs. Swimming times. His life had been formulated, plugged in to an organised cauldron. Sometimes, however, he paused – realised the theatre of Beckett was all around him. And Wagenknecht, a "co-conspirator" – seeing the insanity of man, the craziness, the pickpocketing of brains. When will it stop? he asked himself. Only when there is intervention. You know of one man that needs taking down – his removal an improvement to the world. The Marabou Turd ("a great line in dishonesty and regulation"). Shilp. Would it be so bad? No. I will be carried aloft after the act – *cheered from the rafters.*

A pacifist *and* a murderer? Sometimes the pacifist had to step down, let the harder man play. A pistol or any kind of gun would do it. Wagenknecht had only ever used a cap gun and a pellet gun before, but a trigger was a trigger. And he knew where to go from his paper round days in Choton – knew which pubs had more than drink and food. Yes, it would make him a loser (guns "a fetish for losers", as Breslin observed) but the tide was not turning. Wagenknecht could see no evidence of a much-needed correction.

One man. Just one man. But you take him, and his family react...*Don't think about that!* Just the deed. The simple deed. There will be more happy than sad. And that had to be the measure, didn't it. No – don't stiff the minorities, William! Of course. Sorry. A special case though. This was a special case – his only assignment. A lot of lives would be improved.

Shilp brought stress and upset – and such things caused cancer. Wagenknecht would not be on future adverts extolling the merits of extermination, but he was helping. Yes, he was helping to diminish the poisonous spume.

238 | Jeff Weston

You go home, get your car, drive to the pub, mingle, come away with the shooter and then get in early at work the following morning when only Shilp is around. Park in the underground car park. Take a spot – any spot. Just watch him drive in – his extra-moisturised hand shifting the gear stick like grease on a cogwheel.

"As privates of the industrial army they are placed under the command of a perfect hierarchy of officers and sergeants. Not only are they slaves of the bourgeois class, and the bourgeois state; they are daily and hourly enslaved by the machine, by the over-looker...No sooner is the exploitation of the labourer by the manufacturer, so far, at an end, that he receives his wages in cash, than he is set upon by the other portions of the bourgeoisie, the landlord, the shopkeeper, the pawnbroker, etc."

It feels cramped down there. You hear the giant air conditioning whirling. The thick, circular concrete pillars are many. And the numbered bays seem to proliferate and narrow your spot. Also, the steel ceiling is low.

What is the difference between what I am about to do and the rich, eccentric toe-rags at the Proms bobbing in their seats? Wagenknecht thought. Very little, he assured himself. Except the noise. Mine will be a coarse, harsh sound – yours a bugle-like, drum-banging celebration. And don't forget the little flags!

You sit here and there is a relative hush. It is the scene before the electronic digits, the mayhem, the rows of screens; stockbroking and unimportance made vital. I once thought that it mattered, that values pirouetting before your eyes represented a challenge to the mind - investors kings without getting dirty.

That was not the worst of it though. When a man has no honour, he needs to be shovelled outside. This company, my company, made room for him though – exemplified him, packaged his humour and let it cut through the ranks in the manner of asbestos toxin.

Shilp – to use the old cliché – you would not piss on him if he was on fire. And yet, they had let the irritant roam, promoted him. Does cream rise? If it does, then I am about to douse it in lead. I am about to help the world. Because there is a duty everywhere in this regard. A necessary purge.

Malfeasance, I will call it – Shilp's methods, his getting inside people if he sees dissent. I would pit Godledge against this one – just get him to stare him out. Because Godledge has no sense of when to turn away. He was no superiors in the world. And his seemingly dumb expression (interlaced with an aircraft carrier of grey matter) would confuse Shilp.

Some take everything before them – they are super-adaptors (they go large on the Darwinian pop), people who watch behaviour and adjust their normal pitch. Shilp is one of these – there is nothing of the original man left. He utters plastic words and feeds with the flies. Should they have laughed at Hitler? Would that have helped? Was Wagenknecht to act like The Joker now before firing? Should he engage with the man?

Shutters. Motion. The sound of steel on rubber bounding down concrete. And always a skid. A tiny skid. Was this to be it? Wagenknecht lowered himself a little in his seat – his heart like a band marching through Salchester.

You do this or it never goes away, he thought. You let the menace grow and you change nothing.

Standing on the sidelines lets a lot of things in. If there is not disapproval of some kind then you may as well kiss them.

The head lights swished across him in the manner of a lighthouse's eye. The movement after that appeared to be blocky, the to-ing and fro-ing and bad parking of an amateur behind the wheel.

I didn't imagine you'd nudge about like that, thought Wagenknecht. I assumed you'd swing her in, not care too much if you were slightly over the line.

The car came to a halt but no one got out. 'Come on, come on,' Wagenknecht muttered, his hand near the pistol in the door's well but not on it. 'Too long, too long.' Has the bastard seen me? he thought.

I imagined I would see his hairless and gleaming pate glued to the windscreen, scanning the area, ruffling what he could, but it was as if...

'Jesus, *Hesel*...' He was walking towards him in the manner of a rotund bird. The passenger side door of Wagenknecht's Affordable then opened and the old marriage warhorse got in.

'Why so early?'

'You've just driven in?'

'Yes. I'm here for Shilp.'

Heselglass showed him his piece. It was no bigger than a water pistol.

'A double god-damn hold up!'

'What do you mean...no – you leave this for the oldies, Will...fewer years to burn.'

'Why today? Why have we planned this for today? We didn't even speak about this possibility.'

'I knew I had this in me. Don't forget Spandau, the army. I've handled guns. Where did you even…'

'It doesn't matter.'

Heselglass could see the top of the shooter in the well. He might be an old crock, but awareness, vigilance – he had guarded Hess, been on the world stage. Little things – behaviour, conduct, deportment – he noticed.

'Are you shocked any more, Will? Do things still shock you? Schengen? This?'

'I wish they did, but no.'

'We have a lot of years in us, Will – and it's come to this. Assassination.'

The word sounded unreal to Wagenknecht, like they were just playing, using up a genie's wish. Heselglass, experienced as he was, added sombreness to the occasion though. It was like sitting with an uncle – an uncle reeling off random nuggets about life.

'I know why *I'm* here,' Heselglass continued. 'Shilp – he grabs my snores. He sees that I'm beat from an intense shift but then loads more work on me. He doesn't water his troops, has no grasp of how to run a unit. I've had sergeants that have thrown me into a boxing ring with a skilled fighter – and I've taken a damn thumping – but afterwards they've shown that my welfare is important. A nice nurse. Extra dessert. Gestures. Little gestures. Magnanimity. Have we ever seen any of that in Shilp?'

'No,' Wagenknecht solemnly agreed. 'He's a shitbag.'

'I still have a mortgage, Will. Divorces are not cheap. There'll be the army pension, but ten years to go. Can I take orders off this pisshead for another decade? I don't think I can.'

'How do we do this then, now we're both here? Who gets the longest sentence?'

'It's premeditated. We'll both be inside for a while.'

'*Inside*? We're inside now, aren't we?' Wagenknecht questioned, addressed their predicament in a simple fashion.

'I don't know what it is, but it doesn't feel right.'

'This is Ashpound's Pony moment,' Wagenknecht commented. But *we're* steering, deciding the fate.'

'I sometimes get a twinge from inside my scrotum, my right ball, and think he's responsible. Bad feelings don't just float away. They penetrate a person, run along the nerves, leave the blood cells and genes affected.'

'I know. I agree. But, Hesel – time, we've got to plan this.'

'You don't need to be involved. Will – you have kids. I skipped that. Just me. No one crying over my demise.'

'*I'd* bloody cry. I need someone around to…'

'Is broking really you, Will?'

'Gambling. Gambling. It's *all* that. Why should the daytime be any different.'

'This is what we do, Will. I go back to my car. You exit. Drive out. Get rid of that damn shooter…something you've never held. It'd be like a bad penalty.'

'Or, we could…' Wagenknecht released the handbrake and stepped on the accelerator.

'What are you doing?! Will - what are you doing?'

'Saving a couple of old crocks. We'll figure it out from the outside.'

Wagenknecht took the hairpin and the ramp, knew it would be the last time he was down here. The barrier dawdled – enough time for Heselglass to push at the door – but Wagenknecht held on to his jacket; not a huge grip but enough to signify a re-think.

'No 2nd battalion here, Hesel. Just stay away. We need a rare day to hammer things out. I'll park on the outskirts of the city. We're both sick. Nothing more than that. Tomorrow you decide.'

'The park?'

'Anything. Bench-sitting. Walking. Ice-cream.'

'A new perspective?'

'That's all we can hope for.'

They were silent for a while – Heselglass's bulk contrasting with Tillmann's; his thick spectacles an intimation of trustfulness and being on the level.

What does the Earth give us that is free? thought Wagenknecht. Seed, water, mesmerising views. I have considered killing myself – even plotted the area – but the lack of guarantees from the other side! What if I wake up in Africa? What if the kumboozi overrun me? These thinly-drawn Zola characters that currently surround me though – how has that come about?

Power. Propaganda. 'But Boredman. How did he do it?' Why do I still see the mecca of his old house as uplifting?

'You wanna see Boredman?'

'Yes, but how...'

'Go left, then down Marylebone and onto Bromwich Street.'

It wasn't the out-of-town Wagenknecht had planned. His inadvertent utterance had dredged a candidness in Heselglass that might otherwise have remained still. Here though, along this filthy road with its indistinct phiz they were at least away from perpetrating criminal acts.

'Pull in here. Just at the side.'

There were shattered bus stops, large half-derelict warehouses, humans that resembled sumpters. The concrete hell offered no comfort or inspiration or hope. It was a shuffling patilla of people moving in the poisonous mist of diesel fumes and excrement; a nothing land bordered by grot and feral houses.

'The man there with the walking stick and handwritten sign perched against the wall.'

'What about him?'

Heselglass could say no more. He could only indicate with his eyes that *all* Wagenknecht's peers had fallen. There had been no exceptions. The comprehensive hordes had subsumed them; if not depleted their exam results then planted something that would rot them later.

'It isn't Boredman. Boredman is doing well. I shook his hand. He was buoyant – the great representative of our class.'

'You shook his hand a quarter of a century ago. Just look at the sign, Will. Read the sign.'

Wagenknecht squinted his eyes. His glasses were scratched – had needed replacing years ago. He was looking across, to his right, through the lingering traffic. HELP PLEASE. NO LONGER ABLE.

Able to what? Wagenknecht thought. 'Able?!' he demanded from Heselglass.

'To operate. No longer able to operate, Will.'

'It isn't him, Hesel. You've got things mixed up. I don't see his face in that guise.'

'It is, I'm afraid. This is your Boredman.'

'Hobbling round on a stick? Begging? Nooooo!'

'I've walked past with Routcliff. He mutters things. Refers to the past. William Forrest. Austoff. Godledge. "Fine old chums".'

'The cassette tape, like a skipping rope. What is that? Why does he have his other hand on it?'

'So he can find his way back. He lives a block away. Ties it from his gate to here.'

'No. No. No.' Wagenknecht pushed open his door, stood and stared at the figure just yards from him. The warm eyes, modern chinks, but antiquated richness – surely still there.

He walked across, weaved through the bruising traffic. Heselglass let him go, didn't wish to say any more.

'Boredman? Hey – Boredman!'

The man turned as Wagenknecht approached. Each inch of his frail demeanour seemed to howl.

'Boredman.'

'Don't cross the tape, son. That's important to me. A barrier. A barrier, you see.'

'It *is* Boredman?' Wagenknecht was looking in amongst the fur. So many damn beards these days. Cheeks, a nose and some eyes – that's all they were giving him.

'Who's asking?'

'Forrest, Godledge, Austoff – we're all asking.'

246 | Jeff Weston

'Who and who?'

'Our biology teacher used to perform illegal abortions.'

The bit of knowledge seemed to stun him. His face dropped. The beard sagged around his thicker neck. 'Let me sit, sir. Let me sit please.'

Dear Donna – If I am no longer consistent, it is because I do not have a consistent narrative. Too many things are changing.

Dear Heselglass – We think too much and must stop.

Dear Doc – I came to you with my ears but we couldn't find the deafness. There was no wax. What now?

Dear Lysette – Whatever has come between us, you must know my single aim in life: For the children not to be pushed around.

Dear Leonard – All of my heroes have been poisoned, imprisoned or assassinated (Socrates, Toussaint L'Ouverture, Luther King Jr). Which stop do you suggest I get off at next?

Dear Douglas – Nineteen rooms and you sometimes hesitate with guests. Not recently, I'll grant you, but...

Dear Mum – I'll be OK. You'll be OK. There doesn't need to be professionals. We'll just talk. Sweetly talk. Look back on things.

Dear Lenov – Your house is in a lovely location. But some things cannot be fixed whatever the surrounding splendour.

Dear Jasmine – I don't know anything. How right you were.

Dear Scotty – I once called you the thickest person in the world because of your inability to handle a knife and fork. Despair, my son. Inexcusable despair. A man who once had answers, but who now recoils at everything.

Dear Austoff – Did you ever think we'd see him again? But the circumstances…

'So it is Boredman?'

'I was thinking – it's not money we're after. It's not sex. Just the acceptance that we're "partly fraudulent"; us – the "ridiculous sons of Adam".'

'You're quoting!'

'An excuse to go down. He said I was trying to find an excuse to go down – rely on the state.'

'You got ten O-levels, Boredman. All A's. Before the super A's made their way in. You were up. Firmly up. But never a show off. Braggy – the kids at primary school gave you that name because you were sharp…tenderly sharp.'

'I didn't think they had doctors like that. I thought they were there to help.'

'We can't have had a hardened class. Maybe that's it, Boredman. Winners, but only in isolation. When the real world bit…'

'"Relief from the pursuit of absolutes" though. That's what the 17th century brought.'

'You know about that century? Of course you do.'

'"Something practical was done with thought."'

'But maybe seriousness was replaced by glibness. The teeth of the industrial diggers are wont to grin.'

Wagenknecht wasn't getting through. His old friend had dipped his head into a melancholic reservoir; a late 1990s hoard which was somehow awash with his stronger memories.

So it had turned then – Boredman let down by his GP; the great success story strangled and dumped after seven minutes in a neat, surgery room.

The brown corduroys and worn Hush Puppies now spoke of a man who had never wanted saluting and was on the rocks, gone, gibbering to himself in a higher language.

Where is the centre of things? thought Wagenknecht. After this cataclysm, this disaster. I had hoped to reconvene with Boredman when we hit sixty, talk over the past, our respective lives. But the warden's keys – they seem to jangle. If not an asylum then the regular lockup for a misdemeanour we no longer understand.

The rules - I no longer get them. People stare clear-eyed through me as if my logic is holding up humanity. It is the opposite of what Bellow said. "A curious result of the increase of historical consciousness is that people think explanation is a necessity of survival. They have to explain their condition. And if the unexplained life is not worth living, the explained life is unbearable, too."

Most have stopped doing that. They cut through like mini-fascists. You lean in on your partner at the end of the dance but forget the footwork. The office kails that I now rarely propound to have fetching optimism, but don't ask a thing. History has become three months.

What hope for Boredman then with his Oliver Cromwell essays, his Magna Carta analysis? What hope for any of us?

Wagenknecht looked down. He could see that Boredman was trying – through peeked opportunities

– to recognise him, but was clutching the tape from the cassette ever tighter. A lot was in there swimming around – giant inflatables meeting with navy warships, old bayonets and rocks feeling the force of Willie Pete.

You live too long and the narratives clash. You steam into your second generation or fifth decade and the compulsion to weigh things up tramples you.

'So do we play with the silly little bromides?'

'You're asking *me*, Boredman?'

His life had plummeted into a cartwheel of rhetorical questions. The man with the ginger brown mop had unwittingly signed up to some kind of introspective overdrive. *Careful, Wagenknecht!* You're not far behind. All the lessons you've had with the baseborns and misbegotten that frequented your class!

And Leonard asserts that the playing surface was fair! But I didn't want Leonard's life, thought Wagenknecht. Not eclectic enough.

'*We think* of how to become self-employed. Independent. Like Douglas, my brother.'

But the Ugandan raincoats! You made a mess of it. The voices inside Wagenknecht were like snakes, persecuting and pernicious critics that exceeded anything thrown at him in the real world.

Lenov would tell him not to be hard on himself. You can only do what you can do. Try again. Go slower.

Maybe speed's my problem. Maybe I'm stuck a couple of centuries back. But wouldn't they have thrown chamber pot contents over my head if I'd walked the streets back then?

It's all closing in, thought Wagenknecht. I'm here with the cleverest man I've ever known, but he's had his brain scrambled. Is there an attempt from government to find him and thus re-settle those around him? Do they know how serious this matter is?

With Boredman's unstable meanderings come my own waves lashing the community – bubbles, foam, the fuzz inside, the relentless turning. I never feel still, thought Wagenknecht. In a chair, lying down, walking peacefully – there is something, always *something* nagging at me. If you're up there, then please stop this brutal game! Unplug the currents!

It must be my nerves, Wagenknecht posited. Numerous fuses have blown. Does that come from what you put inside you? Food. Conversation. Sexual wares. Suffering. *Maybe*. But you've never consumed the rich stuff: devilled kidneys; plum and tonka jam; kale pakoras; cured gravlax; matsutake. You've stuck with pumpkin seeds, boneless sardines, risotto, stuffed vine leaves, pasta with green and black olives, and chilli.

Concentrate. Concentrate, he told himself. Is it time to step over Boredman as you stepped over Ashpound? He could pull us both down. People wade in the sea to save an animal and end up drowning themselves. Do you want that?

It would be honourable, glorious in a way, but forgotten. Wagenknecht knew the lifespan of a daily newspaper edition reporting such heroism or martyrdom. Not even 24 hours. In, digested and burped out. And anyway, it was all old people reading print these days. With the younger crowd his face and the accompanying headline would be a mere swipe.

They don't hang around; each savage, dying stroke in that sea hardly justified.

He sat next to you. Boredman sat next to you. Not in chemistry when Austoff was the lonely trellis you shuffled up beside on the laboratory pew, but in form time. Boredman was the August baby – remember! A fellow August baby. But ridiculously ahead of the pack despite his youth.

Some of that playful maturity you soaked in. You owe him in a way. But now, look at us now – mown down on a filthy, incurable road.

Wagenknecht looked over towards Heselglass. He could see the sheepish uncomfortableness, the mortified face. 'In? Can he get in?' he mouthed.

Heselglass shook his head. 'No, he wouldn't want to. That isn't how you save people, Will.'

'But if he goes down, stays here, then I never wake up.' Wagenknecht got a sudden image of his grandfather in the coffin. It wasn't him. It couldn't have been him. He was a puffed out chap, a merry man of solid stature. How could the funeral virtuosos do that – stuff cotton wool inside his cheeks and expect recognition?

Leonard and Douglas knew then. You only do certain things. You don't plumb the depths, risk affliction and show 100% respect. You simply do *enough* – show up, look solemn and roll out a few weighty tears.

Whose rationalism are we wading through though? thought Wagenknecht. Pope worried about English civil society in the 18th century, the French had their 1789, but now – what is this 21st century shebang?

Conscience can't take you into the boardrooms, the high political circles. It can't even stand at the side of an open coffin and eschew the fleeting terribleness set against a largely well-lived life. You're in the moment too much, conceded Wagenknecht. The short term has begun to dictate your ways and habits. Think over the decades that have gone. You were more alive. So hold a few seeds back. Store them up for the hard days ahead.

Think of the child in the crowd "too young to understand the desirability of keeping up the pretence". The Emperor has nothing on! Boredman, in a way, was that Hans Christian Andersen child. And he had the brain and conceptual reasoning to pull it off. Except now, there was evidence of a trip. Boredman had wobbled – fallen off the beam. Do we play the silly little games? If we have no army ourselves, then *yes* I am afraid.

People were realising that the Emperor had his bed clothes on – his undergarments. There was no naked form even if collective denial was high.

You have to run with *someone*, Wagenknecht told himself. If not Hobbes, then *who?* If I cannot trot alongside Boredman then...

Think! Straighten yourself out. Consider this area a hospital. There will be visiting times. As long as the cassette tape does not break. As long as there's a sense of mutability. Boredman came up with some solid lines ("Something practical was done with thought"). Yes – there was disorientation, but he's still in there.

We're all out of our heads, thought Wagenknecht. Why not bow to that fact? Why resist it, try to find the well-tarmacked path? Now, I should walk off, soak in the world, cut out the pride and pomposity.

After Shilp he would have shot himself whilst walking across the station car park. A more suitable place he could not think of. (Nobody wants a bloodied corpse dripping on the house carpet.) Now, renewed by something, a cranking inside, the rich replacement of oil, Wagenknecht studied that before him with a sounder mind.

Leave the car and the iguana Shilp's future to Heselglass, he thought. For a few minutes, moments he wandered the central streets of Salchester asking people to guess his age. He needed the affirmation of something, a lighter aesthetic, the Romantic idyll of that innovator breed.

Wagenknecht's face felt tight yet a slow-release valve seemed to give it life once more. I'm dead without a pen in my hand, or a boob or a bat, he chuckled. *No – I really am.* The plays, Tillmann and sport to sweat out the neutrinos – those subatomic particles they'd assumed had no mass.

One thing I'm only just realising though, thought Wagenknecht, is that words get amplified with kids. I shall be a better father now – from afar with Tillmann in my corner. I shall shine myself up, *look* like a parent. The tailor's! A place I have not been for years.

Wagenknecht pushed his leaden frame through the tinkling door of an old, respected, cobbled backstreet suit shop. A man with customary tape around his neck approached.

'Sir?'

'A nice, single-breasted reasonably dark suit. I'm due to visit my children this weekend and want to…'

Wagenknecht stumbled, but the tailor covered his tracks, softened the pause as was his job. 'You want to look marvellous because with smartness comes proud children.'

'Yes.' Wagenknecht felt taken care of in the company of many professionals – hairdressers, doctors, opticians, tailors, even dentists. Part of him was happy to pull back, feel as if he was with a masseuse.

Money and its tricks! he thought. But I don't seem to care right now. I am an inverse Epicurus. Let the man tape my inside leg, measure my shoulder, do his stuff, anything that makes me feel *half* important, back with the earth.

Wagenknecht walked up and down in an off-the-shelf, brown ensemble that flattered his ageing torso. *Ridiculous!* he thought. Ridiculous that a change of dress can transform a man, but it seems to.

'They're all doing it, sir. Are you ready, sir? I see success. A perfect 40 inch chest, sir.'

Surprisingly, the crass lines – whether about the suit itself or Wagenknecht's future – were sautéed in a gentle parlance. Some people talked and could say anything. It was in the bend of the face, the honeyed agenda.

'Do you have any gloves?'

'*Gloves*, sir! No, gloves wouldn't go with this. Not with the dapper suit, sir.'

You enter the gents at work and your real face appears in the mirror, Wagenknecht mused – often stuck and shorn. What do I see now? he wondered. A desperate man or one just buttoning up a simpler existence?

You know which one it has to be, he thought. Shave off the last two seconds each time you observe something and you'll be OK. Yes. No agonising. Big strides. Onto something else. No more lockdown or black dog.

Wagenknecht shook himself out of the tangled despondency which often smothered him. 'I'll take this and try a blue as well please.'

Prompted in the tailor was a welcome smile. But happy for both parties – not selfish or cunning.

Wagenknecht took a seat. He felt cured of something. Perhaps his previous inability to engage with the real world. Signs flashed in his head – in particular the recent jaunty number in his parents' house (at the top of the stairs): DON'T TAKE LIFE TOO SERIOUSLY - NOBODY GETS OUT ALIVE ANYWAY. Old people needed that, but maybe he needed it now too.

Laugh along, Wagenknecht. Go on – laugh along. He forced a carburettor smile. Practise and it will become natural, he told himself. Yes – I'll try. Try to be merrier, try to see others' wit.

Senses – not the perfect measure of reality, the Transcendentalists had proclaimed. I certainly know that, Wagenknecht thought – especially when paranoia is at play. But look at you now – free for a while, before the Victorians steam in again, before the *Hard Times*.

Go home and prepare a meal for Tillmann. Sit there like an adult with a glass of wine in your hand (consult Douglas if you need to). Consider the renovated garage to be your short-term retreat. The meaning of life might be defined as a bloody struggle, but you can only show Tillmann your better side and hope for a different light in the world.

Wagenknecht stopped off at a convenience store in Choton. Public transport was agreeable to him. The train. The bus. He was mixing with people, not locked up in his can on wheels. From memory he placed the necessary ingredients into the plastic basket swinging at his side: celery, peppers, garlic, stock, rice, curry powder, chilli powder, peas, tomatoes. He had a wok adjacent to the bird house – the feathered friend box his father had worried over.

The dish was simple – no meat included – but Wagenknecht was good with herbs, his nostrils and tongue understanding the infusion. He watched and stirred with an old wooden spoon, imagined the clean white plates and Tillmann sat there gulping modest swigs of wine.

She would be talking about nothing – insignificant wonder, but in her face would be adorable flakes of intrigue and vivaciousness. The attention of *someone* he could truly engage with – that is all he required. And Wagenknecht in a pinny, not giving a hoot – just loving this woman's eyes, her absolute femininity.

In return for her devotion, he would invite her to sweaty ping pong halls, go swimming with her, speak to Douglas about using his side-house at weekends and his Portuguese flat each season.

None of this he had done with Lysette. And that is why they had crashed, fallen into a queer forbearance. Lysette – funny how only *she* lived near lunatics and bad neighbours. So long as Scotty and Jasmine were alright though. So long as *they* saw something fresh in their father which offset their occasional gloom.

Wagenknecht waited for the knock on the door. The well-formed sentences out there in the world could wait. Tillmann. Just Donna Tillmann now. He pushed the philosopher voices in his head to one side and let the butterflies and trepidation guzzle him.

'Hello, William.'

Printed in Great Britain
by Amazon